DOGWOOD

CHRIS FABRY

 Tyndale House Publishers, Inc.
Carol Stream, Illinois

Visit Tyndale's exciting Web site at www.tyndale.com

TYNDALE and Tyndale's quill logo are registered trademarks of Tyndale House Publishers, Inc.

Dogwood

Designed by Beth Sparkman

Edited by Lorie Popp

This novel is a work of fiction. Names, characters, places, and incidents either are the product of the author's imagination or are used fictitiously. Any resemblance to actual events, locales, organizations, or persons living or dead is entirely coincidental and beyond the intent of either the author or the publisher.

Library of Congress Cataloging-in-Publication Data

Fabry, Chris, date.
  Dogwood / Chris Fabry.
    p. cm.
  ISBN-13: 978-1-4143-1955-1 (sc)
  ISBN-10: 1-4143-1955-X (sc)
  1. Married people—Fiction.   2. Triangles (Interpersonal relations)—Fiction.
3. West Virginia—Fiction.   I. Title.
  PS3556.A26D64 2008
  813'.54—22   2008006775

Printed in the United States of America

14   13   12   11   10   09   08
 7   6   5   4   3

For AK, who believed.

"All sorrows can be borne if you put them into a story or tell a story about them."   *Isak Dinesen*

"Eternity is a human stream and our stories are the rain, falling, flowing, surging, searching for an end. But there is no end. Never will be. And that's the great thing about living."   *Ruthie Bowles*

"Many a man claims to have unfailing love, but a faithful man who can find?"   *Proverbs 20:6*

"I think that life is full of pain. . . . It's painful for everybody. . . . Growing is painful. But I think that the only way through it is through it. . . . And anything that helps is a blessing."   *Jackson Browne*

PART ONE

1

Karin

Ruthie Bowles once said I would wind up hating her. She was right.

I met Ruthie on a Tuesday afternoon after a sleepless Monday night in my closet, a space littered with poetry and my mother's well-worn Bible, dog-eared at the Psalms. The poetry kept me sane, and the Psalms gave me hope. NyQuil stopped working long ago.

"Whoever fights monsters," Nietzsche said, "should see to it that in the process he does not become a monster. And if you gaze long enough into an abyss, the abyss will gaze back into you."

I ran across that in a quote book. At 3 a.m. it looked interesting. Ruthie doesn't quote Nietzsche, but the truth is the truth. I am a student of the abyss, but I get no credit. It's a night class I audit.

When I met Ruthie, I had an ache in my heart left by the echoes of friends and choices. Mistakes. I knew women in the neighborhood, names and faces from church and the local preschool, but I did not have what Anne Shirley would call a bosom friend, and there were few prospects.

My husband, Richard, pastor of the Little Brown Church —

though it is not little and more cranberry if you ask me—has been supportive. "Just give it some time," he'll say. "We all go through tough seasons." I've seen him lose a night's sleep about three times in his life, and I fight resentment when I hear his rhythmic breathing. Sleep is a luxury to anxious minds.

Since childhood I have sung about the "river glorious" of God's peace. I hadn't planned on the river running dry.

And the church. I longed for a refuge or oasis. Instead, it became Alcatraz. To me, church has always meant relationships, not a building, but my problems sent me away from people rather than toward them.

In my first fledgling nights in the closet, when sleep and every sense of peace crawled away and hid like a wounded animal, I feared I was losing my mind. I pictured white-coated men strapping my arms and pushing me toward an oversize van while my children screamed and the elders shook their heads. I could hear my husband saying, *"She just needs a little time. We all go through tough seasons."*

Ruthie walked into my loneliness—or should I say hobbled— at a time when God was trimming the nails of my soul to the quick. Angels laughed so hard at my prayers that they held their sides. So many angels.

And God was silent.

One of my mother's favorite songs contains these words: "Then in fellowship sweet we will sit at His feet, or we'll walk by His side in the way . . ." I've felt constantly in his way. He seemed too ticked off to tell me to get out of it, so he kept quiet. The ESO, Eternal Silent One.

My constant companions were fears, not God. I convinced myself he was simply on vacation, out carrying someone else on that beach with all the footprints. My heart had shriveled, and my soul was as wrinkled as the prunes Ruthie loved.

I kept a journal—don't ask me why—and the ramblings tackled these fears and questions. Ruthie was the first to tell me that God hadn't abandoned me but was drawing me deeper, calling me out of the shallows, past the abyss, and into the current of his love and mercy.

Yeah, right, I thought. God hadn't asked me if I wanted to go deeper, and thank you very much, I liked the shallows. It's easier to play when there's no current. In the middle you lose your footing; you lose control.

You lose.

However, something drew me to this old woman. Was she an apparition? an angel in disguise? It would be my luck to get an angel with varicose veins. The sliver of hope that she was from God kept me going, but I did not know she had secrets and a closet full of haunted memories. She had seen the abyss long before me and had wrestled monsters of her own.

I suppose we all do.

I grew up in Dogwood. There are memories and stirrings from some other life. My mother and father, Cecilia and Robert Ashworth, still live here. So do *his* parents. At least, Will's mother does.

Ruthie asked me about *him* at that first meal, what she dubbed our "First Supper." She asked innocently, or so it seemed at the time. Something about her questions should have tipped me off that she knew more. She did not know how many *him*s there had been before the pastor. Or that my mind was drawn to someone I could never love. Could never kiss or hold or touch again.

"My husband is a good man," I said. It sounded appropriate, and I hoped she couldn't sense the hurt behind the answer. I knew I had settled for less. Someone safe. Faithful as an old dog but better smelling.

Ruthie let the answer slip away as easily as my children coming down the slide at the park where we watched them play. Tarin is with me during the day. Darin and Kallie are already in school.

I changed the subject. "Do you have children?"

"Grown," she said. "They fly like birds before you know it. Just when you thought you had the nest figured out. But I guess that's our job."

"Your husband?"

She smiled. "He flew too."

Was he dead? Had he left her? "I'm sorry," I said.

"I remember when mine were your daughter's age. I was different then. Wrapped up in froth."

"Hmm?"

Ruthie scooted forward on the bench. "Like a beer on tap. You spend your life chasing froth and bubbles. I used to think it satisfied, that it could fill me up and make me happy. But froth is froth. Empty. What I needed was underneath, at the root, the soul. Can't find happiness in froth, at least not for long."

She sounded like a preacher—or one of those homespun storytellers on public television, dispensing wisdom one sound bite at a time. I wanted to switch channels or leave. Make an excuse. Head for a fictional doctor's appointment. I needed to get home to the wash. But it was already evening, and I couldn't fool her. Plus, something drew me. Was it her voice, her eyes, or the way she seemed to wallow in life?

"Come to my house for dinner," Ruthie said. The idea came out of the blue, like a magician pulling fried chicken out of a hat.

"That's very kind of you, but—"

"You look like you could use a friend and I love children."

When I was a child, my brother and I wandered near bushes my mother had ordered us to avoid. We were searching for hidden treasure or a lost baseball—I can't remember which—when we stumbled upon a hornet's nest the size of Detroit. Bobby Ray ran, but I stood, paralyzed by the enormity of the nest and all those stingers writhing inside. For a month I had nightmares about hornets covering my face and arms, stinging every inch of exposed flesh.

As it turned out, one lonely hornet snapped me from my stupor, and I ran to my mother, my arm swollen. She grabbed a fresh onion from the refrigerator, cut it in half, and placed it on the sting. The onion felt wet and slick. "Hold it right there," she said. "It'll draw the poison out."

I have been staring at the hornet's nest called life, afraid to live, too stunned to move. Ruthie was the one who drew the poison from my soul. She became my teacher. Our classroom was her living room or the playground at the Memorial Park. Some of the most intense lessons we tackled while standing in line at Wal-Mart.

"Life isn't pretty, so you've got to hug the ugly out of it," she said one day.

She had no idea how much ugly there was.

2

Danny Boyd

My counselor says everybody has a story. Well, here's mine.

I killed my sisters at 7:43 a.m. on a July morning in 1980. I remember it was July because baseball season wasn't even half over, but my father had already given up on the Reds. I remember it was 7:43 because my watch got stuck when I jumped the guardrail. The Focal my dad had bought for me at Kmart just stuck. Little hand between the seven and eight, big hand between the eight and the nine. Closer to the nine.

That was the first thing I told the man who was supposed to help me. He wanted to know why I had killed them. I couldn't answer. I figured he knew anyway. He seemed to know a lot of things even though he just asked questions.

Everyone has a story, he said.

Yeah.

Why don't you tell me the rest?

I don't remember much.

He put a hand to his beard. Why do all counselors have beards? Seems like all the ones in the movies have them. Counselors must take a class in facial hair. You'd think they'd shave or at least trim a bit and wouldn't try to hide anything.

9

You didn't actually kill them, did you?

I did.

That's not the truth.

Yeah, it is.

Then take me back. Tell me what happened that morning.

Why?

I want to hear how you remember it. I want to experience it with you.

I couldn't. Though I had relived the sights and sounds and smells of that day a thousand times. When I was asleep or maybe awake. I don't know. My little sister with her neck twisted—her arms to her side but her neck turned around, like she was trying to be funny. Karla. She had just turned eight a couple of weeks earlier. June 20 is her birthday. It was easy to remember because that's also the birthday of West Virginia. Abraham Lincoln was around when that happened. At least, that's what our teacher told us. Mr. Kilgore told us much more than that, but I don't remember a whole lot except that it was during the Civil War and we didn't want to be a slave state like Virginia. It's hard to remember the little things, especially on a test.

They gave Karla a cowgirl outfit for her birthday, and she would've worn it every day if Mama had let her. She squealed when she opened it and pulled off her clothes right there in the kitchen to put it on. Mama said, Oh, Karla, but she went right ahead and tried it on. The morning I killed them, Karla and Tanny wore starched white T-shirts that smelled like a million cut flowers. Their hair in pigtails. Hand in hand, walking toward a future they'd never see because of me.

When I think real hard or talk about that morning, I can smell the radiator fluid. It was all over the place. And the engine hissed. I never knew a person could do that much damage to a car. A deer, yeah, but a person? Especially a couple of kids.

Then the car pulled back and my other sister was under there, the air coming out of her mouth, puff, puff. And Tanny just stared at me with eyes glazed over like she was sick or something.

Karla and Tanny dead by the road and it was my fault.

The counselor took a long time just looking at me with his lips together. Then he said, Tell their story.

I thought he meant my sisters, so I started telling him what it was like to have sisters and how much I wanted a brother who could play cars or go hunting or ride bikes. The girls could ride bikes—heck, Karla was the first to go off some of the jumps I made. Probably more fearless than a lot of brothers, but I still wanted one. And that made me feel even more guilty for what I'd done.

Then I told him about Mom letting me feed Tanny a bottle when she was a baby. And one time I didn't burp her and she blew the whole bottle on my new baseball glove. I wanted to spank her, but everybody just laughed. Ha-ha. I never did get the formula smell out of the glove. Ruined the leather. Anytime I'd miss a ground ball, I'd blame her.

But my counselor didn't mean that. He didn't mean for me to tell the stories of my sisters.

I told him about how I took them the way we weren't supposed to go—up the dirt road that cut through to Route 60. Mama told us never to walk that way when we were going to Mamaw's. Said it was too dangerous. If she only knew some of the places we'd been, she wouldn't have been so scared, but I guess she was right. When you look back it's a lot easier to tell when people are right.

Tanny and Karla reminded me what Mama had said and tried to get me to go the other way down by the creek, but I grabbed their hands and pulled them through the bushes and out to the gravel and the dust and made them come. I just wanted to walk by her house. The girl with the red hair. She had a horse, and the guys at school said sometimes she'd ride it in the morning before her dad left. I thought he must be a good dad to let her do that before he went off to work, wherever that was. The nickel plant. Union Carbide. I never knew what he did.

The red-haired girl was outside that morning—I couldn't believe it—but she wasn't having fun. She was crying, yanking on her father's arm as he put the horse in a trailer. I thought maybe they were taking it to the vet, but she kept screaming, No! You can't!

And that's when I remembered *Charlotte's Web*. Mrs. Munroe had read it to our class in the fourth grade, and lots of people cried when Charlotte died—I hope I'm not spoiling it for you. I couldn't forget the first few lines—Papa going to the hog house with an ax.

I wanted to help the red-haired girl. I wanted to run in there and save the horse for her so she'd like me and we'd be friends and one day get married. I figured he was taking that horse to the dog food factory or maybe the glue factory. That's what my friends said happened to old horses. I'd like to think that what took place next in my story prevented him from killing that old horse, but I'm pretty sure it didn't.

Her daddy looked at me. I wanted to be the hero, but I chickened out and took Karla and Tanny back toward the road, back the way we weren't supposed to go, looking for the trail that led to the street where Mamaw lived.

The counselor looked at me as if he knew what I was thinking, as if he could see right inside me, though I know that's not possible. Looks that you see in the movies, like a person can tell what's going on in there. Sure felt like it to me.

I'm going to give you an assignment, he said.

Assignment?

Someone of your intelligence should be able to handle this. He turned and grabbed a pad of yellow paper, the kind you tear off and that has green lines on it. He ripped off the top pages that had writing on it and plopped the whole thing on my lap. Start from the beginning, he said. Don't leave anything out.

I can't write.

Just tell it as it comes. As you find out. Don't worry about the spelling. It doesn't have to be perfect.

Do I get a grade or something?

Do you want one?

No.

He leaned forward. What do you really want, Danny? In all the world, what do you really want?

I wanted to scream. I wanted to be forgiven for the awful thing I'd done. I didn't want to feel guilty. It was my fault. If it would bring them back, I'd gladly take their place. I wanted us to be a family again instead of walking corpses. Just going through life like zombies on that *Night of the Living Dead* movie. I haven't seen it, but one of my friends told me about it.

Everyone has a story, he said again.

What good will it do for me to write something down?

He put his hands together, index fingers pointing up like a steeple, and touched his lips. Red lips in the middle of that beard. Nothing good ever hides, he said.

Nothing bad does either, I said. It eventually pokes its head up at some point and bites your rear end.

He smiled. True. But it's best to get it into the open quickly where we can all see it. Begin to understand. Live with it. Work with it.

I wished I could smile like he did, a light coming through his eyes as if you could see as far back as you wanted all the way to the end of something. But behind the wrinkles in the corners of his eyes, I noticed a little sadness. I wondered what his story was. What had he seen and done? Why was he some two-bit counselor in this place talking to a kid who'd killed his sisters?

You were only eleven, you know, he said.

I should have known better. If I'd obeyed, this whole thing wouldn't have happened and we'd be celebrating Tanny's birthday.

He nodded. You made a mistake. You didn't mean to —

I killed them.

He sat for a long time looking at me. I hate it when grown-ups stare at kids. The room felt like it needed music. Something playing in the background. Maybe if he opened a window a bird would chirp or something and break the silence.

He tapped a pencil. Will you write it?

What choice do I have?

He reached for the pad on my lap.

I pulled it away and held on. I can't promise I'll get it right.

Is that what you think I want? I don't want it right. I want it to be good. And true.

I'm saying it won't be any good. How long do you think it will take?

He handed me another pad. Write about them until you're ready to talk.

Wait. You mean my sisters or — ?

Everyone has a story, he interrupted. Tell theirs.

I looked at the pads, the green running across the pages in perfect lines, as if they could go on to infinity. Parallel lines do that. That's what Mrs. Arnold said when we were studying math. They just go on and on and on and never touch. Hard to imagine something going so far as to never touch. Kind of sad, too, in a way. I squared the edges and tucked the pads under an arm. His words echoed in my head, through the halls.

Good things can come from pain, he said. Not all of it is good, of course, but some of it. And the places it leads are good places, not bad. Never be afraid of the places pain will take you.

Like a hospital?

He smiled.

So I left and found out he was right. Everyone does have a story.

3

Will

Clarkston Federal Correctional Institution
Clarkston, West Virginia

I can't stop my hands from shaking. Just like at the trial. Uncontrollable. It doesn't even help if I shove them in my pockets.

With the fluorescent lights over me so strong, I can see a ghost of my reflection. I've avoided mirrors for twelve years. Only two months to go, but I don't think I'll ever look in a mirror again and not remember what's happened. It's enough to turn a strong man's stomach.

Men elected president enter the White House with dark hair, full of vigor, and most leave a few years later looking twenty years older. I would have taken the White House over Clarkston. I entered this white house weighing 195. If I can stay above 150, I'll be happy.

The solace comes when I close my eyes and think of home. What the neighbors are doing. Fishing with Uncle Luther. Or with my dad. I'll never do that again. The excitement of hunting season. There are people up the hollow who were in grade school when I left. They're out of college now or in prison. Maybe out of college *and* in prison.

The chair squeaks as I lean forward and rest my elbows on the

Formica countertop. The letter came a week ago. The explanation was a bit confusing, but it said *she* would visit. And now I sit with my stomach in knots, unable to let the thought enter my mind that it might really be *her*.

My first two months here were spent crafting letters, pouring out my heart, detailing my feelings. Half of them I threw away, convinced I'd said too much or too little. The other half I sent.

Every letter went unanswered.

I heard rumors, of course. Wild ones that she had moved away or was pregnant and had a shotgun wedding. Carson, my brother, called her unspeakable names. But every waking moment of the last dozen years, I've thought of her.

Down the row, a voice echoes off the scratched Plexiglas. Tears. Hands reaching. An inmate falsely accused. A mother weeping. It seems so cliché now.

Yet I can't deny a flicker of hope. After a year I stopped sending letters, but I never stopped writing. Or loving. There are things I have to do once I get out. Hard things. People I have to face. But if I can just see her once more . . .

Every night for twelve years, I've turned off the light and interlaced my fingers behind my head, drifting off to a dream of a house on a hill overlooking a meadow and a sea of West Virginia mountains and trees rolling like an ocean. I'm returning from work swinging a lunch box. I stop and pick up a child who runs to me. Then she appears on the porch, in sandals, relaxed, holding a frosty glass of tea, smiling at both of us. I long for that dream to become reality, but I know it's only a dream.

Someone moves behind me and I jerk around, a reflex developed for survival.

"Take it easy," the guard says, his hands out. "Just got the word that they're here."

I nod. "Thanks."

4

Bobby Ray

This was not what I expected. I walked into the station and found a dark green desk that looked like something shipped back from Vietnam.

"Your uniform is down at the cleaners," the secretary said, a brunette turned blonde turned redhead. Maggie looked like one of those girls from high school who threw herself into food and hair coloring with equal gusto. She could be pretty, but now she is just cleavage and wide hips and jokes about her weight to protect herself. In the days to come, I would learn that she didn't get much help from the others in the office, especially Wes, a patrol officer who worked nights. He was thin, had eyes like a weasel, and walked like he owned the world.

"Ought to come with me tonight over to the Blue Moon," Wes said to her. He winked at me. "They've got a wet T-shirt contest, and there's no doubt in my mind—"

"Just stop it," Maggie said, sorting through the mail on her desk. "You ever heard of sexual harassment?"

"I've never heard a sexual harassment I didn't like."

The door opened and a bell jingled. Two men walked in, the older with the presence of Moses. He had a slick, lizardlike face, and from the Barbasol smell I guessed he'd just had a shave at the barbershop. The silver at his temples gave way to light brown hair that looked like the color of some barn cat I used to toss in the pond behind our house. Something between an orange tabby and the tail of a calico. The man had a chest as wide as the door, it seemed, and he carried himself like a prizefighter.

The second man was younger but had the same barrel chest and stout build. His hair was short, and he had a dark mustache.

"Morning, Chief," Maggie said. "Guess that's the last time I'll be saying that."

The older man put a hand on the counter and leaned against it, draining a spent piece of spearmint gum. "Now, Maggie, I'll always be chief to you, won't I?"

She smiled. "I guess you will."

"You won't mind that, will you, Son?" he said, turning to the man behind him.

His name was Eddie. I'd met him when I interviewed for the job a month ago. He flipped through letters and papers in his mailbox, disinterested. "As long as they up my pay, I don't care what you call him."

The chief turned and smiled, his eyes shining. "Wes? Everything go all right last night?"

"Hardly a peep, sir. Caught two kids going at it in the backseat of their Focus over on Virginia Avenue."

The chief laughed, the gum sticking to his teeth. "Those don't have much room in the back. Sounds painful. You write them up?"

"Nah, it was a friend of mine's little brother. I put the fear of God in him and told him to wipe the steam off the windows and leave."

The chief stepped toward me. "You must be Bobby Ray."

"Yes, sir. It's an honor to meet you, sir."

He shook my hand. His skin was cold and surprisingly soft. "You're Cecilia and Robert's boy, aren't you?"

18

"Yes, sir."

"You have a sister, a little older than you. Right?"

"Karin."

"How's she doing?"

"Fine. Thanks for asking. She has her ups and downs, of course."

"Well, we all do, don't we?"

"Yes, sir. We do."

He took a Hershey's Kiss from a jar on Maggie's desk and unwrapped it. "Well, I'm passing the baton to somebody you can trust. Wouldn't have retired if I didn't know I could leave this place in good hands."

"Got that right," Wes said.

The chief nodded. "Yeah, Eddie here learned from the best, if I do say so myself."

Eddie had his sleeves rolled up, a smirk on his face, as if he wasn't buying the compliments. The tag under his star said "Buret." He had the look of a lone bull in an open field, his upper arms the size of my thighs. He shook my hand—the same grip as his father's. "Good to see you again. Welcome to the force."

The phone rang, and Maggie put her hand over the mouthpiece. "Chief, it's the mayor."

"Better get the office cleaned out, old-timer," Eddie said. "I want to move in this afternoon."

The chief shook his head and closed the door. I could hear his voice through the window. "Mayor, how are we today?"

"Wes, you coming to the breakfast?" Eddie said.

"If you can spare me."

Eddie looked at me. "Figured you could hold down the fort while we say good-bye to the old geezer."

"Sure."

"I'll keep my radio on just in case."

"I don't have my uniform yet."

"That's all right. You'll just be answering the phone. Maggie's coming with us." Eddie opened a desk drawer and pulled out a service revolver, a .38 Smith & Wesson in a holster with Mace, a radio, and a nightstick. Then a silver badge in a leather holder. "We'll grab your uniform on the way back from the restaurant. Any questions?"

"If somebody calls with an emergency?"

He wrote down the number for the restaurant. "Nobody'll call."

I brought in a box of my stuff as the four piled into both cruisers and screeched away. Eddie ran the lights. One last spin for the memory, I guessed.

I settled into the corner desk, going through the drawers to see what was there. Eddie had told me during the interview process that the previous officer had taken a job in Charleston. I must have answered his questions satisfactorily. He knew I was a native and understood the people.

"Dogwood's never gonna be a big city," Eddie had said. "And to be honest, I don't want it to be. I want to keep things quiet as they've always been."

I put out the picture of Lynda and me—a shot we'd taken on our honeymoon at Pipestem, a state park a couple of hours away. Then one from a few months ago, her stomach slightly paunched, my hand on her belly. Another reason I had quickly taken the job. I needed an income and some benefits for the new family.

Another picture showed lots of sand and my buddies looking tough, square-jawed, kneeling near a Chinook. After my military service, I'd gone into officer training and landed a job in Wheeling. With Orson—my affectionate name for our baby—on the way and the grandparents excited about their first grandchild, moving back seemed the best option. Lynda's parents live in Winfield, only fifteen minutes away, so it made sense. We found a house, the old Benedict farm that had been divided into several parcels.

With the money I'd saved and gifts from both sets of parents, we made a down payment and moved in with Lynda's folks until I could remodel. We had a long way to go—the water pipes were worse than I thought and the roof was a sieve—but I was hopeful we could be in before the baby came.

The third and last picture was of Karin and me when we were kids. It was Halloween—I was six; she was ten. She wore a frilly ballerina costume, and I held a motorcycle helmet and had written #43 on a white T-shirt to look like Richard Petty. Our faces were pressed together, cheek to cheek. I'm glad we got a photo of Karin smiling and happy.

The bell jingled and two women entered. The younger one wore tight cutoffs, her shirt tied to show off tight-as-a-drum abs. Her dirty blonde hair hung down, and each time she blinked, her split ends moved. Her lips were pouty, and her teeth protruded slightly. She had a smoker's cough.

The older woman was large with a dimpled chin and gray-streaked dark hair. Her arms looked like the Michelin Man's, and she wore polyester slacks that made an audible whine as she walked.

"Can I help you, ladies?"

"Where's Eddie?" the older woman said.

"He's out for a couple of hours. Can I help?"

"You the new guy?"

I offered my hand and she took it. "Bobby Ray Ashworth. I don't have my uniform yet."

"Robert and Cecilia's boy?" she said.

"That's right."

She looked me up and down and spied my wedding ring. "My, my, Doris Jean. The good ones get taken too fast."

The other woman lifted a hand, her fingers stained yellow. "We're here about my brother Arron."

The older woman introduced herself as Emma Spurlock, the

mother of Arron and Doris Jean. For years I'd heard the family name associated with everything from petty thievery and vandalism to house fires. The Spurlocks had so many kids that it was said you could throw a rock on their tin roof and they'd be running outside for days. Each time a child reached the age where he could strike a box of matches or flick a Bic lighter, the fire department was put on notice.

"I filed a missing person's report on Arron two days ago, and I haven't heard a thing from Eddie."

I found the right cabinet and was impressed with Maggie's filing abilities. I hadn't expected much. But the missing person's file was empty. I asked the two to hang on while I went to Eddie's office and looked through the papers on his desk. The report wasn't there.

"Like I said, it's my first day. Let me take your number and have Eddie call you as soon as he gets back."

"We've got some more information for him," Doris Jean said.

"How long has Arron been missing?"

"Since last weekend. He left work about eight and went over to the pool hall. Nobody seen him after that and he didn't come home."

"We told all this to Eddie," Mrs. Spurlock said.

I wrote down their number and taped the piece of paper to Eddie's door.

"Arron's a good boy," Mrs. Spurlock said. "He works hard."

"Where was he employed?"

"Over at the Exxon station. Been there almost five years now. I'm worried sick."

I nodded. "We'll do our best, ma'am."

5

Karin

Ruthie arrived at the church office, her black purse slung over her arm like she had an appointment with God himself, and asked to see me. I was in a women's ministry meeting mired in the specifics of the spring luncheon, so I excused myself and met her in the hall.

I showed Ruthie to my husband's office—Richard was home working on a sermon or the new budget—and closed the door behind us. We faced each other in chairs near his desk. She stared through me, and I found myself studying the design on the spine of *The Treasury of Scripture Knowledge.*

"Why did you want to see me?" I said.

"You came to my place a couple of days ago. What did you want?"

Ruthie was at least seventy with thinning gray hair and skin that hung from her neck like a turkey wattle. Her eyes had that narrow quality you see in Pulitzer Prize winners who have pain running through their veins, having seen too much of the world, having written about the deeper things of life. Her stare wiped the smile from my face, and I could tell she knew something.

"You were on the list of people to invite, and I was told you didn't have a phone," I said.

Ruthie squinted. "Invite me to what?"

"The spring luncheon. I'm on the committee, and we're trying to come up with—"

"Don't you have that in May? That's months away."

"Yes, we're trying to get the word out early."

I ran down the list of particulars—our special speaker, the menu, the child care.

After I finished my spiel, Ruthie gave me her patented stare. "What's wrong in your life?"

"I'm sorry?"

She opened her purse, took out a tissue, and pulled her glasses off, showing two red marks indelibly left on the bridge of her nose. She wiped the lenses and placed them firmly on the red marks. "Something's going on, and God sent me here to find out what it is."

Oxygen left the room for a second, and I had to consciously open my mouth and suck in a couple of breaths. Of course there was something wrong. Terribly wrong. But only God and I knew it, and he wasn't letting me in on what it was.

"Are you cheating on your husband?" she said.

"Of course not! Why would you ask a thing like that?"

Ruthie stuffed the tissue back in her purse. If everyone lived like Ruthie, Kleenex would go out of business. "It took a lot to get me here today. Ask those ladies. They'll tell you how long it's been since I've been here. And if you don't want my help, that's fine."

"Did Richard send you?"

Ruthie snapped her purse shut and stood, gathering her cane in the crook of her arm. "Not a human alive could get me here, save Jesus himself. You want to talk, come to my place. Tomorrow. Four o'clock." And with that, she hobbled away.

I rejoined the meeting as Constance Weldon read the number of books our guest speaker had written. "What's the matter, Karin? You look like you've just seen a ghost."

I told them Ruthie Bowles had visited me.

The women looked at each other.

Finally, Constance ran a hand across the empty writing pad. "Ruthie is one of our well-intentioned dragons."

"Excuse me?"

"She means well, but she's a few cups away from a full Communion tray."

Lucille Collander, the most compassionate one of the bunch, shook her head until wisps of hair floated onto the table. "Well, she's been through a lot of heartache. I'll give her the benefit of the—"

"Let's stay on task, ladies," Constance said.

The meeting ground on, but all I could think about was Ruthie.

Later that night, while my children were occupied, Richard asked about my day. I told him about Ruthie, and he said he had heard of her. Actually he had heard others talking about her.

"Did you sleep last night?" he said, changing the subject.

"Enough."

"Is there anything you'd like to talk about?"

I yawned. "It's been a long day."

That night was the worst. Some can face sleeplessness with resolve, doing something constructive with the time like Creative Memories. I fell into that long stretch of night thinking I was losing my mind. Then a more horrifying thought. What if I was losing my faith? What good is a mind if you don't have faith?

When I finally fell asleep, I dreamed. It was the same one I had dreamed for years, over and over, like a coded message. . . .

I am standing in front of the house where I grew up, with the black Labrador chained at the front. His fur is the color of dirt, and mud hangs from his jaws. He pants and pays no attention, as if I'm invisible.

I knock on the door and wait, cradling an infant. She is a newborn, pink and tiny, almost weightless. A bird chirps and flits from branch to branch of the three hickory trees in the front. The one in the middle is tall, branches spreading as if it is welcoming something. Someone.

My father opens the door, and he appears older, chubbier, with hair that retreats from a bald spot like soldiers overwhelmed by a frontal assault. His teeth are yellowed from coffee, and his shirt is sweat stained. His eyes are pools of memory. There is an ocean of wisdom in there, if only I could reach it.

He sees the infant and smiles, reaching for her, gathering her in with strong hands. I have never seen my father care so much for anything, and I give the baby freely, almost haphazardly. I am glad to be rid of her. Relieved.

I look for my mother in the kitchen, but she isn't there. The hallway leading to the back of the house is dark. I need to talk. I lean on her at times like this, and she seems to know what to say and what not to say. My mother is comfort and peace in a calico smock.

I return to the living room, where my father is on the floor hovering over my still child, making faces, smiling, cooing, attempting to summon some reaction. A human defibrillator.

I stare at the scene, and a sense of despair, failure, and disgust overwhelms me. I do not care for her. I do not love or hate her. I do not care what she becomes. I have no vision for her future. I have no regret about how she came into the world. She has no meaning to my life, and this horrifies me.

My father is intensely involved. He can't take his eyes off her. He is enraptured with the very thought of this little one.

"I have to go," I choke.

His face softens, mixed with sadness and love. It feels as if he's looking straight into my heart. "I know," he says. I can't recall my father being this loving, this compassionate. "I'll watch her until you get back. Until you're ready."

I turn and, without remorse or pause, abandon them. Past the dog. Through the trees. To the road that stretches farther than I can see.

6

Will

There are dime-size holes in the Plexiglas, and it's all I can do not to put my fingers through them as I consider the list of possible visitors. There have been only a handful in twelve years. Carson. My mother came after my father's funeral to show pictures.

"I suppose you've heard about Karin," she said, shaking her head.

"Mama . . ."

"I know you don't want to hear this, but—"

"One death in my life is enough right now. Please."

She handed the pictures through the small slot at the bottom of the glass, and I felt like a bank teller receiving a deposit.

At first glance, the pictures seemed ghastly. Now, when I feel particularly alone, I pull them out and try to remember names of people with bad suits and oily hair. Farm people. Good people.

In one picture, I recognized a Sunday school teacher from the little white church on the corner. Mrs. Gilfillen challenged us to memorize the books of the Bible, and I worked for weeks only to mix up the minor prophets. And leave out Zechariah. To some, those names seemed from another world. I heard them every day.

Amos. Micah. Obadiah. Names of men my father talked to at the feed store and barbershop.

I tried to hold back the tears as Mrs. Gilfillen handed out prizes, but I snorted so loudly that everyone laughed. It was not the last time I'd have that same feeling.

In several pictures, I was able to see the body of my father. Wrinkled hands folded across his chest. Gone were the eyeglasses that rode down on his nose as he read the morning paper or finished the crossword puzzle. He lay in his only suit, as far as I knew, black with tiny white stripes.

No matter how closely I held the photo, I couldn't make out his face. I had to close my eyes to see that. The gap-toothed grin. Missing teeth in the back.

The man's miserly ways were legendary—5 percent was a good tip in his world. Once, when he was suffering from an abscessed tooth, he reluctantly let Carson drive him to the dentist's office. Carson related the story a year later. I knew it was true. It fit my father's template—the quintessential story of the old man.

"The doctor will have to decide what to do, but that looks pretty bad," the hygienist said.

"How much does he charge to pull a tooth?"

She told him.

"He came home, grabbed the grain alcohol from the cabinet, and went downstairs," Carson told me. "I didn't think too much about it. I was telling Mama what happened, having a slice of pie, when we heard him yell.

"I ran downstairs and found him at the workbench. The acetylene torch was still glowing, and there was a glass of alcohol on the saw. He'd heated up the pliers until they were white-hot; then he'd stuck them in a glass of water to cool, then into the alcohol. I guess to make sure everything was sterile. There was blood everywhere, all over his shirt and pants. Even the sawdust was wet with it. He dropped the tooth in the alcohol and smiled. I swear he was a tough buzzard."

In the pictures, people talked holding Styrofoam cups of coffee. My father lay at the back of the action, much like in life. He had brought people together, unknowingly, unwittingly, and he lay silent over the din of old friends.

In fact, he had been instrumental in bringing Karin to live near us. He saw Mr. Ashworth at the feed store one day and started up a conversation.

"Looking for a new lawn mower?" my dad said.

"Just dreaming," Robert Ashworth said. "Wife and I are talking about selling. Moving back here."

My father scratched his chin. "There's a new development going in near the post office. Have you heard about it?"

"Used to be the old Tunney place, wasn't it?"

A chance conversation. Pieces of information thrown back and forth. How different would my life be if that exchange hadn't happened?

The warden gave me the news about my father. I was escorted to his office, the statue of Christy Mathewson and Rogers Hornsby looking down on us. The warden was not a hardened, immovable man. He even offered me coffee or a bottle of water after he said, "Your father passed, son."

I just stared for the longest time, unable to speak.

"I got the news this morning. I wish I could let you attend the funeral, but I can't. Your brother told me they'll bury him at Mount Pleasant. He said you were familiar with it."

I nodded.

The warden opened a drawer and pulled out a notebook with a Wal-Mart sticker still on the back. $1.97. He ripped out a couple of pages and tossed the notebook across the desk. "We had a counselor here before the state cut funding. When he got these calls, he'd encourage the inmate to write out his feelings. I assume by what your brother told me that you and your dad were close."

"Yeah."

"If you'd like, I can open the chapel. Give you some time in there to remember. I could even call a chaplain if you want."

I gazed at Christy Mathewson's glove and wanted to cry, but I couldn't. "I'd like that. But I'd kind of like to be alone, if that's okay."

The warden leaned forward, his elbows on the huge monthly calendar that filled his desk. "I see a lot of men come through here. Most of them deserve what they get. But I've watched you the past few years, and I swear I don't know why you're here. I read the papers like everybody. I was horrified when it happened." He glanced at his brown, wrinkled hands. They looked like my dad's hands—the way I remembered them. "The guards say the same thing. I know terrible stuff happened in here, but somebody's been watching out for you."

The words washed over me like water. I had struck up a few friendships in Clarkston, but mostly I kept to myself.

The next day, a guard led me to the chapel and closed the door. I stood at the back and studied the crude cross carved into the lectern. It almost felt like I was back at the old white church, hearing echoes of "Standing on the Promises," "Trust and Obey," "'Tis So Sweet to Trust in Jesus."

Hosea. Joel. Amos. Obadiah. Jonah. Micah. Nahum. Habakkuk. Zephaniah. Haggai. Zechariah. Malachi.

I checked my watch. Pretty close to the service time back home. It struck me that it took death to get my mother and father out of the house. Other than doctors' visits and the grocery store, they remained inside, partly by their own choice, partly because of me.

Some couples dream of exotic travel in their old age. Europe. China. A cruise. My parents' dreams were confined to the home they had built together. They hibernated, content to see the world from a couple of La-Z-Boys, underneath a circling ceiling fan, staring at a 25-inch RCA. I had contributed to this choice. My crime was against *them*. I had created the polluted cloud that hung over their lives.

I tried to picture the casket. My father's pallid face. And my voice faltered, only a whisper, as I opened the notebook and read. "'Talk to me of a father's love, and I will tell you of baseball. Tell me of a tender touch or a hug that lasts in your memory, and I will kiss you with stories of our game. Walk with me in moonlight, tell me the ways your father expressed deep emotion, his innermost feelings, and I will tell you of pitchouts, squeeze bunts, and called third strikes.'"

As I read, my voice gained strength, and I settled into the comfortable rhythms of the spoken word, like a leisurely walk in the woods with my father.

"'The women of my life—my mother, my girlfriends—have never been able to touch the part of me that yearns for the fresh smell of baseball. The finely mowed infield. Deep brown dirt and snow-white bases. The tough, pungent aroma of hickory and leather.

"'In the cool of the evening, when his work was done, my father and I played catch to the voices of Al Michaels and Joe Nuxhall. We groaned together through the 1971 season and rejoiced at the next and all the way to Oakland. I still hate Gene Tenace and Joe Rudi for taking that away from us, but it made the experience sweeter three years later when, in spite of Carlton Fisk, we beat the Red Sox in seven.

"'It wasn't the smell of my father's pipe lingering in the air or the winning and losing. It was the game itself, spread out before us a hundred times and more each year, the same yet changing. Baseball cast a spell that drew us together. Baseball was the closeness we shared. We were never able to express ourselves and enjoy each other fully, without reservation, except with baseball.

"'As a child, I had no idea how my father felt about his work at the chemical plant. I still don't know. I knew little about his childhood, the anguish of losing a mother and brother to the flu epidemic that spread through the hills, the abuse of a stepmother, why he chose my mother as his wife, and a thousand other questions I should have asked.

"'But I do know this: I know baseball. I know how he felt about the designated hitter, steroids, and the supposed asterisk by Roger Maris's name. Baseball became our connection, and each spring when the sirens called, I felt the link grow even deeper and stronger.

"'When I was a child and we partook of the blessed sacrament of spring training results, my father and I would coax the sun a little hotter, a little higher and brighter in our West Virginia sky. We trembled beneath that vast, blue canvas, knowing it was the same sky that looked down on the green diamonds of the major leagues.

"'In summer we sweated through each extra inning and blown save. We counted mosquitoes, jarred lightning bugs, and believed in our team. We were separated by years, tastes in music, food, clothes, and politics, but we delighted in baseball. We kept score-cards and statistics ready to recall the previous year's Cy Young Award winner, batting champ, or MVP.

"'Fall came and we praised the God who created pennant races. We cursed the demon of the season-ending groundout or pop fly. Baseball was the glue that bound our lives and kept them coming back to each other. Baseball was each tender word never spoken. It was a pat on the back, a whispered term of endearment.

"'The last morning we spent together, just before my sentencing, my father and I spoke the last words that passed between us. We talked about our walks in the woods—memories of walking sticks and an old dog. We talked about our town and the changes we'd seen, and we talked of baseball.'"

My chin quivered as I recalled his face. "'I have disappointed my father in so many ways. There are things I will never know and things he will never hear me say.'" A pause as a fleeting image floated through my mind, of father and son on a warm summer evening, throwing a baseball back and forth. "'You once said a man's life is a series of choices. Small decisions made every day that don't seem to matter. That nobody notices but you, if you even notice. Over time, those decisions are like raindrops, falling and filling the stream of a life. You believed the big choices were made in the small ones. If I had chosen differently in a thousand ways, maybe I wouldn't be here.'"

The door opened and the guard tipped his hat. "Just checking."

"I'm still here."

When the door closed again, I bowed my head. "'I'm sorry, Dad. I'm sorry I wasn't there to carry you. I'm sorry we didn't get to talk about the play-offs again. I hope one day you'll understand.'"

And then I began to cry.

7

Karin

I spotted Ruthie crossing the long parking lot, her legs moving like eggbeaters, a black purse as big as a small bison over her shoulder. We were in the middle of deciding whether to serve a Caesar or a Waldorf salad at the spring luncheon. I was dying inside. I hadn't slept in several nights, and my mind wandered. My personal Rome was burning while we debated salad dressing.

I excused myself and met Ruthie at the side door and guided her past the atrium toward my husband's office. He was at the hospital on a visit.

"I want you to do me a favor," she said when I closed the door. "I've been thinking about this for a while, and I think it would do us both good. Sit, please."

"Anything for you," I said. A little too quickly as it turned out.

"It's time for a trip."

"Trip?" As far as I knew, she didn't drive and hadn't expressed an interest in going anywhere farther than Wal-Mart since I'd met her.

"I'd like you to go with me up to Clarkston. It'll take us only three, maybe four hours. We can pack a lunch and stop at the Golden Corral for dinner. Wouldn't that be nice?"

The town's name had a faint ring to it, like a distant bell calling children home.

Ruthie squinted, trying to see something in me that obviously wasn't there.

"What's at Clarkston?" I said.

"I'm sure there are a lot of things, but the point of interest to me is the federal penitentiary."

"Penitentiary? Why would we —?"

"I've made the arrangements. We'll go next Tuesday. I talked with your husband, and he thinks it's a good idea."

"You talked with Richard?"

Ruthie leaned close, and I could see my reflection in her Coke bottle glasses. "We've known each other awhile. I consider you a good friend. Do you trust me?"

"Of course I do, but —"

"Then go with me to Clarkston. I'll drive us. There's something we need to find out together."

"What? Are we going to see someone?"

"Not someone. *Him*. This fellow you've talked about. Don't you think it's time you saw him? talked things over?"

My mouth filled with cotton. The meeting about the spring luncheon suddenly had greater appeal. "I don't see . . . I mean, I do trust you, but I don't see what this has to do . . ."

"Karin, there's something missing in your life. Something you're not seeing. I believe deep down you know that. I've known it since I met you."

"I'm a married woman. You know as well as I do that feelings — old feelings — get stirred up if you let them. And the last thing I want to do is jeopardize what I have —"

"You don't have to talk with him if you don't want to. I'll do the talking. You can just sit in the corner and look pretty."

"Talk about what? What possible good could come from this?"

Ruthie drew even closer. "There's something real going on

inside you. Do you feel the unease? I told you God was stirring your pot, leading you into something deeper. Maybe taking you down a road where you didn't want to go."

Of course there was something wrong. Terribly wrong. But only God knew. I was still on the outside looking in.

"You're hiding. You're doing what I used to do when the Jehovah's Witnesses showed up."

"What?"

"I'd see two people heading up the driveway, Bibles in hand. I'd hide in the bathroom and let my dog bark until they went away."

"I can't imagine you being afraid of arguing the Bible with them."

"I wasn't afraid of them. I was afraid of *me*. What I might not know. What answers I didn't have."

What this had to do with me and a trip to Clarkston, I couldn't piece together.

Ruthie opened her purse and pulled out a Kleenex. Then she placed the black behemoth on the floor as a knight might shed his coat of armor and sword and took off her glasses. She rubbed the lenses, then stuffed the tissue back in her purse. "I don't get direct revelation. I told Richard that. I don't want anybody thinking I'm so close to the Almighty that he talks to me, but I got an impression last night that won't leave me alone. A feeling about this fellow. Clarkston's a place you need to go, and I want to be there when you walk in."

I shook my head. "I appreciate what you're doing. I really do. But you know how busy a time this is. And I have children. The responsibilities at the church are enough for me to say no to this, but with the kids . . ."

"I talked it over with the preacher. He said he would work everything out. You can be gone the whole day. Why would you want to pass up such good company? And the trees and hills this time of year are just sprouting green."

I had settled into a good life, a busy life, one that made me feel important, as if I were holding up four pillars of my little world, and if any of them moved the slightest, the whole thing would come tumbling down. But I couldn't remember the last time I had slept the whole night with my husband. I also couldn't remember when we had last made love.

"Well, if you don't want my help, I'll understand," Ruthie said.

"Did he put you up to this? Richard?"

Ruthie pursed her lips and cocked her head at me. "I'm going to Clarkston next Tuesday. I've set up the meeting with the people there. If you want to get on board the Ruthie train, you'd best be making your decision."

"Wait," I said as she reached the door. "If I come with you, will you come to the luncheon?"

She squinted.

"The Lord told me you needed to come," I said, managing a smile.

"You come with me, and I'll make sure it's a spring luncheon those hyenas in there will never forget."

Later that night, while the children were occupied, Richard asked how my day had gone, a fresh newspaper folded under his arm. I told him Ruthie and I had met in his office at the church and what she'd asked.

"I think it would probably be good for you to go," he said.

"You're not jealous? You're not afraid that . . . ?"

He put an arm around me. "I trust you, Karin. Who knows? Old feelings may come up. That's normal. But maybe they need to."

8

Karin's Journal

I remember the first day I saw Will. It was sixth grade, back when that was the top rung of elementary school. My family had moved a few miles east from the country to town. Wild, wonderful Dogwood, the gateway to the end of the world. No stoplight. One grocery store. Two gas stations directly across from each other on Route 60. The water treatment plant that sent a haze over the town.

I wore shiny shoes with buckles, socks to the knees, a ribbon in my hair, and a dress I held down during recess. I was trying hard to fit in with the others, but my clothes set me apart. Most girls wore jeans or shorts. I was so happy in that outfit, so secure and full of joy. Others stole the joy, and I returned home determined to mute my beauty as much as possible.

The instant Will walked through the door of the classroom, my face flushed. He had an air of confidence that none of the others had. A gentleness. An awareness of others. His body already lanky, his fingers already calloused and hardened by farm work, he glided into his chair instead of collapsing like the others.

Will wasn't what anyone would call handsome, at least the way it was defined back then. There were slight imperfections:

his hair was too short, his clothes not in style—a product of life on a farm—and his ears were a bit large. He looked like Alfred E. Neuman without the overbite or goofy face.

But there was something about him that transcended outward definition or judgment. An innate sense of himself. He was the kind of boy who carried dreams in his torn back pocket—dreams others could never hope to see. Other boys fixated on pocketknives and bicycles and minibikes, but Will traded in the future. Whether that future was far away from the steep hills that locked the town in its own shadowy world or just down the road, I couldn't tell. But I had no doubt, even in the sixth grade, that Will Hatfield would grab freedom by the throat and one day travel far. I could tell by the way he thumbed through his math book. I could tell by the excitement in his eyes when we studied science or art or English.

The teachers could tell it as well, and he endeared himself to them by remembering their birthdays and actually completing his homework.

I studied his shy movements around the other girls. He seemed at home on the baseball diamond, not bossing kids around or yelling at inept play but quietly, confidently attacking the game. He ran the bases of my dreams—he still does—his jeans sagging rounding second, tufts of dust pluming from the base paths, perfectly tucking his left leg under his right and sliding under the tag at third.

He looked at me that first day and flashed a smile—and took my breath away. He didn't look again all day. When the teacher, an ancient woman with black cat-eye glasses, called on him to read, I followed along on the page. His voice was strong and deep, and the only flaw I found in it was the high-pitched, cackling laugh. When he thought something was funny, everybody knew it. He'd throw his head back and laugh with abandon. Other kids made fun of it, even imitated him, but he either didn't notice or didn't care.

Two days later, the class bursting at the seams, the principal appeared with a piece of paper and read the names of those who would journey to the new building. An extra class with a younger teacher. Mine was not on the list. His was. It was our first separation but not the last.

Sometimes I saw Will on the playground or in the field, but our paths rarely crossed. He rode the bus, miles back into the hills. I lived three blocks from school. I ate hot lunch or walked home to eat with my mother. He brought a brown paper sack and ate outside between innings, except when it rained and he sat on the steps outside the gym under the eaves.

Though Will seemed mostly disinterested in me, I caught him stealing glances. During games, class performances, or in gym class, which we shared, I saw him look my way and smile.

I thought of passing a note, but that seemed too forward. Maybe I could tell a friend who could tell one of his friends, but that seemed too desperate.

Our silence lasted until the spelling bee. I found myself one row ahead of him, a chair to the left, and saw him in my peripheral vision if I turned my head slightly to the right. Each time I did, he was looking at me, studying my hair, my back, my dress. It would have been even more exhilarating if I hadn't been so competitive. Spelling was my thing. I had a natural sense of words and how they were correctly used, put together. In first grade I could hear a word and figure out how to spell it.

And this crowd wasn't exactly much competition. I had memorized forward and backward the list of words the *Herald-Dispatch* gave out to contestants, knew every word and pronunciation and the origins of most. In the first round, six of the thirty-four participants misspelled their words, and everyone moved to fill in their seats.

Through the fourth round there were only ten of us left. In the fifth round, four more dropped out and Will took his place beside me. I glanced at him, smiled, and focused on the teacher pronouncing the words.

"*Conscience*," the teacher said.

It was the easiest word in the book. Just add *con* with *science*. "C-o-n-s-c-i-e-n-c-e."

"Correct."

Everyone clapped. Then it was Will's turn.

"Your word is *rhythm*," the teacher said.

Sweat formed on the back of his neck, and he pulled his right arm close to his body with his left hand. He seemed almost wounded. "R-h-y-t-h-m."

The audience applauded until it was just the two of us. Chairs were removed and we stood together, closer than we'd ever been before.

"I'm sure you're going to win," I said, smiling. Confident.

Will leaned over and whispered something I couldn't make out over the applause. "What did you say?" But the audience was quiet now, and I focused on the teacher.

I spelled *congratulate* correctly and stepped back.

He smiled at me.

"*Belfry*," the teacher said. "Where the bells are."

"B-e-l-l-f-r-y."

A tinny bell rang.

I spelled *proclamation* correctly and the crowd applauded.

Will didn't slump his shoulders or shove his hands into his pockets. He simply reached out a hand. I offered one in return and he squeezed it gently. "You're really good," he said. "You deserved to win."

"You'll beat me next time," I said.

After school, as I walked home savoring the pleasure of the medal I wore on my sweater, I heard someone behind me in the tall grass.

I turned, saw Will's face, and my heart fluttered. "I thought you rode the bus."

"Need the exercise."

I knew that wasn't true. He would have to walk several miles to get home this way. "You can still catch your bus."

Will shrugged. "Not today."

He caught up with me and we walked side by side past the baseball field, the rusted backstop, and down toward the creek that led to the road. Water lapped over rocks and trickled through the town, and I wondered where the water would stop flowing, if it would find the Mud River and then the Ohio and eventually the Mississippi. Then the ocean. Our lives are like that, filled with thoughts that swim like minnows.

"You knew how to spell *belfry*," I said.

He stopped and picked up a stick, broke it, and handed me half.

I didn't know what to do, so I held it and looked at his eyes. There was something there, something I didn't see in any other sixth grader.

"Got mixed up when the teacher said it was where the bells are," he said.

"No way. You missed on purpose."

Will climbed the steep bank, holding out a hand for me. He moved effortlessly, gliding, his legs as strong as fence posts. "Come on. I'll race you."

"I can't race in these shoes," I said.

He cackled. "No, with these. Throw yours in."

We tossed the sticks in, and they landed in a quiet pool near the metal drain underneath the road. The sticks swirled in the circling water, touching each other slightly, then slowly moved toward the rippling water and rocks.

"I'm going to beat you twice today." I giggled and clapped.

He laughed and we watched the water draw our boats away,

past the sandbar, skittering over rocks and chugging out of sight.

He grabbed my hand and started down the hill. "Following them is the most fun."

But we had been so engrossed in what was before us that we didn't hear footsteps behind us.

"Karin?" my mother called. "You come on home now."

I turned, embarrassed. My cheeks flushed and something inside said I was bad, disobedient. Or maybe that *he* was bad. I grabbed my books from the dirt and hugged them tight. "Mama, I won the spelling bee today!"

She gathered me in and we walked home. I beamed, showing her the medal, and she fawned over it. When we reached the driveway, Mama looked back and stared. I had seen that look many times before. Once in a store in Charleston when I walked too close to some glass figurines. Eyes that communicated what words never could.

Stay away from my daughter, trash, she seemed to say.

It wasn't until I was inside that I looked at the road through the front window. Will had turned to walk the dusty road home. At the top of the hill, he veered left and cut through a field. He would have to traverse a few of them and cross the creek as well. His missing the word angered me, as if he had snatched my victory and was getting satisfaction out of it by following me home.

I went to sleep that night thinking of the bobbing, floating sticks and how they were like our lives. Carried along by a current bigger than either of us, oblivious to the obstacles ahead.

9

Karin

I rolled down the passenger-side window and let the wind blow through the car, fluttering my hair. It gave me a sense of freedom I hadn't felt in a long time. Kids in car seats don't like strong wind nor do husbands with receding hairlines.

In one long conversation we'd had on the lawn, Ruthie, through her genial poking and prodding of the soul, helped me see how much I had become a prisoner of small things. ChapStick. Tic Tacs. A favorite pen. A television program I simply couldn't miss. Air-conditioning.

"You can measure your life by the things that control you. People's reactions, for instance," she said.

At that moment in the car, I did not care a bit about my hair, the way my blouse flapped in the breeze, or that we looked like such an unusual pair. Ruthie sensed it, I think, and smiled as she rolled her window down. It made me think of the tune "I'll Fly Away," because that's what I thought her hair would do.

"How does it feel?" Ruthie said.

"Amazing," I said. "Free. I get so caught up with what to pack in the kids' lunches each day when they usually just throw the whole thing away. Are you sure you don't want me to drive?"

"Just relax for a while. I packed us a nice lunch. But we do need something to drink, and I see the gas gauge is a little low."

The Exxon station was just ahead, and Ruthie pulled up beside an empty pump. I got out and started the pump while she headed for the convenience store. She asked what I wanted to drink and I told her.

"I'll pay for the gas," she yelled over her shoulder.

I pressed the right buttons, and the pump numbers sped by. I collected some trash out of the backseat. The garbage can was full. A few ambitious bees flew sorties around a Dairy Queen cup, reminding me of the hornet's nest when I was a kid.

"The can over here is empty, ma'am," someone said behind me. "I can take that for you."

It was a thin man in a gray shirt, his hands and fingernails dark and grimy. He reached for my trash, and something passed between us, a recognition.

"Karin? Is that you?"

I handed him the trash. "Yes. I'm sorry; do I know you?"

"Arron Spurlock. You used to—"

"Arron?" I gasped.

"You used to babysit my little sisters, Doris Jean and Judy." He touched my shoulder and smiled as wide as the New River Gorge.

Being the oldest, Arron should have been named after his father and grandfather. In some families, names are passed down like old socks and whoever seems to fit them best keeps them. But Arron's mother was the biggest Elvis fan on the planet, and though she had trouble with her spelling, she named him Arron Pressley Spurlock. He had become "Elvis" for obvious reasons.

"I remember it like it was yesterday," I said, looking from head to toe. "It's been so long since I've seen you. You sure have grown up."

"Yes, ma'am, I guess so." He looked at me curiously, as if

becoming a mother or the wife of the local pastor was as foreign to him as Thai food.

"What is it?"

Arron waved a McDonald's bag and smiled. "It's nothing. I just didn't expect to see you here. I'm glad I did."

"How are your parents? They well?"

"Tolerable, I guess. At least my mom. She has pleurisy, so it keeps her inside most of the time. Dad passed a few years ago."

"Arron, I'm so sorry. I hadn't heard."

"Well, he had the black lung."

"And your sisters?"

He rolled his eyes. "She's still Doris Jean. Always will be, I guess. Judy's married and moved to Akron with her husband. She has a couple of kids now."

Ruthie came out of the store carrying a plastic bag that weighed more than she did. She listed to the right, and I was surprised she didn't tip over. I introduced Arron, and Ruthie smiled and shook his hand. He wiped his hands on his pants twice before clasping hers, but she didn't seem to mind.

"Let me help you put those things in your car," he said, opening the back door and taking the plastic bag.

"They don't make any like you in a slightly older model, do they?" Ruthie said.

Arron blushed. "No, ma'am, but I got a few uncles."

"Maybe I should meet them."

"Yes, ma'am." He shut the door and stood back, nervously looking at the two of us. "So where are you lovely ladies heading today?"

I answered before Ruthie could open her wrinkled mouth. "We've planned a day trip to Clarkston. It was Ruthie's idea."

At the word *Clarkston*, Arron looked like I had said Auschwitz or Hiroshima. "That's about four hours from here, isn't it?" he said, quickly recovering.

"Not the way we drive," Ruthie said. "Three and a half at the most as long as the smokies don't get us."

There was an awkward silence, and Arron glanced at his watch, then at the tinted front window of the store. "Well, I better be getting back to work." He touched the brim of his hat. "Nice to see you again, Karin."

We were a mile down the road, almost ready to hit the interstate, when Ruthie asked about Arron's family. I told her about Mr. Spurlock and how mystified I was that my mother hadn't given the news. "She usually tells me about every birth and death in the county, or I see it in the paper."

"Maybe she did and you just forgot," Ruthie said. "You were probably busy with those babies of yours. The whole world could have exploded when I was in the middle of my pregnancies and I wouldn't have known it."

She was right. I seemed to have the ability to focus fully on one thing, to narrow my life to certain tasks. At times I had to turn the radio off just to do the dishes. "Do you think that's why I have such a difficult time sleeping?" I said after we turned onto the interstate. "I focus on one thing and can't let it go until I'm finished?"

Ruthie shrugged. "That's one way we cope with life. Makes it a little easier, I guess. Breaking it down to bite-size portions. You could have a lot worse things, if you ask me." She opened her purse and pulled out a PayDay. I pulled the wrapper off for her, peanuts dropping on the front seat, and she picked at them like a bird taking communion. "One of life's little pleasures. You want half?"

I shook my head and marveled that like a child she could take such delight in the candy bar. The night before, Darin had run into the kitchen and hugged his father. "I got new toothpaste!" he yelled. You would have thought he'd just won a trip to some exotic island. Later, he begged and whined, "But, Mom, I'm hungry for brushing my teeth!"

"You get much sleep last night?" Ruthie said as she chomped, the nougat sticking to her uppers and making her sound like some cartoon character.

I watched cars speed around us as Ruthie stayed about 20 mph under the speed limit. "No, I spent the night with a quotation book and Max Lucado."

"Don't tell his wife."

I laughed. "You know what I mean. I get so tired that my eyes droop. I feel like I can't stay awake another second, and then suddenly I'm awake and all I can think about is falling asleep again. By then, it's over. I've lost the battle and have to do something else."

"I don't think I've ever met anyone yet who's died of lack of sleep. Do you have a lock on that closet door of yours so nobody can walk in on you?"

"When it's really bad, I'll lock it, but most of the time I want to be available in case the kids get up and wander. That's one good thing about it. I'm always available."

"Your husband ever stay up with you?"

"He's such a heavy sleeper. I don't think he understands. It's like trying to explain the ocean to someone who's never seen it. How can you describe something so immense? or the way the sand feels?"

We eased into a rhythm of driving and talking and silence. I tried the radio once, an AM station giving the news about a highway fund being blocked at the capitol. The former governor was under suspicion of fraud. An investigation into three robberies at gentlemen's clubs in the valley.

Our tires hummed on the road and provided the soundtrack for our trip, background music for the conversation. As we passed another of the seemingly endless patches of green trees coming to life, Ruthie began singing. I thought I had experienced it all until I heard her blast out "Take Me Home, Country Roads."

I joined in, which is what you have to do as a native of the Mountain State. Some people stand at the singing of the "Hallelujah Chorus." West Virginians stand, at least in their hearts, at the singing of "Country Roads." I remember the first time I heard it on a radio station, though the song seemed like it had always been there.

There's something peaceful and melancholy about the way the words and the music coalesce, like the dirt roads that crisscross my state, that wind through the hills and rocks and trees and make their dusty way home. West Virginia has a soul that remains untouched by the outside world. No matter how many chain stores and restaurants try to take up residence, they seem strangely out of place. There are parts of the state where it seems no human being has set foot. Arrowheads still wash up on creek banks, remnants of life burrowing deep into the land. Take a lungful of air, especially in the spring, and you take in a fecund aroma of history. This is not the tidal plain smell of shrimp and salt water but an ambrosial aroma of manure and wet, fertile ground waiting for someone to turn it over and plant. The ground screams to be worked by farmers, yearns for the violation of the till and plow. To have seeds planted deeply in verdant soil.

Most people know West Virginia from news stories of tragedy. The torch the state holds is alcoholism and the lottery, and those who take but a cursory look will see only the vacant stares of children from a front porch littered with washing machines and spare tires. A bad Foxworthy joke. A redneck, hillbilly, barefoot, incestuous, drunk, blaze orange, country music, cigarettes-rolled-in-your-shirtsleeve, tobacco-chewing, NASCAR-loving cutout.

The Deep South has its poster children of Confederate flag-wavers and men in white sheets. West Virginia, since its inception a state not allied with the South, carries its emblems on its sleeve, the curving, unending back roads that seem to lead nowhere to those on the outside.

But not every road has an end.

A state defined by its political divisions—a Democrat, union stronghold for economic reasons, but flag-waving, committed to any war our country decides to fight.

Some think of West Virginia as a place they need to escape. But most people here, if they have a steady job, a good church, and a satellite dish, wonder why anyone would want to leave.

"You thinking about him?" Ruthie said, snapping me from my self-induced trance.

I told her my thoughts about our state, the people, the past, and the future. I should have known Ruthie was more concerned about the present.

"What's your heart telling you right now?" she asked.

"That what we're about to do is scaring me half to death. When I think of actually *seeing* Will again after all this time . . ."

"You told me about him watching out for you once. Were there other times he helped you?"

"I suppose there were. I think he was always watching out for me."

"And you were attracted to him?"

"Yes and no. He seemed safe. He had a certain promise when he was younger, but as I compared him with others in high school, he seemed more like the kind of guy you went for if you wanted two kids and a trailer. You know? I measured people by what kind of chances they'd take, how far I thought they'd get out of the hollow."

"He didn't look like he'd move far?"

"Right. We talked once on a school trip—he drove his dad's car and I didn't want to ride the bus. He wouldn't turn on the radio. He wanted to talk."

"What did he want to talk about?"

"Plans after high school. College, that kind of thing. I said I wanted to go as far away as possible."

"To get away from your parents?"

"From everything this town had done to me. Stifled me. Held me back."

"Isn't it interesting this is where you wound up?" Ruthie said. "Do you see it differently now?"

I checked the side mirror at the cars in a line behind us. "It's ironic that I'd end up in a church I hated as a kid, yes. It's ironic I'm fighting the same type of ladies I remember my mother fighting. But I kind of feel like I've come full circle and I'm not afraid to . . ."

"Face the truth?" Ruthie said quickly.

I looked in the mirror again.

Ruthie craned her neck. "What is it? What do you see?"

"There's a dark car hanging back a few hundred yards. I thought I saw a car like that at the Exxon station—around the side."

"You sure you just don't want to answer my questions?"

I smiled and watched her give the gas pedal a slight touch.

Ruthie ran her hands across her knees, knocking peanut crumbs to the floor. "Are you afraid you'll still have feelings for him?"

I glanced at her and frowned. "I have children. I have a good husband. And my rear end is widening. Oh, and I've made a promise to be faithful. You know, as much as the rest of the world says it doesn't, that still means something. I don't care if I had so many feelings my toes curl—it doesn't change the facts or my choices."

"I'm glad to hear you say that. I wouldn't have encouraged you to come with me if I didn't know it."

"You would have come by yourself?"

She nodded. "There are some things I have to find out."

"What?"

Ruthie turned. "You know, I think that *is* the car from the Exxon station."

"Stop it!" I laughed. "What horse do you have in this race? What do you get out of it?"

"I know some old women who can't keep their traps shut for

two minutes, but not this old bird. There are some things you'll just have to guess." She adjusted her seat belt away from her wrinkled neck and sighed. "At what point did you give up on this guy?"

I reached up and grabbed the handhold above the door. "I guess it was right around the time of the accident."

"Did you go to his trial?"

"No. Mom and Dad didn't even let me see the paper. They were really shaken. That someone we knew could do such a thing was a shock."

"Your parents knew you and Will were friends."

I chuckled. "He used to come by the house and talk with my dad about cars. He even helped install a back patio once. Oh, Ruthie, you should have seen that boy without a shirt on. Even his abs had abs."

When we'd had a good laugh, she tilted her head back on the headrest. "So they liked him?"

"They were a bit wary of him. I don't think they ever considered us a match. There were a lot of other prospects, boys with brighter futures and ambitions. I think they saw his road a little limited."

"A dirt road that led back into the hills."

"Exactly."

"Well, sometimes you can be right about that. Did he ever say what he wanted to do with his life?"

"I remember him talking about a piece of land his father had given him. Back on top of the ridge. He said it would be the perfect place for a house and to raise a family. I thought it was strange at the time that he was talking that way, thinking about a family and a house instead of going out and conquering the world."

"Some people know what they want early."

"I guess. But look where it led him. Look where he is now."

Ruthie pulled off the interstate. "There's a rest area here. I have to tinkle like a big dog."

While Ruthie went to the bathroom, I found a phone and called home. I already missed my little family. The morning is always the most difficult, with backpacks and lunches and assignments. It's so hard for me to throw away any of the papers they've worked on, and half the ones I toss I wind up fishing out of the trash and putting in their baby boxes. I want them to remember these happy days trying to learn the alphabet or struggling with spelling.

The phone just rang, and I pictured Richard at the store with Tarin, buying diapers and applesauce. *Such a good man to let me go,* I thought. *But why doesn't he feel threatened?*

Ruthie returned and soon we were heading north again, into the teeth of a budding spring and new life everywhere we looked.

"Busting out all over, isn't it?" she said.

"It's beautiful." The smell of lilacs was overpowering.

We arrived at Clarkston a half hour early and parked near a small roadside picnic table surrounded by maples. It was one of those flat scenes, almost like a picture in some newspaper report about government-subsidized farmland. Through the trees I could make out the hazy silhouette of the prison, surrounded by fences and razor wire. I expected something bigger, I guess. A complex of buildings or guards with dogs, but the structures looked prefabricated, like they'd been thrown together in a few days.

Ruthie walked carefully over the uneven ground carrying a brown paper sack of chicken salad sandwiches and fresh greens. She sat daintily, propped her cane against the end of the table, and opened a plastic container of cucumbers in white vinegar.

I watched her enjoy the food, standing because I was tired of sitting, but she patted the bench and wiped a bit of potato salad from the corner of her mouth. (It was the best potato salad in history—I found out by spreading some on a saltine.) I sat, my back against the rough edge of the tabletop. Limbs hovered over us like arms reaching down.

"I've been thinking about that dream of yours," she said.

I faced her. Thoughts of the prison and my family and how far from home we were and who was waiting on the other side of the fence melted away. "What dream?"

"The one you told me about. With you and the baby and your father."

It had been nearly a week since I'd had that dream. It only changed in small ways. One night I would notice a picture on a table or the upright piano in the living room. Another night I would catch a shadow of someone slipping out of sight into a back bedroom.

"Do you think you know what it means?" My heart would not have beaten harder had a serial killer escaped through the razor wire and headed straight for us.

Ruthie crossed her legs in that prim way, nearly wrapping the left completely around the right like a wisteria vine. "What is it that bothers you most about the dream?"

I closed my eyes for a moment. There was no sense in being aloof. By this point I was convinced she could see into my thoughts whether I wanted her to or not. "It's my indifference. That I don't really care for the child. I love my children. That's what bothers me most. I'm not really ready to have another, but if that's what God—"

Ruthie held up a hand. "Don't jump the gun on me. And remember, I'm not saying this is the best interpretation or the right one. But I'm convinced God sometimes wants to communicate outside the usual box."

"Tell me."

"Have you ever thought that maybe this baby might be something else entirely? something other than a child?"

I hadn't. It seemed so simple and clear that this was about a real child. "I'm listening" was all I could say.

She folded her hands, as if she were about to pray. "What if this child represents something else about your life? Would you be open to that?"

"Yes, but what?"

"Think about it. You bring a child to your father. He nurtures it, cuddles it, holds it, and you walk away."

"Ruthie, would you just—?"

"What if this man who is supposed to be your father is not really your father?"

"My husband? Richard? Could that be it? That I don't really care as much for my children as I thought? I don't understand. . . ." A new thought crept in. "What if it's Richard? What if it means he's only interested in new things? I've grown up and the baby . . . You don't think he's having an affair, do you?"

She howled. When she was done, she wadded up her trash and stuffed it back inside the paper sack. Then she stood, using her cane, and walked to the waste can.

"That's it? You're not going to tell me?"

Ruthie pointed a crooked finger at me. "I want you to use that head of yours. Think about it. The baby is not a baby, and your father is someone else."

"But if you—"

"You can't rush these things, Karin. You've had this dream for a long time, and the ground has been stirred up even longer. When you're ready to hear it, when your head and your heart come together, you'll know."

"That's not fair. If you know something, why won't you tell me?"

"I know enough to know this is not the right time. I'll let you noodle on it a little more. Besides, there's a fellow in that building over there, and I don't want to keep him waiting."

I couldn't help staring at the building and wondering. "I'm not sure this is such a good idea."

She patted my shoulder as she passed on her way to the car. "You'll be fine, girl. We've come this far. Let's see what the old boy has to say."

10

Danny Boyd

What's the hardest thing about losing your sisters? my counselor said. He had come out with me to walk the hills where I felt a lot more comfortable. I don't much like rooms inside anymore.

I guess it's the silence, I said after a while. Not hearing all the squeals and the fighting over who owns which doll and stuff like that. Comparing Christmas presents. None of my mama's high-heeled shoes striking the hardwood floor when they get into her closet and dress up. And not hearing Mama laugh while she's standing at the door looking right at them and then hollering at them to get out of there.

I don't know what it is about walking that kind of loosens up the tongue, but it does. We hiked up a ridge overlooking the town, and I got a feeling in the pit of my stomach that things were going to change. That everything was going to be all right with some time and distance. Then I saw the road and what my mother had done.

He must have seen something come over me because he asked what was wrong. He said the word *troubling*—which has to be a counselor word. I would have said *bothered* or *who put the burr under your saddle* or something like that.

I pointed to the curvy black snake that slithers through our town—the main road leading in and out. In a clear spot where no trees blocked our view was a kind of a shrine to my sisters. Friends of the family and people who knew about the accident had started it. Little kids brought stuffed animals and flowers and made signs saying We Miss You. Every few weeks the highway department came and took it all down, but Mama would be right back there the next day. On Valentine's Day, there were red hearts and roses. At Christmas she wrapped up fake presents and tied them to the guardrail. Their birthdays were the worst. She'd put the number they'd be that year on a poster and draw a cake.

Some people probably thought Mama was losing her mind, but I kind of think she was trying to keep it. Others probably thought she wanted everybody to remember her babies and how old they'd be. To keep it before them and remind them that it could be their babies under the earth. But I don't think so. I think *she* wanted to remember. I think she was worried she was going to get busy and look up one day and catch herself not thinking about them for once.

One day I heard Mama talking with a lady who came over just to sit on the couch and drink coffee. Mama wasn't bawling or nothing. She was talking like she'd talk about what kind of meat she was going to cook for dinner or who was getting married or getting a divorce.

I swear, sometimes I forget and start worrying about how we'll send them to college, she said. And then it'll hit me fresh. It's all I can do not to bust out crying when I see a school bus. All the kids in their classes are growing up and having parties, and it's like my kids are stuck in time, their faces never changing. She was holding Karla's picture in her lap, rubbing her face with a thumb.

Maybe you should move away from here, the other woman said. I can't remember her name. Put some distance between you and the memories.

Sometimes I think that's a good idea. I really do. But then I think that there's not a place on earth where I could get away from the memories. There's no island far enough away that I could forget my kids and what happened.

Maybe it would help your marriage.

There're some things that can't be helped. They just are. You either live with them or you don't. Simple as that.

There's nothing simple about it.

You got that right. You certainly got that right.

11

Karin

Slowly, over time, I told my story to Ruthie. I did not reveal the conglomeration of boys I had known too well but the one boy, who seemed so right and so wrong. Ruthie said the tongue held the power of life and death, and it felt like if I didn't tell all, I would die.

"Tell it, then," Ruthie said.

It was a scene that came back all too often—a scene I would rather forget, but it does show Will. In my mind were images and bits of conversation from the high school homecoming dance. Junior year. I wore a billowy, pink dress with lace above my cleavage. Not that there was much but just above what there was. My mother had helped pick it out, thrilled I was going with Eddie Buret, the son of the police chief and a respected family in our community.

Eddie stood next to me in front of our fireplace, both sets of parents clicking cameras, lights flashing.

Eddie's mother smiled and shook her head. "She looks so much like you, Cecilia."

"Do something funny," Eddie's dad said.

"Kiss her," my father said.

Everyone laughed when Eddie did. Everyone but me. On the outside I smiled, but on the inside something died. I did not want to ride in the same car with him, let alone kiss him. I cursed myself for agreeing to go, but I was a good girl and didn't want to hurt his feelings.

Things didn't get better at the dance. Eddie kept getting too close, dancing faster and with more intensity, sweating, looking at me knowingly, like we both wanted the same thing. I was glad when he asked if I wanted to go for a walk. Our gymnasium was an oven of hormones. I wanted to go home, but I settled for a stroll.

Eddie went to get us drinks and Will appeared.

"I didn't know you were going to be here," I said.

"Student Council has to set up and take down," he said, smiling. "Thought I might as well have some punch."

He had let his hair grow longer. He wore an old black-as-night suit that could have been his father's or brother's. Shoes a little big, probably his father's. His tie was out of style by at least ten years, and he wore a little too much cologne.

"You want to dance?" he said.

"I just want to go home." I glanced around for Eddie. "I'm with this creep who thinks —"

"Ready, Karin?" Eddie said, coming up behind Will and bumping his shoulder. "Sorry about that. Clumsy me. Didn't realize you'd been let off the farm. Git all yore chores dun in time fer the big dayunce?" He snickered.

Will smiled, as if the words were toothpicks thrown by a two-year-old.

Then Eddie squinted and turned up his nose. "Do you guys smell something?" He looked down. "Hey, Will, you better check your shoes and make sure you didn't step in some cow pies on the way over."

By now others had gathered. A few girls who worshiped Eddie stared at me like I was the luckiest person on the planet.

"Come on, Karin. Let's get out of here," Eddie said. "The smell's getting to me."

Water rippled in the river by the baseball field, and the moon was a crescent shadow above. We walked in the muted light along the line of parked cars, Eddie waving at some football buddies who catcalled and whistled.

"Go get her, Eddie!"

"You kids be careful now."

"Be good or be good at it."

Eddie put his arm around me and guided me toward the covered bridge, a historic structure the town had placed on postcards for visitors, as if anyone in their right mind would sightsee here. Eddie was oblivious to my feelings, perhaps thinking geography could change the unease I felt inside.

He held my hand and pulled me onto the walkway attached to the bridge, overlooking the water. The handrail was rickety and looked as if any pressure would splinter it. This was a favorite spot of couples sneaking away for privacy during school hours, and I was surprised we were the only ones here.

Eddie spun me around and held me an arm's length away, gazing at me as if I were a steak smothered in barbecue sauce. "Karin, you're the most beautiful thing in the gym tonight. Do you know that?"

I tried to smile, tried to push my feelings down, but they kept coming up, like the gorge in my stomach. I rubbed my arms. "Can we go back? It's getting chilly."

"I can warm you up. Come here." He drew me to himself and kissed me for the second time that night. This was not the polite kiss at my house in front of our families; it was the kiss of an untamed tongue on an altar I had never knelt at before. His hands moved over me, and he shoved me against the bridge, his tongue inside my mouth.

I struggled to breathe. I tried to push him off, but his two-a-day practices over the summer and weight training in the fall had made his arms rock hard. "Stop!" I managed to mumble as he reached for the bottom of my dress.

A pair of headlights turned away from the road, and I realized why it was so quiet. Eddie had orchestrated the whole thing. His friends were keeping watch, turning people away so we could be alone.

I felt like a cornered animal, like a snake in one of the minnow traps we'd set in the creek. Bobby Ray and I would put pieces of bread inside, submerge the trap in a slow-moving part of the water, and come back a day later to pull up the fluttering, flicking minnows. But several times we found a snake inside the trap. It had eaten all the minnows and suffocated by its inability to escape.

"I'll tell your parents," I said, struggling.

"Hey, your dad *wanted* me to kiss you. I'm just obeying my authorities." He leaned in again, pressing me hard against the wooden slats, wedging a leg between both of mine.

A shard of wood pierced my dress and the skin underneath. I focused on that pain, shutting out the rest. Why had I gone with Eddie? I didn't even like him.

I tried to bring my knee up in a last, desperate attempt to get a point across. He locked his legs, and I wondered if this was a move his coach taught in the locker room.

"Feisty," he said, a guttural, earthy sound to his voice. "I didn't know you liked to play rough."

I struggled, telling him that God was watching us and trying to remember some verse to say that would get him to stop. Before I could, a shadow passed and Eddie fell back against the bridge. I caught my balance and turned away before hearing a sickening, bone-crunching sound. Then came a thump on the rickety boards.

I ran, hobbling on the asphalt with one shoe, one broken heel trailing.

When I reached his friends, they looked surprised. "Where's Eddie? What did you do?"

I kept running toward the gym and looked back to see guys on the bridge, gathered around a body. They helped Eddie up, like they were carrying him off the field after a broken play.

I opened the door and noticed a silhouetted figure on the hill overlooking the bridge. Clouds swept over him as he turned and walked into the night.

"Did you tell your parents?" Ruthie asked when I finished the story.

"I didn't tell anybody. I got a ride home from a girlfriend. Told her I didn't feel well."

"You had to see Eddie the next week."

I nodded. "He acted like nothing happened, although he had a hard time explaining the missing tooth and the bruises to his coach."

"Did you ever figure out who it was? Did Eddie figure it out?"

I turned from her, a wave of memories washing over me.

Ruthie put a hand on my shoulder. "I don't know what happened, Karin. I don't know the things you've seen, the roads you've stumbled down, but I do know God has brought you here and he's given you a desire. The old adage is to write what you know, and what you know seems pretty painful. Well, if that's what you've been given . . ."

"The memories take me places I don't think I can go. Things Richard doesn't even know. I could never tell."

"You have to face them at some point. Otherwise you'll be running the rest of your life. Is that what you want to do?"

"What if he finds out?"

"The preacher?"

"Yes. And what if—what if *he* comes back? Will. If I write the things I know, it might bring him back, and if that happens . . . Oh, Ruthie, I don't think I can look at him."

My body shook. We'd hit something subterranean with only one memory, and if this happened with each new chapter, I was going to die paragraph by paragraph.

"You need to stop worrying about everyone else and how they're going to react. You have to get that demon off your shoulder that's telling you what's safe and okay. Just open a vein. Let it spill out and we'll be the judge of it."

I remembered the quote by Nietzsche that I'd found in my closet, the one about looking into the abyss. I did not count on my memories being the monsters. I did not want them looking back at me.

I spent that night sobbing into my pillow, trying to muffle the anguish, unattended by my husband. Could he begin to understand? Would he have it within him to walk through this valley? Some people weep for things they don't understand. I weep for things I do and wish I didn't.

12

Will

I was staring at the clock in the visitors' room, watching the second hand glide along, but I was somewhere else. Funny how prison can confine you but can't make you live there. I've read *Rita Hayworth and Shawshank Redemption* fifteen times if I've read it once, and each time I cry. Not for myself or Andy Dufresne but for the lack of dreams in here. People live day to day, counting time until it's the only thing to count. Most people outside these walls live the same way. They wait for something to happen, something that tips them over the edge so they can start living. "When I finish school . . ." "When I get a new job . . ." "When I get a little more money . . ." The goals are endless. School. Marriage. Children. You can wait your entire life for something and when it finally comes forget why you wanted it.

It took time to adjust, but once I saw the possibilities and embraced Clarkston, I tried not just to exist but to *thrive*. Some saw it in me. Others resented the life in my eyes. The guards called me Will instead of by my last name like the other inmates.

A black guard with a thick African accent once said to me, "You seem freer in here than half the people I know out there."

Now the air felt stagnant and hot. Spring was on us and the

sun baked the room. It would be several weeks before the warden relented and turned the air-conditioning on in the newer part of the jail, and the men would complain and sweat and thrash against the unwritten rule that it wasn't turned on until mid-June.

Some men count the days until their release. I don't waste my time crossing squares off a calendar. I have an internal sense that things are changing. Soon I'll have paid my debt, and other than my mother, there's only one person I know I have to see.

You're going to be a great mom to your children when that time comes, I had written Karin in the first week. *Whoever marries you is going to be the most fortunate man on the face of the earth, and I can only hope that you'll wait for me. I'll understand if you don't feel the same way. I release you from any promise you've made, any unspoken desire, anything said in haste or in an unguarded moment. It sounds trite, but I will truly be happy if you find happiness. If you decide to wait for me, my joy will be doubled. If not, I'll still pray your husband treats you with gentleness and respect and will always realize that you are a treasure.*

My face burned when I thought of her reading those words. I wanted to crumple the paper and write something else, something about her counting the days until I was free. But that wouldn't be fair to either of us, and I knew, like with the farm kittens I held as a child, the more you cling to an animal, the more it wants its freedom. I have claw marks in my memory to prove that.

So I released her. Not as a calculated plot or ploy, not because it was the only way to get her to return, but because it was my true heart's desire that she be happy, fulfilled, and loved.

I reached an understanding there on that bed, listening to the sounds of men in the night. Like a burning campfire, I was either in or out. I would be either her passionate lover or nothing. I could not settle for some platonic friendship that danced at the edge of the truth. If I had to love her from a distance, I would. But if she allowed me in, I would love her wholly, with every fiber.

I clung to a dream — a vision of Karin, wind flying through her hair, her pale, freckled face upturned to the moonlight. Deep in the still West Virginia night, with the crickets chirping and fireflies rising from the earth, beacons to a new season of life, one night came back to me when we had been close.

She had unlocked a door and defenses had fallen. Maybe because she was so vulnerable and fragile? Whatever the reason, I held on to it as if it were life itself. Her laughter, her voice singing along with the radio, songs I would always associate with her, the hum of tires, the rush of wind, a touch. Lips pressing. Eyes closed. The soft hint of wine on her breath. The smallness of her back and shoulders — I had never known anything could feel so delicate, so alive.

My dream, my vision, ended there. I never received a reply to the letters. They dropped into a void, a bottomless pit, and never returned. Writing those letters was my first act of release, the first of many, ridding myself of the feelings and passion. It was my first act of love toward her. I hoped it would not be my last.

13

Karin

Palms sweating, I walked behind Ruthie through the metal detector. She had to put her cane through the machine and hold on to the sides. The machine beeped, and the guard made her go through again. When the alarm didn't stop, he used the wand and centered on a spot at Ruthie's side near her waist.

"You have anything under your dress, ma'am?" the guard said.

Ruthie had an attitude, and I was concerned she might say something we'd both regret.

She gave me a playful look, which was not a good sign. She looked straight at the guard and said, "I had my hip replaced a few years ago, young man. My doctor said there's a good chance it would drive security people crazy if I ever started traveling. Guess he didn't take prison into account."

"I'm going to need to frisk you, ma'am, just to be sure." The guard said it apologetically, like it was something he really didn't want to do.

Ruthie held up her arms, and soon we were both through.

"Do you need a wheelchair, ma'am?" the guard said.

"I'll let my feet do the walking, thank you," Ruthie said, but when we were at the other end of the hall, she looked like she wished she would have said yes.

Another guard led us to the visitors' room, but Ruthie couldn't keep up with him. Finally the guard just pointed. "Take a seat inside there. Your party will be on the other side of the glass."

"Is he there?" Ruthie said.

"Waiting on you, ma'am."

I took Ruthie's free arm and walked with her. Having her close gave me comfort, and I wasn't sure who was steadying whom as we walked.

We were halfway there when Ruthie spoke. "Been thinking it might be time you know my interpretation. Of the dream. You and the baby and your parents."

"Here? Now?"

"Good a time as any, don't you think?"

No, I don't think so. I'm about to see someone I haven't seen in more than a decade who changed the life of our town forever, who took my heart, my very life with him as he walked into this prison, and you pick now to . . .

"I guess so," I said.

Ruthie stopped and looked at her watch. It was a minute before eleven according to the gray clocks in the hall above us, but Ruthie ran on her own time.

"There's a reason your mother isn't in the dream," she began. "You and your mother are close; it would cloud things. But your father is more aloof in your life, so the fact that he's there for you and inviting makes it easier to see."

"Easier? What part of this is easy?"

"Have you ever seen the baby's face?"

I thought for a moment. "No. I can hear it. It coos and giggles and makes baby noises, but it's covered with a blanket when I'm holding it, and when it's on the floor, I never see its face."

She nodded. "It's not your child. Not one of your children or one of your future children."

"How do you know?"

Ruthie skirted the question. "It's just a theory, mind you, so I'm not saying—"

"Would you just tell me?"

She sighed. "What if the baby is you? Or better yet, what if this child represents your soul?"

I stopped breathing, dead in my shoes. The hallway spun with some realization. But what?

"Your father is intensely interested in your soul, even though you don't seem to be. You wrap it up and hold it tightly, not because you want to nurture it but because you don't want to see its reality. That it really is there."

"Soul, as in my spiritual side," I said, gasping the words.

"Soul, as in your being. What's at Karin's core. It's clear you don't care much about it, at least in the dream. If it weren't your father, if it were some babysitter or drug dealer, you'd hand it over. You think?"

"I don't know," I said, my voice catching. "What about my father? Who is he?"

"I think you know."

I struggled to swallow and choked out, "God?"

Ruthie nodded. "He cares a lot for that soul of yours. More than you know. More than you ever will or could. He's the one who made it in the first place. Makes sense he'd want to care for it, nourish it, cherish it. And he's willing to wait until you're ready, until you can bring everything to him. In the meantime, whether you realize it or not, he's there, acting like yours is the only one in the world."

My knees felt weaker than hers looked. "Why now? Why *here*? Why did you wait until—?"

"Timing is everything, my dear. It's no coincidence I waited till now because I didn't think you were ready before. I knew you weren't. That you came with me to this place, that you're willing to see this scoundrel or devil or lover is proof you're willing to open up a little and take a chance."

I recoiled from the thought. "Take a chance on what? On throwing my marriage away? my children? my life? I don't even know what I'm doing here. What *we're* doing here."

Someone stepped up behind us. A guard. "Is there a problem?"

"No," I said. "Just a discussion before we go inside."

"Better hurry it up." He pointed at the clock. "Time's wastin'."

"Ruthie, this whole thing scares me. What if I get in there and . . . ?"

She patted my arm with an arthritic hand that could have passed as the talon of some ancient bird. "Karin, do you trust me?"

"I have up until now, but I'm beginning to wonder why."

"Then you're going to have to trust me when you don't feel like it."

"I don't know if I—"

"I do." Ruthie said it forcefully, eyebrows furrowed, like she meant for it to sink deep into my soul. "I've divined the one dream you told me about, but I haven't figured out the other one."

That took my breath. "How do you know about the other one? I never told you."

She waved a hand. "Some dreams are written on our minds, and it takes years to figure them out. Others are written on our hearts, and it takes someone who loves us deeply to read them and tell us what they mean. There is a language on your heart I've been trying to translate ever since I met you. At first, it was just curiosity. Then the more I got to know you, the more I came to love you, the more I wanted to know." She pointed at the door. "There's an answer sitting in a chair in that room, separated from us by a thick wall of plastic. I am going to find out what is written

74

on that heart of yours because it's the only thing that will truly set you free. At least that's what I believe."

My heart would not be still. Something told me life would never be the same once we faced Will.

"Karin, I know this is good, but there's something I need you to do."

I wasn't sure what else she could ask. She had already driven me from my comfortable life. What more?

"Can you open that door for me?" she said.

14

Karin

Children are unaware of thorns.

I pushed Tarin's stroller to Ruthie's house, and Tarin caught sight of a rosebush in bloom and reached to grab it. I held her hand but picked a bud so she could smell it. "That'll hurt you if you touch the sticky parts," I said.

Ruthie's house was nestled in a sea of stucco and hot tubs, and its simplicity struck me. Ivy wandered around the chimney, and violets bloomed near the concrete porch. Inside was unbearably hot, but she didn't seem to notice. She had bathed before dinner and smelled of sweet talcum.

Ruthie poured two glasses of sparkling wine, and we ate a mouthwatering Parmesan chicken recipe she said had been in her family a hundred years. I think it was the first time I truly savored a meal.

"Food was never meant to be gulped," Ruthie would later say. "Food and family and friends are meant to be enjoyed *slowly*. Meals are a lot like life, fresh and hot and inviting. If you run through them, you miss a lot."

At some point in the evening, Ruthie asked about my love life.

"I'm married. I don't have time for love."

I thought she would laugh, but she waited, drawing me like some ingrown tide. Though I could not speak his name, I told her of a young man I had known, and the feelings I had pushed away suddenly returned.

"What happened to him?" she said.

"He went away and I settled for a good man."

"Have you ever spoken with him?"

I shook my head. "It's too late."

Somehow we got onto the topic of writing, something I had done in childhood. Ruthie handed me a leather-bound notebook and said she wanted me to fill it with everything I could remember.

That night I began writing again, but I mostly filled the book with her words, her homespun wisdom. When I met her for lunch and forgot the notebook, I wrote on paper napkins or on the backs of children's menus. I could not get enough of her words, and there didn't seem to be anything she would hold back from me.

Some time later she asked what I'd written, and I opened the book to her words and shared my thoughts.

Ruthie laughed from the gut, put her elbow on the table, and propped her chin on the back of her hand. "I think we've finally found something."

"Really? Like what?"

"Finally hit a nerve. All this time we've been dancing around the edges of your life, and we finally find it in this journal of yours."

"You mean, writing? You think—"

"It's never only one thing, honey. It's not just writing or the idea of putting something on paper for others to read. There's something more here."

The wrinkles on her face came into focus as she leaned forward. "You struggle. You fight and you claw inside that head of yours. You wrestle with God, with the idea that he actually cares for you, with the place your children have brought you, and a thousand other things. There's something about your struggle others need to know. That they'll benefit from."

"I don't understand."

Ruthie stood and picked up one of the glass objects her husband had created. A dogwood bloom. Two long petals, two short, like the cross. A bloodstain on each. At the center, a crown of thorns. Our town had embraced the story of Christ crucified on a dogwood tree. The legend said it once grew straight and tall. Jesus promised it would never be used for executions again, and as the poem went, "Slender and twisted it shall always be, with cross-shaped blossoms for all to see."

Ruthie cradled the glass gingerly, studying it and holding it up to the light like a priceless gem. "God puts every one of us here for a purpose. There's some pull on our lives that draws us toward that purpose, and the farther we go away from it, the more unhappy we are. The closer we get, the more we yearn and desire it."

"I'm a mother and a wife. I don't have time for purpose or desire or being drawn to anything but sleep and laundry."

She smiled. "There's a reason you spend nights in your closet. I think you're there because you're not even close."

"Close to what?"

"To what you were really put here to be. Not to do. To *be*. *Doing* is overrated. *Being* is where God works. What he's most concerned about."

I frowned. "What, you want me to start an orphanage? run for office?"

"Nobody knows that but you and God. And you don't even know the half of it. You see, he looks at our lives as a whole, not just today, tomorrow, yesterday, and next week. Not even this year and next. He's not counting your failures and your mistakes and keeping a running tab like heaven's waiter. He sees the end just as well as the beginning. He knows about the pit you're in right now."

"The closet."

"Exactly. He knows where you're headed. You'll get there if you keep struggling. Most people think the struggle means failure. It's actually the best thing that could happen. That struggle will pull you out on the other side a lot stronger, a lot deeper. It's like cooking a good meal. You don't do that in a microwave, my dear. You let it simmer and boil and simmer some more until it's right. And you do that in an oven over lots of time and some high temperatures. Life is a process without a timer."

It was a stretch to believe my nights in the closet weren't worthless siftings of the mind. "So you think I'm supposed to write?"

Ruthie rolled her eyes. "It's not a *supposed* to. And, yes, you will find whatever that thing is."

"But how do you know?" I said. "What was *your* purpose?"

Her eyes twinkled like I imagined Santa's would the night before Christmas. "When I was little, times were hard. I grew up along a creek, and I'd spend hours walking up and down it, surveying the flow of the water, just like you used to do. One day I was looking into the water and saw the reflection of a young girl across from me. From that day on, I knew I had a friend. We spent hours together. Talking. Laughing. Having tea parties. Every time we were together, it was like pouring water from an endless pitcher. Her life into mine, mine into hers. Over the years, I've replaced her with others, usually younger women."

"Like me."

Ruthie nodded. "Water that's not moving becomes stagnant. And if there's not someone pouring into you, the pitcher gets dusty. A person is most satisfied and most useful when she is both giving and receiving. In marriage. In life. In friendship. With God too."

A few days later Ruthie and I talked as I pushed Tarin in a stroller along the sidewalk. There were moments talking with Ruthie when things became crystal clear, as if my life's clouds suddenly broke and brilliant sunshine streamed through, illuminating the countryside.

"I went to the kitchen the other night for a glass of water and grabbed a mug from the cabinet," I said. "It was dark and I felt my way along until I found the sink and turned on the tap. But I had the mug upside down. I didn't know it, but I was trying to put water in an upside-down mug."

"What happened?"

"Water went everywhere. My nightshirt got soaked. It just struck me: I've lived my whole life like that—upside down. God has tried pouring things into me that I had no capacity to keep."

She smiled and wobbled to a stop. "Karin, here's the hidden truth about that. He's the one turning your life upside down. He has you in that closet for a purpose."

"But I don't like it. It's not fair."

Ruthie put a wrinkled, arthritic arm around me. "One day you'll be right side up, and the water will go where it's supposed to. You'll be filled." She spread a hand out and motioned toward an imaginary window. "One day there will be a display at Books-A-Million. It'll fill a whole window and they'll have to stack them on top of each other and people will push their way through to get at them. Oprah will call and you'll be too busy to talk."

"Right. And what will my books be about? What's the subject that will draw me again and again?"

"It'll be about struggle and finding your heart. It's really what you're all about."

"What do you mean?"

Ruthie didn't speak for a long time. When we made it to her porch, I took Tarin out and let her play with a shoe box filled with toys Ruthie kept out for her.

Finally she spoke. "We do almost anything not to struggle. We take the easy path because it makes us feel better. We think a smooth road will get us to the destination quicker. And that's our problem—we're not at all concerned about *where* we're going but *how fast* we can get there." She sat in a rocking chair and wiped her brow with a paper towel. "That has been your full-time job for a long time."

"Taking the easy way out?"

"Choosing to feel better instead of growing."

I wasn't sure I agreed, but I decided to follow her lead. "Why do you think I do that?"

"Because growing is painful. Most people work overtime at the Make Me Feel Better Chapel. Something bad happens and they throw a verse at you, like a fish to a walrus. That makes *them* feel better, being able to pull something out of a hat they hope will make sense of the pain. But if you're on the other end, it doesn't matter that the verse is true; it still feels like a fish because the person had no intention of entering your struggle. Of just sitting with you and moving through it like those Old Testament boys did or the man in the parable. It never occurs to them that you need them to bend down and help you up, take you to a doctor, try to bandage your wounds. They throw a verse, cross to the other side, and they're on their way."

"But I don't blame them. Struggling is hard. You can't really enter into another person's pain like that."

Ruthie drained her glass of iced tea and tossed the remaining ice cubes onto her zinnias. She took my glass, turned hers over, and poured a small amount of tea on the bottom and watched it pool. "You were telling me about living upside down and trying to pour water on the bottom of a mug. It's possible to hold a little water here. That's the way I tell if my dishes are clean in the dishwasher. Most times I can't remember if I've done them, so I pat my hand there to see if there's any water. You can't get much, but there's some."

Then she turned her glass over, grabbed the pitcher of tea,

and poured with abandon until the glass overflowed, ran down the sides onto her hand, and spilled onto the porch.

I picked up my feet as it gushed past Tarin, who looked on in amazement.

Ruthie's eyes were on me, burning through. "Which do you want?" she whispered. "Do you want to live on the surface of the bottom, as shallow as the bottom of this glass? Or do you want something else?"

"I want to be filled. I want to overflow."

Tears rimmed her eyes and ran down her cheeks. "Good. You struggle and fight with everything in you and don't take the easy way out. Wrestle those demons in that closet and don't stop struggling until you've written it down for every one of us."

It took a long time to digest that.

Later, when a cool breeze had blown past us, carrying the scent of dinners on the wind, Ruthie spoke again. "Most people have given up on their heart. They've settled for less. Like a married couple on treadmills, both working hard, spewing out sweat, but never getting anywhere. They're content to sit on the porch in rocking chairs and watch life. At one point they had some vague sense when something deep down inside called to them and they wanted to follow, but the ticking clock and the kids and the mortgage drowned it out. It's a rhythm, a beat in the background you have to strain to hear. You have to push things out of the way to really listen."

"I think I know what you're talking about," I said reluctantly.

"You hear it clearly when you're young. There's a freedom when you're a child that sets the heart on the right path. But something happens. Especially with girls. We sense something. We feel uneasy in our gut because of someone's words or an action, something that doesn't feel quite right, but then we push it down. We don't listen."

"Why?"

"For a million reasons. We don't want people to think we're judgmental. We don't want to hurt another person's feelings. We're afraid of what others might think."

"Example," I said.

"When I was younger, I sang in a church group. We'd travel around to different places. There was something about the leader, though. It was a gut reaction—stay away; don't get too close. But I didn't listen."

"Did he ever do anything to you?"

Ruthie bit her cheek. "Yes. And here I am an old woman, and I still remember that night. Like it was yesterday. To this day I feel vulnerable around people who are supposed to be spiritual leaders. That's the terrible thing. You stop listening to your heart and you become a shell of who you were meant to be."

Exactly what I felt like. Empty. "Can you ever get that back? regain the power to listen to your heart?"

"You bet. That's the great thing about God. He can restore the broken places. It's really what he's all about. Beauty for ashes."

If you've ever had a friend who cares enough about you to get down in the dirt and roll around, to cry and laugh and shovel the manure of life, you'll know how I felt when Ruthie leaned forward. I still get shivers thinking about her words and how true they were. How true they are.

"God is taking you somewhere, Karin. Someplace deep. He wants you to go with him. Most people never hear that call, never follow. They're too busy or too successful or have just stopped listening. He's making you uncomfortable. He doesn't want to let you settle for chicken feed, where you hunt and peck what you want and leave the rest. I don't know where you'll wind up, but I'll bet it's going to feel a little bit lonely. He probably won't take away your sadness. In fact, he might add to it. But when you're closer to God and the things he cares about, there's no better place."

"I'm not sure I want to go. I'm not sure I can."

"You can. You've been given a gift. Most people never get old enough to let go of the illusion. . . ."

"Which illusion?"

"The one that says you can have a perfect life, a perfect marriage, a perfect child, or whatever else you dream of being perfect. That you can get to a point where there's no pain. That you never lose sleep." Ruthie put her head back on the rocker. "Basically life is a dance through a field full of cow manure. Most people won't even go into the field; they go around it and pretend. Or they try to tiptoe here and there and stay close to the fence. They never see that all that fertilizer creates some beautiful flowers and some of the greenest grass you'll ever see."

"So you what, wallow in it?"

"No, girl, I put my hip boots on and waltz through the cow pies."

15

Will

I tensed as the door opened, not knowing whether to sit or stand. I put my palms up, pushed the chair with the backs of my legs, and stood as a withered ghost hobbled into the room. She looked a thousand years old. Her leg bones appeared as thin as straw, her knees just bumps, shoulders stooped.

She transfixed me with those eyes, as if she were an aged vampire ready to suck the lifeblood from me. I doubted her false teeth were up to the task, but the ferocity of her stare left no doubt she had the willpower. I sensed strength in her. You develop that in prison — knowing the ones who will make it and those who won't.

She stopped to catch her breath, looking like a battle-worn soldier who had come out stronger on the other side. She seemed familiar, but I couldn't place her. Was she from Dogwood? one of my mother's friends? a teacher? She glanced behind her and motioned.

All music that had been the soundtrack of my life in Clarkston faded. The world stopped turning, stars fell, and the sun stood still as *she* entered the room.

"Karin," I whispered. The word I had spoken only to myself

the last twelve years. The name on my lips as I went to sleep each night. The face in my dreams. I hadn't dared believe it was true, that she was really coming, but here she stood.

She moved tentatively, as if something in the room might swallow her whole if she made a wrong step. What these two had in common, what drew them together and to me, I couldn't fathom.

Karin's face had aged gracefully, unlike my own. I could feel a new line or wrinkle every day I washed my face. Her skin still looked as I remembered in my dreams. Cute freckles just above her cheeks—like someone who studied a map of home and tapped a pencil on a familiar spot—long eyelashes, and milky white skin.

Her eyes, however, betrayed a hard road. I remembered them as deep blue pools, moons circling an unknown planet, full of life. She was thinner, too, and I recalled the fears she used to have of growing up and inheriting her mother's hips. She hadn't.

Here was the answer to my prayers, every longing of a dozen years, standing half a room away, and yet so far.

Karin glanced to her right, and the old woman waved her forward. The woman spun to the back and with a grunt sat in a chair shoved close to the wall.

For the first time, Karin's eyes locked on mine, and she smiled and glided to the chair across from me.

I leaned forward to speak through the holes, unable to quell my excited laughter. "You came. You really came to see me."

"It took me a while. I'm sorry, Will."

The mention of my name gave me chills. "Did you get my letters?"

Wrinkles formed at her brow. It looked like confusion. "I don't think so. At least I don't remember any."

I let it drop, but I wanted to tell her I'd written her every day for a year, that some of the other inmates had called me Letter Man.

"How are you?" Karin said.

Did she want the truth? "I'm looking forward to getting out," I managed. "I'm okay. Really."

"I heard about your father. I'm very sorry."

"Yeah. Are you still living in Dogwood?"

She nodded and a shadow crossed her face. "I'm married now. We have children."

It was like a hand grenade to my heart, though I had heard all the rumors. I didn't want to believe any of them. I tried to recover quickly. "That's great. I'm happy for you, if you're happy."

"Well, I love my husband. I'm devoted to him and my children. I hope you'll understand."

I looked at the old woman in the shadows, trying to figure out this meeting. Why were they really here?

"Can you believe I actually have kids?" Karin said. "You'd think there'd be a law against it or something."

She told me their names and a little about each. I could tell how much she loved them by the way her eyes twinkled, and she used her hands to reach out and caress their faces in the air. "Darin is a handful. He's just the most adventurous, playful thing in the world. I swear he's going to be an astronaut someday. And Kallie is . . . well, I don't want to brag on them too much."

"I'll bet she's as pretty as her mother," I said.

Karin grinned and looked away, embarrassed.

"That's really great. I always thought you'd make a good mother. What about your husband?"

"He's a pastor. There's another shocker. Can you imagine me a pastor's wife?" She made quotation marks with her fingers. "In ministry together."

I shook my head.

"We're at the Little Brown Church. You remember it, don't you? Richard likes it. The people. The challenge of it all."

"Those people would be a challenge."

"Yeah." Karin laughed. "It's kind of a day-to-day thing. You can't plan what's going to happen long term, but Richard says, 'Faithful in the little things will work the big things out.' I can't believe we actually wound up back in Dogwood, but I guess the Lord's ways are mysterious."

I stared into Karin's eyes, searching for the girl I'd fallen in love with long ago. I had pictured us growing old together. All the romances that lined the bookstore shelves would pale in comparison to our story. "Is he good to you? I mean, are you really happy?"

She chuckled, and a bit of the young girl shone through. "A lot better than some of the other guys I went out with. He's a good man, Will. He's kind and caring, loves the children. His schedule is a little crazy visiting the hospital and some of the older members, but I'll take it. I could certainly do worse."

"And what about happy?" I said. "Are you?"

Karin studied her hands and fiddled with a scrap of newsprint so thin you could see through it. When she looked up, there were tears in her eyes. "I'm not sure I know what *happy* means. And I'm not sure it's as important as I used to think, you know?" Her voice was pleading, whining. Tears fell and ran down her cheeks. She wore no makeup that I could tell.

She continued. "I used to dream of getting out of our skanky little town, of going someplace and becoming somebody. But that was all so I could come back and prove to people that they were wrong about me. I'm not sure it's important what those people think. I'm not sure that being happy is a good goal."

It sounded like something someone had told her. Something she'd learned in a Sunday school class and was now parroting to me.

"I'm glad you've found someone," I said, trying not to show the hurt.

"What about you?" she said.

I wanted to say I'd been waiting for her, praying she would wait for me, hoping against all odds that there would be a future for us. "It's kind of hard getting dates in here. At least with the opposite sex."

Karin laughed and squinted, taking me in with new eyes. "Will." She said it like a prayer. Like *I* was the mystery. Then she scooted closer to the glass and put a hand gently on the table, her skin pale. "Remember when we were kids? the day you walked me home?"

"Racing those sticks in the creek," I said.

"Boats," she corrected. "And my mother came out."

"I remember like it was yesterday," I whispered.

She turned and looked at the old woman, then back at me. "You said something to me. When we were at the spelling bee. Whispered something. I was thinking about it the other day. Do you remember what you said?"

I could almost hear the water trickling over those rocks. I had been there a thousand times in my mind. When the heat of the summer or the smells and sweat of prison overtook me, I retreated to those hills, that water, the sound of the frogs and crickets filling the night, the buzz of june bugs, diligent bees spreading pollen. I had replayed the look of her hair, the smell of elementary school perfume.

"I just said you deserved to win," I lied.

I have read the story of Joshua and how he prayed until the sun stood still. If God could do this, whether causing the earth to stop its spin or the whole universe to freeze, could he not turn back the clock for me? It seems plausible to a person of faith, whose soul has awakened, to ask and receive. Believe and be given.

I tried to believe and ask, but there must be prayers that amuse God. The Ancient of Days and Giver of Life is also the Laugher at Men. I had harbored a secret hope all these years, like a child who is too afraid of asking for what he truly wants at Christmas but blurts it out at the last minute on Christmas Eve and receives nothing but blank stares and chuckles.

If God sees the beginning from the end, if he knows the secrets and dark avenues of the heart, surely he must know what hope he steals when something like this happens to one of his children. Surely he must grieve as the wound-up world spins like a top, knocking against the dreams of his creation.

To say time stood still as I looked at Karin would not be accurate, because time had no consequence at that moment. I could see myself aged, living alone in some cabin on a hill with nothing but jerky and a bottle. Maybe a dog. Women would take their children by the hands and lead them to the other side of the street when they saw me coming. From this one visit, this one revelation by Karin, I had been banished to my own Patmos.

I closed my eyes and thought of that childish moment long ago. I had thrown the bee, had misspelled the word on purpose, had taken the fall for the lovely girl who needed something good in her life.

"One day I will marry you," I had whispered. I had held on to those six words for most of my life, certainly since the day I set foot in Clarkston. I had planned the very spot I would build our home, the playground in the backyard, even the sandlot where our boys would bring their friends to play baseball. We would hike in the woods together, pretend we were great explorers, greet trees and animals that had never met a human being. When our children were exhausted, when they lay sleeping soundly in their beds, I would take my wife to the room that had come to life from my own imagination—with a fireplace near the bed and a skylight above so we could make love watching the moon and stars.

One day I will marry you.

It was as certain in my mind as anything I had ever believed. My father's love. The 1975 Reds. It was more certain than my conviction or incarceration.

All my life, if I could see something in my mind, I could make it come true. I could take that idea and create. It didn't matter what the object was — a cradle, a chair, an end table — if I could see how to piece it together in my mind, I could accomplish it.

That was what I had tried to do all these years at Clarkston — piece together the two separate parts of Karin and me. I had conducted this conversation a thousand times. Perhaps a million. I would make her laugh, her laughter would turn to love, and I would see in her eyes that she truly felt the same for me. We would embrace somehow, if only with our eyes, and she would promise to be there on the day of my release.

One day I will marry you.

I whispered it as a prayer as a child. I whispered it to myself in regret, as praise to the One who knows beginning from end, east from west, freedom from captivity. I whispered it to myself because I could not bring myself to believe the words.

One day I will marry you.

16

Karin

Will whispered something, his head down, eyes closed. It seemed like he was working on a sentence he could not bring himself to utter.

"What is it?" I said. "Did something happen in here? You're not telling me something."

"I'm not telling you a lot of things," he said. "Karin, you can only care about so much, and then it just becomes overload. They call it compassion fatigue."

"You're not some third world country."

"Maybe I am." He looked away. "An island."

"Maybe that's where you'll go when you get out," I said. "A place where the sun will keep you warm all year long and you won't have to worry about seasons."

Will faced me. "I like the seasons. I like the change, the currents of life. I couldn't live on sand or in a place where the sun doesn't go down or come up. As much as I complain, I don't think there's another place on earth I want to exist outside Dogwood."

I smiled and pointed a finger at him. "You keep talking like that and we'll be seeing you at church with some young thing on your arm, walking into worship like you own the place."

"I don't know that I could . . . I hope your husband won't be offended if I hang out with the snake handlers."

I snorted and laughed, and he looked at me like he remembered the old Karin. Carefree and young, nostrils flaring, sucking in air. There was life in my laugh, and it took control.

Someone coughed and I turned. Ruthie pointed to the clock as if I didn't know our time was limited. She wobbled and stood with the help of her cane.

"I have a friend who wants to meet you," I said. "Would that be all right?"

Will glanced at Ruthie and lifted an eyebrow. "Is she single?"

"Very." I laughed. "Ruthie is wise beyond her years, if that's possible. And she's become a good friend. I think you'll like her as much as I do." I put a hand out and touched the glass.

"For now we see through a glass, darkly; but then face to face," I thought. It was a Scripture I had memorized as a kid from the King James Bible, and I knew even then that I couldn't fully understand it as a child. Now, looking at Will, I felt I understood it less.

Will touched the other side of the glass, and we both smiled.

I lingered a moment, and something passed between us. There had been a connection long ago, but that had been severed. Something in me wanted to hold on, to roll back the clock and never let him go, but I had made my choice, as he had, and we had to live with our choices.

I pulled myself up and held the chair for Ruthie.

"Thank you, dear," she said.

I hovered there, gazing at these two souls I cared so deeply about. You can pick your friends and choose who surrounds you, but family is something you cannot choose. That's the way I felt about Will and Ruthie. They were the family that I hadn't chosen but had found me.

"We need to be alone for a moment," Ruthie said, breaking the silence.

"Of course." I walked to the other side of the room where Ruthie had been.

The two stared, as if sizing each other up for a prizefight.

I folded my arms and sat back against the plastic chair, thinking of all the choices, big and small, that make up a life. Ruthie once said that eternity is a human stream and our stories are the rain, falling, flowing, surging, searching for an end. "But there is no end. Never will be. And that's the great thing about living."

I wanted to frame the picture before me. Two strangers united only by their love for me. One whose love I could return. The other's, I could not. And never could.

I guess that's the sad thing about living.

17

Will

"The name is Ruthie Bowles," she said. Her teeth seemed to get in the way of her upper lip, or maybe it was the other way around. Her pupils were the size of stickpins. In fact every part of her seemed closed tight, even her heart. "You recognize that name?"

I nodded. "I recognize the name, but I don't think I've ever seen you before."

"I was at the trial. I figured somebody should be there since *they* never had the chance."

"How do you know Karin?" I said as even and measured as I could.

"She comes to visit me. You could say we're in the same boat, though maybe it's the same river. I'm just a little farther along than she is. Sweet girl. She's talked about you for a long time. I thought it would help her to come here."

"So it was your idea?"

"Yes. Richard and I both thought it might help. But I'd be lying if I didn't tell you I have my own reasons."

"You're not gonna attack me with that cane, are you?"

Ruthie didn't laugh. "I've thought about it. Then I wonder if it's not better to wait until you get out and come looking for you with my Confederate pistol."

I stifled a smile. I could believe she actually had one.

"You know there are people waiting for you," she continued. "Waiting for true justice." She passed her hand across the desk, as if she were smoothing an invisible tablecloth. "But part of me thinks you need to be forgiven by someone. That you need to hear the words."

"Which part usually wins?" I said.

"Depends on the day. Seeing you here, seeing you with her, I can imagine what it's been like. You've paid a high price for your mistake. Almost makes me want to forgive you. Then I look at the pictures I've stored in the drawer, the futures cut down, the pain you brought to that whole town. To me."

"Were you there for the sentencing? when I spoke?"

She nodded, and because of the way she held her mouth, the lower jaw jutting out like Larry King listening to a call, I thought her teeth would simply fall out. "I saw the tears. Heard your quavering voice. I suppose it must have made you feel better to—"

"I didn't mean it. The part about being sorry for what I'd done. It was an act."

It seemed like Ruthie had aged another ten years when she looked at me squarely. "What did you say?"

"There are things you don't know. Things I've never told anyone."

"Are you asking me to feel *sorry*? For *you*? Do you think after what you've done that anyone could feel sorry for you?"

"I don't need your sympathy. I don't want the town's embrace. I don't care if you forgive me or not. I just want to be left alone. I've paid the debt, and I want to live my life and put this behind me."

"There's a cloud a mile wide and darker than this prison that will hang over your head, son."

"Maybe. But clouds can move, can't they? The sun eventually comes out no matter how dark it gets."

There was something about this old woman I knew I could trust. If she had walked into the belly of the dragon and faced the beast head-on, she deserved answers.

"Waters recede after a flood, but that doesn't mean the earth isn't changed. There's a Grand Canyon of hurt back there. And it's not leaving easily."

"Doesn't sound like you're in a forgiving mood," I said.

"Doesn't sound like there's any remorse."

I stared through her, catching Karin in my peripheral vision. "I have lived every day of my life with one regret, confirmed by this visit. I should have taken Karin away and married her. I should have told her how I felt. It would have changed everything."

"How?"

"I've lost her. She's gone now. Forever."

Ruthie shook her head. "You don't know the whole truth. There are some things I came here to tell you. Things you should know before you come back, if that's your plan."

"My roots are there. Everything I love is there. I won't let those people have my soul."

"Everything you hate is there too."

The guard walked into the room on Ruthie's side, tipping back his hat.

"I just need a few more minutes, young man," she said.

He looked at his watch. "I'll give you ten."

"Thank you kindly," Ruthie said, turning back to me. She scratched her ear, as old people do, finding one spot on their head or the back of their hand to focus their energies. My mother had a spot on the back of her neck, a stigma of nerves and scaly skin. She was at it constantly while she visited, like a dog that can't stop licking a paw.

"What is it I should know?" I said.

"I'll tell you on one condition. That you tell me everything. No holding back. In a strange way, that girl over there needs you. I know it in my heart."

"Needs me? She has a husband, a family. The only thing I can bring her is confusion. If I even try to make contact, I know that her family—her mother especially . . . well, it'll be ugly. And that's not counting her dad."

"You wrote her, didn't you? I heard you tell her that."

"From over there? You must have a good hearing aid."

She chuckled. "If I turn it up and hold my head just right, I can get three radio stations simultaneously."

We both laughed; then I folded my hands and looked at her. "I wrote her every day for a year. Never received a reply. I figured she didn't want anything to do with me. That the memories were too painful."

"What memories?" Ruthie said.

I held her gaze and let the question sink deep. Could I really trust this old buzzard with the secret I had bottled up and thrown into an ocean of memory? If I miscalculated, if she was not who she said she was, I was opening myself up for more anguish and hurt. But there was something otherworldly—some would say angelic—about her face. She labored under the lie I had lived, the one I had allowed so many years ago.

"I can tell how much you care, Ruthie. But what if I told you that what I have to say would affect your friendship with Karin?"

"I could never love her any less than I do. She's like a daughter to me."

I nodded. "That's what I thought you'd say."

So I quickly told her. I told her everything.

18

Karin

"What's wrong?" I said as we made our way to the car.

Ruthie seemed distant. She walked through the prison like a zombie, her cane striking the tile floor with abandon.

I guided her past a cement post outside — she was going to run right into it.

She eased herself inside the car and placed her cane and purse in the backseat. "Just tired," she said, buckling her seat belt and staring straight ahead.

A half mile past the front gate, I couldn't hold my excitement any longer. "This was such a great idea! I can't remember having such a good day. It's as if I can start over again. You don't know how long I've dreaded seeing Will, thinking he would get out and I'd pass him on the street someday and be paralyzed. Maybe this is what's been keeping me up at night."

"I'm glad you enjoyed it."

"What about you? What did you two talk about?"

The wrinkled skin under her neck worked like a snake downing a rabbit as she swallowed spittle. "There are some things girls have to keep to themselves."

"Oh, come on, Ruthie. I didn't go all this way to have you clam up on me. What did he say?"

"He said if you weren't available, he was going to ask me out when he came back."

"Oh, please . . ."

"It's true. He said he was so hungry for a real woman that it was all he could do not to break the glass between us and kiss me right there."

I plugged my ears and rocked back and forth. "La la la la."

"Settle down," Ruthie snapped when I brushed her shoulder. "You want to get us killed?"

Her sharp tone startled me, and I felt like a scolded child. "I'm sorry. I didn't mean to scare you."

Ruthie stared at the road, refusing to make eye contact. "I just don't want you to get hurt. Those children . . ."

My mind ran to my children. It was early afternoon, and Tarin would be sleeping if Richard had done his job. If not, she would be cranky until we put her to bed later. My love for them over-flowed—and meeting Will had touched something, had almost given me a new lease on loving them, a freedom to abandon myself to my family.

Still, I couldn't break through to Ruthie. When both our stomachs growled, about an hour from home, I looked for a place to stop. She had mentioned the Golden Corral, but the one she remembered had closed. Instead, we found a Shoney's strategically placed between a Sam's Club and a Wal-Mart, and she parked as close to the front as she could.

"I don't think I have the energy to go inside, honey," Ruthie said, a hand on her cane.

"It'll be relaxing," I said. "We'll get a booth, and you can com-plain to the waitress about the food."

Inside, Ruthie excused herself and limped past the salad bar to the bathroom.

I watched a family with two young children. The kids were more interested in their crayons than the food. At another table was a young woman with a baby in a car carrier. She had put the child in the seat opposite her in the booth and propped the carrier against the wall so she could watch the sleeping child. Ruthie's words came back—the child in my dream was my *soul*. My father cared for it even more than I did. He was waiting for me to return.

Tears came. The events of the day were almost too much to take in, and I wondered about Will. Was it difficult for him to see me? to discover the truth about my marriage? Did he still harbor some hope of love between us?

The waitress came and I realized Ruthie had been in the bathroom too long. I hurried to the restroom, thinking she might have fallen. The bathroom appeared empty except for one closed stall. I tiptoed in and spotted Ruthie's orthopedic shoes. A low moan echoed through the room and I moved closer, peering through the crack in the door to see her sitting fully clothed, her head in her hands, rocking and shaking, emitting a mournful cry so heartrending that I thought she was going to die.

"Ruthie? Are you okay?"

"I'm just finishing," Ruthie said, blowing her nose. "Be out in a minute."

"You want me to wait?" I said.

"No, I'll be all right. You go ahead and order."

"What can I get for you?"

The tears came again, and it was a few seconds before she choked out, "I can't eat anything. Just some coffee."

I paused at the door. "What is it? I want to help you."

My heart nearly burst when Ruthie wept again. "Oh, Karin," she wailed, half whisper, half cry. "Karin."

Everything Ruthie had said to me echoed in that cry. She had every reason to give up on me, to leave me in my closet and my darkness. She hadn't given up. But something about her cries now changed that. What had she discovered? What had Will told her?

When she finally emerged, still dabbing at her eyes, the waitress met her at the table, turning a white mug over and pouring Ruthie some coffee, about half a cup. It's the same thing I do for Darin, not filling it too full of lemonade or milk, knowing I might be pouring what I'll have to clean up.

"Thank you," Ruthie said.

"You sure I can't get you anything?" the waitress drawled. She sounded like a transplant from farther south. Maybe Georgia. South Carolina. "A muffin? Some toast?"

"I'm all right." Ruthie smiled.

"Well, if your tummy gets to feelin' hungry and you change your mind, let me know."

Ruthie sipped her black coffee while I ate a salad with a few bits of chicken and croutons thrown on top. The muted conversations and clinking silverware were drowned out by an instrumental version of "Y.M.C.A." I didn't want to close my eyes for fear I'd see the Village People dancing.

Glancing out the window, I noticed a car slowly pass. It looked like the same one I'd seen in the side mirror earlier this morning. Tinted windows didn't allow me to see the people inside. I didn't want to mention it to Ruthie and alarm her, but I was sure someone was following us.

"You seemed to enjoy meeting him again," Ruthie said.

My fork shook and I had to put it down. "I dreaded it at first, but you were right. It was so good to see him. Now tell me, what did he say to you?"

"Nothing you'd want to announce at the spring banquet," she said wryly. "You realize when he's getting out, don't you?"

I craned my neck to see the car. Brake lights flashed and my heart fluttered. "What was that?"

"July 2."

"Right," I said, my face flushing. The room spun. I'd eaten bad chicken years before and this was the same feeling.

"Does that date ring a bell? July 2?"

"Should it?" I said, feeling my gorge rising. Ruthie leaned closer as I blinked, trying to focus.

"Is she all right?" someone said.

I was down. On the floor. The tile felt cold. A baby wailing. A child's red shoe lying on the floor in the corner. The parents didn't see it.

Two eyes looking back at me. Leaning down. Swirling lights outside.

"I thought it would be different," I managed, my breath faltering. "That seeing him would change things. Make me fall out of love with my husband. Make me want to leave. But it didn't."

"It's okay." Ruthie touched my shoulder. "Help is on the way."

I closed my eyes because my demons were back. Swarming, accusing, mocking—their knees drawn to their odd, bloated stomachs. They had introduced themselves without a welcome long ago and had sent me to my closet. I had chased them away, but like bees to an abandoned hive, they returned.

"Oh, Karin," they seethed. "Poor Karin. So delicate."

All I could think of was sleep.

I thrashed, trees and rosebushes a blur outside the window. My mother and father. Will being led away.

And then there was silence, as if someone had spoken peace to my soul. A pinch of the arm and my muscles relaxed. I drifted away, free from the stares, free from the mocking, but not free from the pain.

PART TWO

19

Danny Boyd

My mama still sits in the living room and stares at the pictures on the mantel over the fireplace. Mornings are the worst, so she lies in bed as the sunlight streams in the window. My daddy is up before the sun, so his side of the bed is cold. He reads the paper and lets the dog out and checks the tomato plants and leaves footprints in the dew on the grass before she even knows what time it is.

Mama turns the Westclox alarm around so she doesn't have to look at it because she remembers what time it was that she heard the sirens. She had a sick feeling as soon as the fire whistle blew, and she ran outside to see the smoke. I've heard her talk to her friends about it on the phone. In fact, I overheard her telling one of her friends that she prayed somebody's house was on fire that morning.

Isn't that awful? she said. That I would pray such a thing.

I don't think it's awful. People can get out of a burning house.

That first winter the sadness covered my mama like a blanket of snow, and she gazed at the closet full of coats and scarves and empty gloves. In the spring, the Goodwill truck came and took a bunch of sleds and coats and other clothes away. The neighbors helped gather it all because she couldn't bear to do it by herself.

She stares at those pictures on the mantel and thinks about her two little girls who will never sleep in their beds or hop out the door going to school or cry when the soap gets in their eyes or snuggle up to her late at night because some boy broke her heart. A mother's grief is the worst because it's always there in front of her. She carried the children, saw them come directly out of her body, nursed them from her own breasts, and then cared for them, kept them safe.

A father's grief stays hidden. You have to look a lot harder to catch it. I've seen my daddy pause while looking at a school bus, and I wondered what was going on inside him. When he's alone on the porch, his pipe lit, rocking back and forth, I think he's thinking about Tanny and Karla and how they used to crawl up in his lap and go to sleep to the sound of the crickets and the whip-poor-wills and the soft light of the fireflies coming up from the wet ground like the prayers of parents for their kids. I don't know if he ever prayed for them, but if he did, it didn't do him a lot of good.

It was late one night when I saw him sitting in the corner of the living room, looking out at the darkness. Before he went to bed, he'd been drinking some of the stuff he keeps in his special cabinet over the refrigerator. When he got up, Mama didn't stir and I stayed as quiet as I could and just watched as he poured another glass and downed it. Something was bothering him. He got into his gun cabinet and fumbled for some shells.

Then he headed for the car. I made it there before he did and hid in the backseat. It was an old Chevy Malibu that he said I could have when I got old enough, and there was a lot of stuff in the backseat, so I pulled a cover over me and stayed there. He turned left at the end of the driveway, but after that I kind of got lost as to where we were. I peeked out the window a couple of times to see a gas station and then some streetlights in a parking lot, but it was as dark as pitch. I don't know what pitch is, but I've heard him say that.

He pulled over to the side of the road, and I heard the rose-bushes scrape against the car. It was then that I knew where we were, and I wondered if there was a way to stop him.

Then I wondered if I should even try.

20

Bobby Ray

Eddie Buret tried hard to show everybody he was a strong-armed, no-nonsense chief, even though that seemed to come naturally. He'd nitpick, stand over my shoulder as I wrote up my traffic tickets and daily reports, and basically let me know I was on probation. So much for the peaceful little town police force he was trying to assemble.

On my first day, when they returned from the retirement party for Chief Buret, Eddie was already tipsy from a few beers and Wes could hardly stand. It was a good thing Maggie had gone with them because she was the only one who didn't need a Breathalyzer. I mentioned that Mrs. Spurlock and her daughter had been by, asking about the missing person's report, and Eddie lit into me. He said I shouldn't give preferential treatment to "skanks" like that. It seemed extreme, but I learned that any mix of alcohol and police work caused Eddie to get mean.

"Don't worry about him," Maggie whispered when his door was closed and he and Wes were inside. "He don't mean nothing by it. Tomorrow he won't remember a thing he said."

But Maggie's prediction turned out to be wrong. The next day he threw the missing person's report on my desk. "Here's your report. I told you I filed it."

I tried to talk sense into him, but he seemed put off by the whole thing. "If you're not going to respect my authority, we're not going to be able to work together."

"Yes, sir."

"You gonna let this happen again?"

"No, sir."

"Good."

But it did happen again when I brought up the possibility of adding Kevlar vests to our inventory of equipment. He hit the roof, asking if I wanted to pay the cost. I'd seen them work while in Iraq and had several friends live after being shot.

Eddie wouldn't listen. "Plus, they're heavy and hot in the summer. You know how many shootings there have been in this town since I've worked here? That's right, a big, fat goose egg. And I aim to keep it that way."

My routine became regimented. I'd work early mornings, relieving Wes and patrolling neighborhoods and school zones. After work, I'd stop at The Home Depot, eat dinner with Lynda, then head to the old Benedict place and work on the roof or drywall. We spent a ton of money for a plumber to rework the pipes that had rusted out, but the rest of it was pretty straightforward.

One Saturday evening I told Lynda I had a surprise for her. She thought I was taking her out for dinner, but instead, we drove to the house and I put a blindfold on her, which made her laugh. She was scared that she might fall, with her belly poked out and off-balance, but I held on to her and led her up the rickety steps. At the top of the stairs we turned right, and I brought her into the little bedroom and closed the door.

I took the blindfold off and watched. Her face lit up like sparklers on the Fourth of July. Then the tears came as she surveyed the room. Her parents had given us a crib, and I'd set it up in the corner. Beside that was a nice rocking chair. I'd painted the room the color she'd picked out at Sherwin-Williams and glued the Noah's ark border with all the animals on it just below the ceiling.

The rest of the house was a pure mess with creaking floors and missing railings. Paint chips littered the kitchen, and the old refrigerator smelled like something had died in there. But this room, our baby's room, felt brand-new. I'd redone the windows and the trim, added new hardwood flooring, and hung a new six-panel door. Standing there with the door closed, it felt like a kid's room in some ritzy neighborhood in Huntington.

"Bobby Ray, it's beautiful," Lynda gushed. "Is this what you've been working on?"

"This and the roof. Just want you to see what it's going to be like when it's finished. Stay right here." I hurried to the car and retrieved a basket and a blanket from the trunk.

Lynda was in the window on the second floor, still looking at everything, her hands over her mouth in a posture of awe.

I made her sit in the rocking chair and pulled the crib mattress out for me, and we ate fried chicken, biscuits, and cole slaw.

In the middle of the meal, she got down on all fours and planted a greasy kiss on my lips. "You've heard what happens to pregnant women, haven't you?"

"They get strange appetites for weird foods, right?"

"Not just that. Their hormones rush around, and you never know what's going to happen."

"Is that so?" I wished I'd hung curtains on the window.

She kissed me again and then pulled away, sitting with her back against the wall, her knees drawn in.

"What? Did I do something wrong?"

A tear escaped. "I'm worried. What if something happens to you? What would *we* do?" She put a hand on her stomach.

I placed my hand on hers and kissed her again. "Honey, there's nothing that could take me away from the two of you. We're going to watch this little guy grow up together and have a bunch of sisters and brothers. Besides, what could happen in a sleepy little town like this anyway?"

She lay back on the mattress and embraced me while the chicken got cold.

21

Will

The bus that picked me up in Clarkston originated in Pittsburgh. Every time I hear the name of the city I think of October 11, 1972, and the final game of the National League play-offs. The last pitch. Bob Moose falling off the mound, letting go of the slider. Dust kicking up by Manny Sanguillen as he threw off his mask and hustled to the backstop. George Foster loping home from third base with the winning run. My father and I dancing around the Curtis Mathes TV.

Roberto Clemente, the best right fielder ever, would step on a plane to Nicaragua that winter and would never return. One decision changed the course of a life.

The bus driver that day looked like he needed convincing that the sum of our state was equal to its parts and not a hole. To most, West Virginia is a place you go through or around to get somewhere else. It is wide, hand-shaped, and filled with mythic beauty and unadorned, unending poverty. Its boundaries hold unparalleled beauty and danger. It is a redneck opera. The driver glanced in the mirror periodically, reading the past on my face and my newly purchased khakis and Carhartt T-shirt. The fact that I was heading anywhere from Clarkston betrayed me. Unlike Hester Prynne, I didn't need a scarlet letter to prove I had done something terrible. He no doubt thought I was some convenience store robber whose plan had gone awry. Maybe I'd wounded the clerk or stolen a few pickups. He had no idea the crime I paid for was much worse.

I stared out the window, trying to calculate the cost of the diesel against the sparse occupancy of the Greyhound. I counted maybe ten people in front of me, though I couldn't see children with the high-backed seats.

We passed a bloated deer wrapped around a mile-marker sign, its eyes open and tongue lolling, wounds stuffed with gravel. The legs rose at a weird angle toward the sky, as if in petition to erase the grotesque pose.

In a flash I saw my father's boots and a gun held at his side as he climbed over the barbed wire fence, then lifted the wire in the middle for me. Our first hunting trip. Squirrel season.

He sat me on a stump and put one knee to the ground, scanning the trees. He could shoot the eye of a squirrel at fifty yards with a .22. "This is a good spot—saw five or six the other day gathering for winter. They'll be up with the first light."

Hunting, like vacations, required an early start. Shuffling around in the dark, looking for an extra coat, calculating shells, keeping the dogs quiet. By this time, Carson could hunt on his own and had chosen the back side of the property, where not even a No Trespassing sign was needed.

An orange stripe lit the tops of trees. A red-tailed squirrel stretched his head out of a hole. The tree before us had grown sideways and up, like half of a football goal post, and the hole was right in the corner, where the tree took a turn toward the sky.

"You ready?" he whispered, not taking his eye off the twitching tail that circled the trunk and inched closer to us.

The .410 passed down to me was rusted on top and had a stock that pulled away from the barrel if you didn't hold it right.

My father whispered the squirrel play-by-play. "Here he

comes now. Get that gun ready and aim just a little to the right. That sight is off a bit."

My thumbs were cold as I placed one on top of the other and edged the hammer back. Like a shelf too high for a child, one he has to pull a chair over to reach, the hammer was too much for me. I had it halfway back, struggling to hear the click as it lodged in place, gritting my teeth and mashing, when it slipped through both thumbs and struck the shell.

A thunderous roar. Leaves shook. A hole big enough to bury my squirrel opened in the earth by my feet. I was so shocked by the blast that I didn't realize blood was pouring onto the white laces my mother had bought the week before when I told her I wanted new shoes.

I felt life leaking from me, but my father put a finger to his lips. "Put another shell in."

"Daddy, I'm hurt," I whispered.

I remember little about the downhill trip. He left our guns by the stump and wrapped my foot tightly with something, cradling me in his arms, my arms and one leg flopping. He held my injured foot in the air and gripped my ankle so tight I was sure he would pinch it off.

It was that foot that an inmate pointed to in the shower, asking me what had happened. It was not an observation from a concerned friend.

"You headed to Charleston?" an old woman in front of me said. I'd been watching her in the reflection of the window, knitting a hat. She was diminutive, with a finchlike face, a nose so pointed she looked like she had it sharpened for special occasions.

"Huntington."

"You live in the city?"

"Actually east of there. My brother's picking me up."

"That's nice of him. What's he do?"

"He was in the military. I'm not sure what he's into now."

She shook her head. "So many people out of work these days. What do you do?"

"I'm actually looking for something."

She craned her neck over the seat, and her eyes roamed over my clothes. "You just get out?"

I nodded.

"Well, bless your heart. A new start. How long were you in?"

I told her and she invited me next to her. We settled into the easy conversation of strangers, revealing enough to keep the banter going while the road beneath us changed.

The rolling hills were the same, spreading out like an ocean of green. Each spring when my father turned over the ground, my brother and I would find evidence that we stood on defiled soil. Those who had gone before us had touched the land and brought it under submission. Once, Carson found an arrowhead stuck in a tree. The arrow's shaft had weathered away, and all that was left was the hewn rock. He left it there, saying we would bring our children back someday and show them, prove to them that we were not the first to walk those woods.

My new friend's name was Mrs. Meyers, though she hadn't been a Mrs. in a long time. "You have someone waiting for you? Other than your brother?"

"My mother." I smiled. "She lives alone. Had a fall last winter and is still on the mend. You headed to Charleston?"

Her fingers worked like a spider spinning a web. "I'll switch there. Headed to see my sister in Lexington."

I knew the road well. Interstate 64 cut a swath through the southwestern part of the state, crossed the Big Sandy River, and flattened as it rolled into the land of Daniel Boone and the Kentucky Wildcats.

"This is for her. Cancer, you know. Too proud to buy a wig, so I make her these. Stage IV. I scraped up enough for the bus ticket because it might not be much longer."

"I'm sorry to hear that."

Mrs. Meyers dipped her head. "She's had a full life. A lot longer than some. Did you hear about those kids playing at the reservoir the other day?"

She told me the story as a hawk flew across the road and lit on the branch of a pine. It fluttered and held on, the wind blowing it back so it had to adjust its grip, while scanning for prey.

"It's sad when a child dies," she said. "So much potential lost. I'll bet those parents never get over it. First thing every morning they'll wake up and remember what used to be. Can't imagine that, can you?"

"No, I can't."

We rolled toward the capital and it grew cloudy, then began to rain, pelting the bus and sending drops of water running down the glass like tears.

Mrs. Meyers grew quiet, humming to herself, turning on the light. "There we go," she said, fitting the gray beanie on her head. "How does it look?"

"I think your sister is going to love it. I can't believe you finished."

"I got a head start a few days ago." She stuffed the knitting needles into her purse. She could have fit a person inside.

The Kanawha River lay below us as we exited the interstate, a mud-caked snake where my father had worked for more than thirty years. The city had changed—new hotels, restaurants, billboards, big box stores—but the river was just as brown, just as lazy.

"It's none of my business," Mrs. Meyers said. "You don't have to tell me, but why'd they put you in Clarkston? You seem like such a nice young man."

"I made a big mistake."

"Sold something you shouldn't have?"

I smiled. Seeing an old woman probe like this gave me an indication of what was ahead. "It was a costly error."

She turned and patted my hand. "Well, you just remember it's behind you. You've paid the debt, and the Lord's given you another opportunity."

There are losses that mark a life forever, that in simple terms define that life and everything around it. Dropped passes in the end zone. A wild pitch in the bottom of the ninth. But there are also collective losses shared. Blurred images of a grassy knoll. A child's salute to a flag-draped coffin. A body on a balcony, men pointing. A space shuttle soaring, then exploding into smoky trails.

These losses provide borders for our collective territories and set life's cornerstones. The locusts of time devour, and we are left with stalks. I was banished to a wasteland outside that territory, and reentering would cost. But I have to pay. For her. For me. For our future. I still had hope that our lives could be salvaged from the past.

As we neared the station, I opened a closed and locked door. I allowed myself to dream. Ruthie Bowles had given me permission. As discouraging as the visit had been, as the news Karin had shared, I took heart in Ruthie's revelation.

Before she left, Ruthie had said something that sealed my decision to return. "Your heart is good, Will. I can see why Karin still talks about you."

"How much has she told you?"

"Enough to know that I want to see your children before I die."

I had felt free to open my own doors and tell her things no living soul on earth knew but me. She had taken my words, processed them to the bitter root, and turned them back to me, giving hope and a mission—to rescue the heart of the woman I loved. I knew the road would be difficult and I had no idea how long it would take—who knows the ways of the heart?—but I was prepared to stay and work to help her heal.

Ruthie had opened the door for us both. It was my job to walk through it.

I waved at Mrs. Meyers and she rose, giving me a peck on the cheek.

"My best to your sister," I said. "I hope you have a good visit."

"Good luck, Will." She didn't continue, but it felt like she wanted to say, *You're going to need it.*

Clouds hugged the landscape as the bus chugged west toward Huntington. The road had been cut through the hills, so I mostly saw rocks and trees, but what I could see from that rain-splattered window surprised me. Big box stores and restaurants dotted the landscape between exit signs. I expected things to be different, but what I saw was shocking.

Huntington was a mixture of the new and old. We passed Marshall University and the new football stadium. At the bus station I had to resist the urge to remain inside. An appointment with my parole officer helped ease that, and I walked the two miles from the station, up Fourth Avenue past the shops I recalled from childhood.

The parole officer was a middle-aged woman who didn't fit the profile of what I expected. She commended me for my quick reporting and laid out the guidelines, most of which I'd already memorized. I had to find a job. I couldn't possess firearms or weapons of any sort. No alcohol or drugs. No bars. Of all the conditions, the employment scared me the most.

"You'll be staying at this address?" she said, looking over the form I'd filled out.

"With my mother. It's the house I grew up in."

She handed me a packet of information and said she'd see me for my next report.

I walked back to the bus station looking for my brother, checking the clock and glancing at a bank of pay phones. I had vowed not to call him. The warden faxed the information of when to meet me along with a note asking him to come alone. Dealing with Carson was hard enough. Adding others to the mix was a relational accelerant, and I knew there were things we needed to deal with. The warden said Carson had agreed.

After years of looking at walls and staring through bars, it felt foreign to walk outside without permission. I knew that would change. I couldn't wait to go back on the hill and explore the old haunts I had visited every night as I went to sleep.

I had a ritual in Clarkston that eased me into each long prison night. I read at least half an hour, sitting on my bed with my back against the wall. At lights-out, I would lie down and make the long trip in my memory out of the house and up the hill, past the barn and pond, the woodpile, and the abandoned station wagon. I would pass my father sitting on his tractor, a rake or baler attached, his Cincinnati Reds hat planted firmly on his balding head.

I walked the graded path, stepping from one limestone boulder to another. The path snaked up the hill and curved to the plateau of the tree line. My father had constructed the road the summer I was born. He was always a believer that animals knew much more than we did about ingress and egress, so he followed the path cattle and deer had made over the years, with a few variations, and the project was completed before the first snow.

Acres of grass began at the tree line, and I walked the rolling pastures where I had played as a kid, built model rockets and set them off from Carson's launching pad, built forts, had campouts, and ran a dirt bike ragged. The property was punctuated by two gently sloping mounds that rose high over the valley.

In Dogwood, a town surrounded by hills, there is limited vision. Even from the tops of mountains you don't see for miles because there is little break in the trees. But from this spot the world spread out in extravagant ways. Industrial smokestacks to the north, the lights of TV and radio antennas to the west, swirling smoke from chimneys, and a sky so close you could touch it.

Above the easternmost knoll rose another hill with the tallest pine trees on the property. The ground was littered with pine needles most of the year, and in the fall the pinecones fell like snow, creating a warm, rustic bed for woodland animals.

This was my nightly routine—exploring the landscape of my youth, retracing angles and slopes I had searched and now savored. It was part worship, part salvation—a city of refuge in a world that screamed for safety.

I saved one leg of the trip for last. As I felt my eyes sting and give way to Clarkston's restless sleep, just before I let myself drift the rest of the night, I turned to face the wall, took Karin by the hand, and we strolled up an imaginary stone walkway. In my mind, she wore a thin, white nightdress that fluttered in the breeze and clung to her legs. Her hair shone in the gloaming and blew across her face and neck, tendrils cascading along her shoulders in the evening breeze.

The stairs led to a brick walkway above the tree line. I put an arm around her, and we turned to watch night descend on this world atop the valley, oblivious to the shadows below. In the summer and fall we sipped tea or she carried a glass of wine as we gazed at the beauty of the mountains. In winter, snow formed a white blanket that covered creation, making everything appear new and fresh and real.

The final ascent took us to the highest point, where I had built a home. Huge windows on either side of the front door stared as we approached. I saved most of the trees and let them buttress and accent the house, perfectly framing it.

"Will, it's beautiful," she would say.

"It's ours. We'll love each other here. We'll have children and raise them on these hills and watch them fly."

In my life, in the actual real world, my lips have touched Karin's only twice. But in my dreams, I have kissed and made love to her a thousand times. I do not know if that dream will ever come true. Perhaps we will both be too old to fall into each other's arms before she is ready, but I am willing to wait.

True desires of the heart are worth the wait.

"Hey, gimp, get up," a voice said from some distant hill.

Coming out of the fog, I looked into the face of my brother. At six feet one Carson is a little shorter than me, but what he lacks in height he makes up in brawn. His muscles looked tight, his neck as thick as a bowling ball. His arms were tree trunks, his legs massive. He's a linebacker on steroids with a little less rage and sunglasses to hide sleep-deprived eyes.

His voice has always been a cross between my father's and a bear's. He has a deep, resonant quality with an edge of authority, and I imagine tawny young men with shaved heads following him into the mouth of hell itself if he beckoned. Though I had tried to smooth out my upper-Southern accent, pronouncing *i*'s like "eye" instead of "ah," he had done nothing to lose his. He always said the way he talked was fine and people up north sound "uppity," and people down south sound like they talked around marbles.

"You *reddy*?" he said.

I sat up and snapped my eyes open. I didn't recognize anyone in the station, and when I looked at the clock, I realized why. It had been three hours since I'd returned from reporting to the parole officer.

"Got the car double-parked. Come on before I get a ticket."

I grabbed my Clarkston-issued overnight bag and followed.

Carson had that same familiar gait, like a farmer carrying a little too much on one shoulder, both feet striking the heel and going all the way to the toe. His arms dangled, and he moved with confidence. "You bring me anything? License plate or something?"

"That's funny."

"I's just asking."

"I brought you a present for every time you've visited in the last year."

"This is it here," he said as we reached the car. He opened the trunk, but I threw my bag in the backseat.

It had been years since I'd ridden in a car. The leather seats smelled new, and it felt good to stretch out. I'd seen this car in commercials, as sleek as a race car but a bit more practical. The front panel looked like a cockpit for a jumbo jet, and his audio player was placed in the radio compartment.

"This thing looks like it could cook your breakfast for you," I said.

"Lots of things have changed since you went away. We have running water now. Can you imagine that?"

I smiled. "And you don't have stripes on your shoulders. What happened?"

"My feet. The army nearly ran me to death, and my arches fell flatter than Susie Wilcox's chest."

Susie was one of Carson's old flames. After they broke up, she was a target for criticism.

"How is Susie?" I said.

"She married some old boy out on Barker's Ridge. Probably met him at the dog track on one of the days she wasn't running. Heard tell she had a bunch of kids and got big."

"How big?" I said, biting at his joke.

"Not sure, but they say she's supersize now. I swear, Will, that girl was so bucktoothed she could eat a cantaloupe through a picket fence. Every time I kissed her, it felt like I was getting a tonsillectomy."

One thing that did not come easy to Carson was the subtle put-down. I knew as long as we kept the conversation "out there," among people of the community or in Congress or the military, we were all right. But there was always the point when we ran out of other people to talk about and he turned his salvos to our family.

"I need a drink," I said, my throat parched like fire. "Not a drink drink, just something wet."

He turned into a gas station near Cabell Huntington Hospital and filled up while I went in and bought a bottle of Mountain

Dew. I had exactly $34 in cash and a check for the money I'd made working at the Clarkston heavy machine refurbishing plant. I had made about a dollar a day, but some of that was taken back because of fees. It was enough to get me started with a few months' rent in some other town, away from the memories and the stares and the talk behind my back.

"Is Mama planning on me living with her for a while?" I said as we pulled away. "I assume she could use the help around the house."

"You sure you want to take that on?" Carson shook his head. "Jenna has a hard time going near the place. Says it clogs her sinuses. She thinks there're dust mites in that house older than we are."

"She's probably right."

"Jenna offered to go over and do Mama's hair for her since she doesn't get out much. Told her she'd do the biggest dust mite's hair for free."

As I discovered, Jenna worked at Eula Johnson's salon, the only one in town, if you didn't count the barbershop where all the men got their hair trimmed if their wives didn't do it for them.

"How is Jenna?" I said.

"Tolerable." He merged onto the interstate, ascending the ramp and reaching the speed limit quickly—something I could never do in the car I drove here as a teenager. "We've had our share of problems, but . . ."

"But what?"

He shrugged. "Nothing. That's all."

"Anybody that would stay with you for this long deserves a combat medal."

"You got that right."

I looked for familiar sights along the road. When you've been away from home, especially in forced exile, you lose the signposts of *place*. It only took a few—one advertising the news team at

Channel 3, another showcasing the shops at a new mall in the area. I saw the holy grails on the hillside—a Sam's Club, the sacred shrine of life in the hills. My theory has always been that West Virginians like Wal-Mart because it returns them to their roots. Our grandparents and great-grandparents planned their trips to town, riding on wagons pulled by horses, then bought their supplies for the month. Wal-Mart is just another general store where you buy in bulk and prepare for the apocalypse.

Carson punched a couple of buttons, and classic rock filtered through the speakers. Grand Funk Railroad, the Who, Styx, and Kansas. The songs took me back to days running the interstate, living life as fast as I could, as if it might end the next day. I'd learned that speed and a little bad judgment can change life in drastic ways.

Carson turned the volume down on "Sweet Home Alabama." "Looks like you stayed in pretty good shape inside. Little on the puny side, but Mama's cooking will fatten you up."

"Didn't have much else to do except stay literate."

"You make it out of there okay? You know, you didn't get hurt or anything, did you?"

I had prepared myself for three questions. This was number one. He wanted to know if anyone had gotten to me, if I'd been violated by some inmate. "I did okay."

"It's harder when you go in young, I guess," he said.

We passed a splattered opossum with its unmistakable long tail and sharp nose amid the viscera, blood, and intestines. On the hill above stood a white church, as familiar as Wal-Mart. The opossum almost looked like a sacrifice.

Two songs later Carson dropped the second question wrapped in a tone of concern. "You've got an uphill battle coming back here. I don't know why you changed your mind about heading up to Morgantown, but people have been talking ever since they ran that newspaper story a couple of weeks ago. Mama can't even set foot in Foodland. I have to drive her down to the Kroger in Barboursville because she thinks nobody will recognize her. Still, she wears sunglasses and a scarf."

"I'm going to play it low-key," I said evenly. "I promise not to put a sign around my neck that says, 'I'm Will Hatfield. Hate me.'"

"You don't have to wear a sign. Your face is enough to bring down the judgment of God for the people around here. I get enough of it at the office."

"What do they say?"

"You hear it on the grapevine. Passed along at church picnics and bars and the produce section at Big Bear. How you really didn't pay the price. That what you did deserved a lot worse than just being locked up a few years."

I had prepared for this, but the words stung even worse coming from my brother. Not that I expected understanding and compassion.

"They're saying that they're gonna get justice their own way. That's what bothers me the most. And Jenna . . ."

"What about her?"

"You know how it can be at a beauty salon. Those people talk it up like it was the second coming of Lucifer himself, you moving back here."

"How would they know I'm coming back?"

Carson shook his head and waved off the question. "She comes home crying sometimes. Those people have judged us, tried us, and hung us a thousand times."

"What do *you* think?"

"About what?"

"About me serving my time? Do you think I paid the price?"

"Aw, I'm not getting into it. That's between you and the law. From that perspective, you've fulfilled every requirement they made. What you have to live with inside is another thing. I expect that'll stick with you a long time. Longer than those people want to know."

"Why did *you* come back?" I said. "You could have lived just about anywhere."

Carson turned off the music and we rode in silence. The verdant hills rolled past like postcards of our youth, and it seemed he was loading his cannon and aiming at something. When he had the target in sight, he began.

"This place is in my soul, deep down to the bone." He cursed. "It's like some people look at Jerusalem or Mecca or one of those Middle Eastern countries where they make their women cover their faces with towels or veils or whatever. That's what this is—a hillbilly holy place. Doesn't matter how far I traveled, Europe or Africa or South America or Asia—what a hole that place was—I always knew I'd come back here, being close to Mama and Daddy and the family. The whole screwed-up, dysfunctional family."

I had never seen Carson so impassioned, unless it concerned sports or his beer brewing. He was an amateur brewer and had mixed his hops and barley in our garage when he was eighteen. How he kept it a secret from my mother is one of the mysteries yet to be unraveled. He didn't keep it a secret from our father because he and Dad had taste tests and even entered competitions until Carson went to college.

"I've never tasted a tomato better than one grown in Uncle Luther's garden," Carson continued. "I've never seen a hillside you can put seed into year after year and watch it grow the sweetest corn, the greenest, most delicious beans this side of heaven. I've been to Paris—what an awful, rat-infested slum that place is. They took us to Versailles and let us walk around in gardens with every imaginable flower in the world, and I tell you it doesn't hold a candle to those three weeks in fall when the leaves burst into a rainbow along the hills around here. It's like living at the end of the yellow brick road."

We passed another exit and a blighted strip of homes. "Bet Versailles didn't have as many trailers. Or liquor stores."

"This place owns me lock, stock, and barrel, Will. And I own *it*—we've got a big piece of it coming to us, you know. The roots go deeper than any ocean on the planet. I don't want to live in any city you could name. I don't want to live down south, where the bugs are bigger than our dogs or cats. I don't want to live out west, where the earthquakes and mudslides bring houses down or the Midwest, where tornadoes chase you into hiding. Name me one place on God's green earth that's better than right here and I'll kiss your rear at midfield at the next Super Bowl."

"Only if I get to sing the national anthem too," I said.

The closer we came to the Milton exit, the tighter my shoulders became, a slow-moving ache that coursed through my body. I sensed a shortness of breath, as if I were climbing into the thin air of an unwelcome mountain.

"That's the way I feel about this place," Carson said. "But no matter how much I love it, if I had your history and if the people there would rather see me dead—"

"You think that's what they want?"

"Some of them, sure."

I wanted to say I'd fallen in love with an Appalachian girl and that truth pushed me forward. I wanted to tell him I was a soldier on a mission, a ranger dropped behind enemy lines whose only weapon was my love for Karin and that I would leave no comrade behind. He would understand that word picture. Instead, I sat, silently listening to the unnerving quiet of his car. We had to yell at each other to be heard in every vehicle I could remember from my childhood, but this was pure silence.

"After Dad died," Carson said, "I thought a lot about you. How close you two were. I think he always felt bad about your foot, that he had caused it."

"Wasn't him. It was my cold thumbs." I asked what the funeral service was like.

"Terrible. It's hard enough to take it in yourself, but to hear

Mama wail like that and have to be carried out to the hearse, I almost wished I was with *you* that day."

"I could have used the company."

"You hear about Elvis?"

Arron Spurlock was someone I'd tried to stay in contact with while I was in Clarkston. He was a year older but had been held back in the third grade. We were instant friends. I'd tried to help him with his homework, and he'd tried to get us kicked out of school.

One hot Fourth of July when it hadn't rained for weeks, Arron lugged a five-gallon bucket full of fireworks to a field near our house. It was mostly cherry bombs and firecrackers and a few bottle rockets. He challenged a group of us to help him light the whole batch at one time, but none of us would bite. Elvis cursed us, and because of his father, he had a pretty good repertoire. He crumpled up some newspaper, set it on fire, and walked over to the bucket while we watched from the hillside.

"That boy's gonna blow himself up," Carson said.

He wasn't far off. The explosion knocked Elvis back, and everybody laughed but me. The fire in the field spread quickly. By the time I got to him, his clothes were ablaze. I dragged him to the creek, coughing and sputtering through the smoke and heat. I can still hear his screams. Carson ran and called the fire department. I thought Elvis was dead because he was just lying in the trickle of water, smoldering. You could smell his burned skin from the field, and the firemen made us go home so they could care for him.

Elvis carried the scars of that day on his body. It took months for him to walk again, but he did. And every time he came around the corner of the road, walking to our house for a pickup game of football or baseball or just to have a watermelon seed–spitting competition, he'd be singing "Hound Dog" or "Blue Suede Shoes" or "Heartbreak Hotel." You could hear his voice ring off the mountains, a bit off-key, but still alive.

"He's not in trouble again, is he?" I said.

"No, he just disappeared. They put out a missing person's report on him, but there's been no word. I'm figuring somebody gave him a recording contract."

Carson told me where Elvis had been working and about his exploits. A DUI two years ago and a breaking and entering at his former boss's house. (Elvis claimed the man hadn't paid him his wages when he quit, so he broke in and took a few items for fair compensation. After Elvis returned the items and fixed the broken window, the man decided not to press charges.)

I was enjoying the conversation because it didn't focus on me. "Any idea where he might have gone?"

Carson shook his head. "Every time I saw him at the gas station he'd ask about you and when you were getting out. Said he couldn't wait to go fishing or hunting with you. You hear anything from him?"

"He came up a couple of times, but I don't think he liked being inside Clarkston. Reminded him too much of what could happen."

"It's a big mystery around town. The Exxon station had a devil of a time finding somebody to replace him. Say what you want about his character but he was a wonder with a wrench and a socket set." Carson exited the interstate where I remembered gas stations and the Mountaineer Opry House. There was now an adult bookstore and more gas stations.

My head ached as the light faded to the west. "Before we go home, could you run me by the cemetery?"

Carson looked at his watch and gave me a furtive glance. "Sure thing."

It wasn't until we were on a two-lane country road that ran deep into my history that Carson asked the third question. He mentioned Karin as "that girl you liked."

But before he could continue, I held up a hand and let him know this was the only No Trespassing sign I had erected. The hunting in the rest of the forest of my history was open, but this section was posted. "I don't want to talk about her, okay?"

His face softened, as if some measure of understanding had invaded his heart. "You're not holding on to that, are you? Tell me you're not coming back for her."

"I said I don't want to talk about it."

"Will, she's—"

"I know everything you know and more," I said, the emotion welling up and overtaking the tightness. "I know, okay?"

Like a persistent lineman, he wouldn't give up. "I'm just trying to keep you from more heartache. That girl—"

I whirled in the seat and grabbed his right arm in a death grip.

Carson overcompensated and jerked the wheel left, weaving into the next lane. A horn honked and rose in volume as we locked eyes. He finally swerved back, regaining control and narrowly missing a pickup that ran off the road and threw gravel and dust into the air.

"Are you crazy?" he shouted. "You almost got us killed."

I stared, jaw clenched. "I'm asking one thing. You don't have to like it that I'm here. You don't have to pretend you're glad to see me or make your wife keep quiet about me, which I know she won't do. But you will *not* talk about Karin. It's a closed subject. You understand?"

"It's your life. You want to throw it away, go ahead. You seem to have done a pretty good job of that, little brother."

A graveyard, particularly one in a small town, provides more than a plot of ground to place remains. It endows a history to its residents, a memorial of the past and their place in it. Years ago people came to graveyards to remember, to honor. Graveyards are not as popular today. Perhaps we're too busy to remember or the exercise is too painful. Perhaps it's simply not convenient for our fast-paced society. But I suspect most people don't care as much. We have chosen to shun the pain of the past and ignore the dead, as if they can't see what we're doing with our lives and their legacy.

Mount Pleasant Cemetery is a small town of its own, sitting on a hill, surrounded by leafy trees that give shade and shelter for inhabitants. I remember coming here as a kid, visiting our grandparents' graves, distant uncles and aunts and cousins taken too soon. We'd mow, weed, plant flowers, and lay wreaths. The oldest graves date to antebellum days with headstones that crumble at a hint of wind. There are men buried here from every conflict in which our country has called poor, young white men to file out of the hills and take their place in the ranks of patriots.

As a boy I quickly learned that a graveyard is no place to play. One leapfrog over a child's headstone was all it took to send my mother flying after me, her eyes like fire. "Will, we respect the dead. We don't dance on graves or use this as a playground. Understand?"

"Yes, ma'am."

Carson's was the only car in the parking lot. A small, white church stood at the entrance to the cemetery, its steeple casting a cross shadow on the length of the yard. The doors to the church were closed, but I could shut my eyes and bring the smell of the wooden pews back from memory. The stained glass was still there, faded and dull now. The concrete steps had weathered and cracked, and I imagined older men and women clinging to the iron railing running up both sides and the pastor in his suit from Sears or JCPenney.

The graveyard rose in the middle and sloped at either side. It was like walking on top of a well-baked pastry. The oldest tombstones were in the middle, flanked by the younger dead. I noticed they had cleared a patch of the woods at the end to make room for more of us, and there were several fresh graves, the ground still brown and grainy from recent burials.

I turned left and made my way to the edge of the woods, respectfully staying true to the lines and angles of the deceased. I stood before a headstone that said *Walter E. Pfelt*. Carson walked up beside me as I said, "Is this . . . ?"

"You didn't hear?" Carson said, dropping his head. "Of course you didn't. He passed a couple of months ago. No, just before Thanksgiving, I think it was. Just dropped dead at the A-Z and plowed into a big display of gherkins. I heard it was a real mess."

For as long as I could remember, Carson and I had pronounced the man's last name "Pee-felt" even though the *P* was supposed to be silent. We even said it to his face, and he never corrected us. He managed both our Little League teams, our jerseys emblazoned with the word *Dodgers* on the front and *Mohr's Tire Farm* on the back.

"He always had a flair for the dramatic," I said.

We stood looking at his headstone a few moments until Carson broke the silence. "Remember that stop sign you ran through?"

"I didn't know you were there."

"We were at practice at the other end of the park, and I wandered over. You got thrown out at the plate by about half a mile."

I remembered like it was yesterday. "I just made up my mind from the moment that ball was hit that nothing was going to stop me until I got home."

"You were flyin'," Carson said.

"Unfortunately that kid in right field had a cannon for an arm."

Carson laughed. "Didn't even bounce. Threw it right to the catcher and he just stood there and waited, like a cat coming up on a mouse in a trap. Shoulda seen your eyes."

"I was going to bowl him over like Rose did Fosse in the 1970 All-Star Game, but it didn't work out."

"What'd Peefelt say? He chew you out?"

I chuckled and shook my head, patting the tombstone. "He knew how bad I felt. He grabbed my arm and helped me up, then dusted me off. The other team was jumping up and down like monkeys at feeding time, hollering and falling on each other by the pitcher's mound. Everybody else wanted to kill me."

"I remember. I turned around and went back to practice so I wouldn't have to claim your body."

"Peefelt bent over so I could see into his eyes and he said, 'You know what I like about what you just did? I like the fact that you didn't slow down once you'd made up your mind. You threw everything you had into that. You live your life like that, Will, and you're gonna go places.'"

"He sure was right," Carson said with more than a hint of sarcasm.

"He made me want to be a Little League coach. All the other coaches would have yelled at me or turned and walked away, but he met me at home. It was almost like he took the pain away when he did that."

"You still remember it."

"I remember blowin' most of my foot off too, but it wasn't half as much fun as that game." I nodded toward the grave. "So long, Mr. Peefelt."

We moved down the row, passing familiar names that brought faces to mind. Chaney. Ullom. Hall. Black. Meadows. I could give addresses and phone numbers for most of the families laid to rest here because they had lived in one place their entire adult lives.

Under the fading shade of an oak tree I found my father's grave. He rested beside his mother, father, two sisters, and a brother. The final plot was for my mother—her name already etched in the stone with only the year of her death left blank. The grave was well tended, as he had done for his own parents, and I assumed Carson paid Jasper Woods to keep it. Jasper was

a grizzled old man when I was a kid, with a perpetual stream of
tobacco juice running down his chin and a pack of Pall Malls
rolled into his shirtsleeve. He moved like a phantom around the
grounds, cleaning and mowing even those graves he wasn't paid
to care for.

"Jasper's still around, isn't he?" I said.

Carson pointed to a small, metal trailer parked behind the out-
building that held the mowers and garden equipment. "A bunch
of us pitched in and bought him a new trailer after his other one
burned. Even has a toilet hookup and running water so he can
take a shower."

"What did he say when he saw it?"

"Just mumbled a few things and spat. Same old Jasper."

No one could understand Jasper better than my father. He was an
interpreter of the strange language of the toothless, bespectacled
nomad who had lived at the cemetery as long as anyone could
remember. In that sense he was not a wanderer, but one look at
his disheveled clothing and rattletrap truck led you to believe he
was trying to escape something or someone. He lived in blessed
seclusion, among the vagaries of the human mind.

I often wondered if the reason I was drawn to certain out-
casts in prison was because of the example of my own father. He
showed a love and compassion for Jasper, and the man returned
his kindness with almost caninelike obeisance. My father was the
alpha, Jasper the pack dog. Every year my father filled in the
man's meager income on his 1040 form and mailed it, using our
address. When the refund invariably came, I would accompany
my father to Jasper's trailer. Jasper would stare at the check and
mutter something, at which my father would laugh and clap him
on the back as if he were a professional comedian.

On Thanksgiving and Christmas my father and I would drive
to the cemetery carrying plates full of turkey and ham and stuffing

and cranberry sauce and all the fruits of our holidays covered with
Saran wrap. We'd make the long walk, angling through the graves
until we came to his place.

Jasper's eyes would widen with excitement when I'd say,
"Happy Thanksgiving" or "Merry Christmas." My mother always
fixed the best desserts, and though I could not understand many
of his words, I did understand the emotion he expressed when he
mumbled about her rum or carrot cake.

The only time I ever saw my father at odds with Jasper was
when the people of the church complained about Jasper's dog. He
was a short-haired mongrel that loped through the cemetery like it
was his own, with the proclivity to lift his leg on some of the most
well-to-do members planted in the ground.

My father was elected to tell Jasper the bad news that his
dog—unnamed by Jasper but Carson and I called it "Urine"—
would have to go. I was with him, skirting the edges of their lop-
sided conversation. "We just can't have a dog peein' and poopin'
on the graves, Jasper. It's nothing personal."

Jasper mumbled louder than I had ever heard him. His sen-
tences were filled with *n* and *h* sounds, punctuated with the dribble
and spit of the tobacco juice. He pointed past the church toward
the road. "Nat daw obaan mmhn behh ahhn moh kihh huh cuh
aroh heeh," he yelled.

Afterward, with my father's help, I had pieced together his
argument and that one sentence: "That dog obeys me better than
most kids who come around here." Jasper was right. The dog did
obey, but when Jasper wasn't around or was tending the back
plots, the animal had a mind and direction of its own.

Jasper seemed perplexed that anyone could feel his dog wasn't
hospitable. In fact, he was known to nuzzle the preacher's hand
when he read, "Ashes to ashes and dust to dust . . ." The mongrel
seemed to have an uncanny ability to pick out the most bereaved
in the crowd and sit at their feet.

"I'm sorry," my father said. "I really am. The people are serious about this. They say if the dog doesn't go, you'll have to leave."

"Wheh I goh tah hmn?"

"I've got some friends on a farm over in Hamlin. I can ask them if they need a good dog. Maybe they'll take him."

The next day I rode in the middle of the truck, my father to my left and Jasper to my right. The dog sat between Jasper's legs, sniffing at the wind blasting through the cab of our truck, watching the trees go by, licking and sniffing. They say a dog's sense of smell is a lot more sensitive than a human's, and I figured that was why the dog liked Jasper. The man was a veritable olfactory smorgasbord. His clothes hadn't seen the inside of a washing machine except for the few times he allowed my mother to do a load for him. His boots were caked with the mud of the dead, his armpits smelled cadaverous, and I could only imagine the inside of his home, his bed, his kitchen. I couldn't even think about his toilet.

Two weeks after Jasper dropped the dog at the farm and waved good-bye to him in that field, Urine returned to the cemetery. I suppose Jasper's scent was just too strong. Jasper tried to hide him at first, but soon someone from the church called my father, and I accompanied him on one of our longest rides together.

"Why can't Jasper tie him up?" I said, stating the obvious.

"I've told him the same thing, but Jasper says tying up a dog is a sin. I guess he tried it, and it nearly broke his heart to see it run back and forth, wearing a path out beside the trailer."

"It's better than losing him, isn't it?"

"Will, it's hard to understand some people. Why they do what they do. With Jasper, it's easy. Because of what he went through as a child, he can't bear to see an animal caged."

"What happened to him?"

My father clenched his teeth and thought for a long time. "Let's just say his parents weren't the most well-adjusted people on the planet. His mama loved him, but she had other kids to care for, and when she died, his daddy kept him locked up so he wouldn't go roaming at night."

"Locked in his room?" I said.

"Something like that." He shivered and shook his head. "I'll take you back to their place someday. Maybe. But don't be too quick to judge Jasper about his dog. Have you seen the way animals sidle up to him?"

"I figured it was because Jasper smells more like a dog than a human."

Another father would have shamed or scolded, but my dad smiled, his eyes crinkling. "You may be right. But I think it might have more to do with his gentle spirit. Jasper has every right to be angry at the world, but somehow he turned that meanness into goodness. There's not a soul on earth as close to God as that old boy."

"I've never seen him in church," I said.

Daddy nodded. "I don't think he'd be welcome. People would be more concerned about the way he smelled than the state of his soul. But I've seen him in the summer standing outside an open window, staring off into the sunset. Seems to me he's praying. Some people are given a great gift of not caring what others think or about anything but being faithful to what they're called by God to do. I think Jasper is one of those people."

We pulled into the church parking lot, and as soon as we closed the doors, Jasper was outside his trailer looking at us. He lived about a hundred yards from the church, and as we came through the main gate of the cemetery, he darted inside and emerged with something black in his hand. The dog jumped up on him and followed.

"Oh no," my dad said. "Jasper!"

A shot rang out. It was the only time I ever saw my father step on a grave. He bolted for Jasper's trailer, and I caught a glimpse of the young man he once was, fast and lean. The wind whipped his hat from his head, and it landed on a fresh grave. I grabbed it, and when I caught up to him, he and Jasper were standing over the dog's lifeless body. Blood splattered Jasper's coveralls, and he said something through an expressionless face as he turned over the first shovel of dirt. My father put a hand on the man's shoulder.

"Mind if I have a minute alone?" I said to my brother.

He checked his watch again. "Yeah. I'll head back to the car. We should be getting home soon. Jenna —"

"I'll only be a minute," I interrupted.

I knelt and studied my father's stone. It was gray, the kind Daddy said he liked as he roamed the grounds. Not too big. He always had a problem with people or families who thought they were important enough to take two parking spaces. It was the same in death.

"Well, I made it, just like you said," I whispered. "I came back. I'll take care of Mama now, for whatever time she has left. I wish I could have been here for you. I wanted to at least say good-bye."

His face swept through my mind like a flash flood. Pictures of him younger, a sepia tone to his skin. Him asleep on the couch, me watching a game. Him and his father standing by an awning, near an old Chevy, squinting into the sun, a foot apart, hands clasped in front of them, not touching. A grainy video played in my mind, with yellow streaks running through it, the kind you see of those famous stars when a find is made in their basement. Only these movies would never be seen by anyone but our family. My father riding the tractor. My mother in the kitchen. Carson and I called her "Our Lady of Perpetual Baking Soda." Shep, our white and brown collie, panting in the summer dust and my father sitting beside him on the porch, a blue sky framed in the background. Those were the images I carried of my father and a thousand more.

A car door slammed, and Carson started the engine.

I patted my father's headstone in the same way he had patted my head so many times when I was younger. I found a path and walked it, looking from side to side at the graves. Most were early 1900s here, but I was surprised to see one newer stone. At the bottom, under the names and near the ground line, were the words, *"Jesus said, 'Let the little children come to me, and do not hinder them, for the kingdom of heaven belongs to such as these.'"*

I stood transfixed. Children's lives taken at such an early age. Lives forever entwined with my story.

Carson honked and I joined him, knowing I was about to enter my hometown, free-falling into a life I had left so many years ago. Fear—metallic and strong, tasting like blood—bubbled up from somewhere under the earth. I had navigated the years away, avoiding taunts and threats and indescribable evil, but this new voyage, coming home, somehow scared me more. I felt out of control, tossed on unending, unforgiving waves. Life has a way of doing that. At one moment you're moving in a direction that seems sensible, even exciting, and the next you're hurtling, breaking from orbit, wondering what forces caused gravity to loosen its hold.

What would I say to people who asked what I was going to do with my life?

Carson cut through the belly of Hurricane and under the railroad until he found Virginia Avenue, a familiar stretch of back road that had strangely narrowed in my memory. The homes seemed closer to the road, and I could almost read the fine print in the satellite dishes that dotted the double-wide trailers and small homes. As kids we would travel this road in search of an open tennis court. There always seemed to be someone on a front porch, kids swinging in a tire suspended from a walnut tree branch, but now the porches were barren and the front windows flickered the light of big-screen televisions.

I remembered when this road was unpaved and the ruts from the trucks taking the back route were so deep that we had to ride the side of the hill, the car pitched precariously at a seventy-five-degree angle. Those were the days before mandatory seat belts and air bags.

We drove in silence, the chirp of crickets and a soft humidity settling over the fields and meandering streams. I had heard the same at Clarkston, a faint, muted melody that somehow seemed too far away to grasp, but here I felt I could reach out and touch it. Grab it with a fist and hold on tightly.

Fireflies—we called them lightning bugs when we were young—drifted up, their rears flashing yellow, as if something was approaching, some unstoppable train that was bearing down on them, and there was nothing they or any of the rest of us could do about it.

Railroad tracks ran to our left, an old freight line that chugged through every evening about this time. Later in the night it would pass the other way, coming and going, a cycle of the hills.

"Think I might find an old Ball jar in the basement tonight and fill it full of those lightning bugs," I said, breaking our silence.

Carson glanced at me like I was roadkill, a mess of blood and guts by the curb of some five-star restaurant. "Why would you do a fool thing like that?"

I closed my eyes. "Just to see what it feels like. To be a kid again. To get excited about something innocent and pure."

"Go ahead and bring a big jar of bugs into the house and see what Mama does," Carson said. Then he thought a moment. "On second thought, after what you've been through, it would probably be better to do that the first night and get it over with. She ought to know you're crazy from the get-go rather than getting her hopes up."

We crossed under the I-64 bridge, and I read the same spray-painted message I had seen every day on the way home from school twenty years ago: "Dogwood Sucks." A newer message was written on the other side, where my family could see it every time they drove past: "Fry Will Hatfield."

Carson frowned. "I asked them to come wash it off or paint over it, but it didn't do any good."

"It's okay. Good to know what I'm up against."

"Listen, that's not the half of it. There are some things you're going to have to get used to. One is that the people around here have good memories. A bunch of them are still fighting Vietnam. Some are still fighting the Civil War, for crying out loud."

"I know this will be an uphill battle," I said.

"Yeah, but you don't know how uphill. That sucker is tall and these people hold a grudge as well as anybody on earth. I don't know that two lifetimes in jail would satisfy them."

Telephone poles carried the outside world into the hollow, and electrical wires looked like lifelines. I expected everything to look smaller as we rounded the final turn and saw the house. Instead, the rosebushes and shrubs seemed to have taken over. Trees grew over the road, dangling limbs and branches reaching out to intercept us.

I glanced at my watch and calculated the time it had taken to get from Clarkston, and I figured it was twice as long as if I had driven myself. It was just one more thing I hadn't done since I'd been arrested—cared about time.

Jenna was at the door as we stepped from the car and made our way to the concrete path. The huge windows of the great room, an extension Carson had designed and helped build, reflected the golden glow of the evening and the lightning bugs ascending into the mist.

"Hello there, stranger," Jenna said as she opened the creaky screen door. She gave me a weary smile as my mother appeared, older than I'd expected—grayer, more thinning hair, her face puffy, her hands frail. She took a high step, lifting her leg twice as high as she needed to clear it, then grabbed Jenna's arm. Jenna gave Carson a look.

"Aw, honey," my mother said, her eyes filling with tears. She held my face in her hands and shook her head. "I never thought I'd ever see you again."

"I know, Mama."

I held her a long time. Finally she pulled away, grabbed her glasses, and wiped her eyes with a paper towel. "Your father would have loved to see this day."

"I wish he were here."

"I didn't sleep at all last night. Was up the whole night praying. Just hoping everything would go okay." She looked at Carson. "Did you find him all right?"

"Yeah, Mama, he was right where I thought he'd be."

As Carson helped her inside, Jenna turned and draped an arm over my shoulder. She wore a low-cut blouse and perfume that wafted like a cloud of nuclear waste. She licked her lips, leaned forward, and whispered into my ear, "I'll bet it's been a long time since you've been this close to a woman."

I leaned back and tried to smile. "They don't have many dances up there, if that's what you mean."

I took her arm from around me, but instead of moving away, she reached behind me, put both hands in my back pockets, and pulled me close. "Your mama's a lucky woman to have a man like you around again."

"Yeah," I said, stepping back. "I'm not sure she should be all that excited. You know as well as anyone what people will say."

Jenna crossed her arms. "Nothing they haven't said for a long time. When my customers find out my last name is Hatfield and who my husband is related to, they get sick and have to cancel their appointments. Most never come back."

"Why do you stay? Why don't you move someplace where this whole thing doesn't hang over you?"

She leaned close again, and I wondered if every man who got a haircut had the same view. "Give me a reason to leave."

Carson cleared his throat. "You two come on in — Mama has supper ready."

She had made my favorite salads, macaroni and potato, along with her famous chicken and rice dish. As kids, Carson and I had fought over the leftovers like they were rare baseball cards. The rice and chicken blended perfectly, the chicken falling off the bones in homage to my mother's intemperate ability to take a few pots and pans and mix them with heat and come up with food that would literally make you want to not stop eating.

There were green beans from the previous canning season that tasted like they'd just been picked. Rolls that melted like manna in my mouth, slathered with "cow butter," as she called it. No margarine for her. And a pitcher full of sweet tea and lemonade — something we discovered long before Arnold Palmer ever did. The only thing missing was my father's sweet corn, and I figured I'd plant that as an offering to his memory and enjoy it in the summer.

"Bet you didn't eat like this at Clarkston," Carson said.

"You're looking skinny compared with how I last remember you," Jenna said.

"Now leave him alone and let him eat," Mama said. "You look good, Will." She jumped up, if you could call it that, her languid arms firmly pressed on the table for support, as if some intestinal pain had hit her.

"What is it?" I said.

"Sweet potatoes. You always liked sweet potatoes, and I cooked a whole dish full and forgot to get them out of the oven."

I made her sit and searched for an oven mitt in the drawers by the sink. I opened the silverware drawer by mistake and noticed cloudy forks and knives, the tray edged with dirt, spoons caked with splotches. Her eyesight had become worse in her old age, but she still worked hard trying to keep the place clean and I couldn't help but love her for it.

I brought the CorningWare dish, covered with foil and bubbling like lava, to the table. She cooked the potatoes cut in half and soaked in a perfect juice—some concoction of her mother's filled with brown sugar and cinnamon and other spices.

To my mother, cooking was not just an exercise in survival. It had been growing up in the hollows of Camel's Creek. Cornmeal and molasses for breakfast and dinner—no lunch. The smell of her mother's iron skillet cooking a squirrel or rabbit her brothers had killed or a fish they'd caught in the stream. At some point in the abundance we enjoyed when I was a child, cooking had changed from an avoidance of hunger to an act of worship. She worked as a high priestess, toiling and sweating before the altar, combining ingredients, and eliciting unforgettable flavors.

I never marked Xs on a calendar at Clarkston, but I did count down the meals at the end, knowing it would only be a year before I had a taste of her pecan pie. Or the rum-laced pound cake. Or blueberry crunch. To me, grace is my mother's sweet potato casserole—undeserved, unmerited favor lavished on children who have no idea what it took to achieve.

Jenna brushed her foot against mine under the table, and I finally rose and held my plate in my hands, leaning against the oven.

"Why don't you sit?" my mother said.

"I've been sitting all day."

Carson laughed. "Yeah, and he can pack more in that way."

"Where are you going to work, Will?" Jenna said.

Carson gave her a halfhearted scowl.

"Well, he doesn't want to sit around here all day," she said.

"I've been thinking about that. I figure I need a long walk or two before I go down that road."

"Carson can find you something, can't you?" my mother said. "You've hired a ton of people."

"Government would have trouble with me hiring a convict. Besides, Will doesn't want to work indoors and stare at a screen all day. He's been cooped up enough to last a lifetime. I mean, I could help you get back on your feet —"

"It's okay," I said, less annoyed by the conversation than the feeling of being trapped again. I had spent years in a cage, working off my debt by listening to conversations I didn't want to hear and breathing air forced on me. Sweat and odors too foul to describe. Now I felt I had walked back into another prison. A prison of childhood memories and words I didn't — or *couldn't* — accept.

"Think I'll take a walk back on the hill before dessert," I said.

"But it's getting dark," my mother said.

"And we have to get going," Carson said, pushing back from the table. "Got an early morning tomorrow."

I smiled at them. "I made a promise — to myself and the Almighty — that if he got me out of that place, the first thing I'd do when I got home was go up on that hill and thank him." I kissed my mother on the forehead and grabbed a black flashlight my father kept by the door. "Thanks for the ride," I said to Carson. "Jenna."

"Don't be a stranger now," she cooed. "I could probably ask the owner at the shop if she knows of anything."

"I appreciate that, but I'll be okay."

The flashlight was a black behemoth my father would take on early morning hunting and fishing trips. It weighed five pounds if it was an ounce. I could hardly pick the thing up when I was a kid. Now it almost felt light.

The barn lay in ruins at the base of the hill. It had fallen midway through my tenure at Clarkston. The mass of wood and tin was probably worth a fortune at the flea market about ten miles down the road, and I laughed as I thought about how much money I could make selling knickknacks from the basement and out of the rubble here.

Weeds and brush grew around the shell, and the barbed wire fence had succumbed to rust. I moved past the hulk of my father's hay rake, a rusted, spiderlike metal sculpture with red fingers pointing toward the sky. My father would hook it to the tractor, Carson or me perched precariously on the metal seat, and when he gave the word, we would kick a pedal in front of us. The fingers would lift, leaving behind a perfect row of hay for the baler a few hours later; then the fingers descended, catching dried grass and pulling it to the next line where we would kick again. On a flat piece of property it was actually fun, but our land was marked with rolling hills that looked innocuous and gradual.

As we rode, the back of the rake filled us with dread. It was like hanging on to the side of a listing ship, and when my father stopped the tractor to avoid a rabbit scurrying for its life, we hung, suspended in the air. I was sure the feeling was the same one astronauts had while waiting for the lunar module to fire.

I used the flashlight to guide me up the hill. To my left the moon reflected on the surface of the pond. Water had changed the slope of the graded pathway, revealing new seeds of limestone I'd never seen. But I remembered the trees, a mighty oak at a curve that held back the shifting earth, and a fecund smell engulfing me. Halfway to the top I turned and saw the trail of headlights snaking down our driveway toward the road and the soft, yellow glow of the light at the end of the walk.

Home. It hit like a wave and the emotion was strong. I was finally home.

The rest of the trip was blurry, a mix of regret and emotion at what I'd lost. The feeling of simply walking up a remote hill, alone, no guards, no one watching. When I made it to the field at the top of the path, a cool breeze met me, and I ran my hand through the growing hay, recalling the faces of cattle and our old mule, Pet.

Stars reached out as I moved toward the plateau of the two hills. A little farther, I could see the outline of the tall pines.

I found remnants of campsites of my youth, a ring of rocks where we'd kept warm through the night, sharing stories, trying to scare each other. Once, we'd seen a light moving through the darkness, and Carson told me it was a headless hunter looking for his gun. It turned out to be our father and the big flashlight I now carried. At the moment he reached our tent, the wind picked up and blew like some Appalachian hurricane. He helped us gather our things, extinguish the fire, and hurry back down the hill. That night the maple tree behind our house fell, a victim of lightning and a fierce storm.

I sat on one of the rocks, clicked off the flashlight, and stared at the sky. The moon was a crescent, and I traced Orion with a finger and found the Big Dipper. My father had instilled within us a love for places we would never go but could only see.

Below me, half-hidden in the treetops, were the lights of our town. Though it had grown since I had left, it was still small, and I could pick out the lamps over the Foodland parking lot and the flashing yellow at the railroad tracks.

"I do thank you for bringing me back here," I whispered. "You've been faithful to me and I'm grateful. Now I just have one more thing to ask, and then I'll leave you alone and never bother you again."

My voice drifted down the hill and into the woods. I closed my eyes and thought of Clarkston—I'd seen this in my mind a thousand times. If this could become a reality, why couldn't my dream of Karin also come true?

Through the trees walks a figure in white, her skin milky and ghostlike. She glides along, her skirt touching the grass top as she sways to the beat of unwritten songs. As she nears, I stand and reach for her. Her skin is soft and warm, and she envelops me with her arms.

"Karin," I whisper, "I've waited so long."

She pulls away, and there is nothing but the sky and her smile and the curve of her lips and the softness of her back.

"I will build our house here," I say out loud, for no one to hear. For everyone. "I will marry you. Our children will roam these hills, our laughter will bounce off the walls, and our love will grow."

I could almost hear her laugh. The weight of the task is heavy—not just building the home or grading the road or the thousand things it will take to make the dream come true, but the wooing, the process I am about to undertake with *her*. How it will be accomplished and how long it will take I don't know.

But I do know this: I love Karin. She is the unsung song of my life. I long to see her smile again and hear her laughter. I long to sit on this very spot and watch the sun go down over the hills, watch the fireflies rise, and enjoy our children. We will sip tea, hold hands, make love, and give life where there's been death.

"Karin, I've waited a long time. But I will wait longer. I will wait for you."

I camped there that night, returning to the house for a piece of pie and digging an old sleeping bag out of my closet. My mother had kept the room virtually the same as when I'd last slept there—the innocence of the walls and bookshelves shocked me. It was like walking into a stranger's life.

My mother caught me sneaking out the back, and I told her I didn't want to wake her.

"Why would you want to sleep up there on the ground after all you've been through? I made your bed."

"It's hard to explain, Mama. I guess maybe it's because I can. Inside, they told you what to do and when to do it. This is the first thing I can do without anyone having a say in it." I moved toward her. "You'll be all right, won't you?"

She recoiled at the notion of being needy. All her life she had presented a can-do attitude, never asking for help. The very suggestion that she *needed* me in the house was anathema to her. But it was the easiest way to be released. She had taught the art of guilt and manipulation well.

"I'll have your breakfast cooking tomorrow morning," she said, closing the door.

I ate some pie on the way, the moon higher and brighter now, and carried the flashlight along with my grandfather's old quilt. I also found a small shovel, some old newspaper, and a box of matches. After I cleared the fire pit, I dug enough grass away so the fire wouldn't spread and moved the rocks into a complete circle. It took three trips to get enough wood to burn through the night. I used the newspaper to start the fire and spread the quilt and sleeping bag on the ground.

With the stars set perfectly above, I laid plans to work my way back into the world. Her world. Sleeping outside cleared my head and energized me the way it had when I was a kid. It was my hope to build a house on this spot and, as simple or as crazy as it felt, begin an adult life.

The fire caught, and soon yellow tendrils of flame licked skyward. The smell of woodsmoke brought back nights Carson and I spent with my father at the lake or hunting. I could almost feel my father's touch. It was during those long, languorous nights that I learned the most from him and about him. He would teach something new about himself or reveal something about me with each outing, not in a planned, scripted way, as if he had an agenda, but in a loving, more natural way that flowed like the laughter we shared.

I often imagined his reaction to what I'd done—did he stare out at the yard and anticipate what lay ahead for us? Did he weep or was he resolute, unmoved in his compassion for me?

"How do you know the right person to marry?" I asked one summer night as we lay by the fire, our hands behind our heads, our bellies full of fish and baked potatoes.

He answered as if we were talking about catching a fish or shoeing a horse. "You never *really* know who the right one is, if there is such a thing. I've always thought it was more important to *be* the right one than to find her."

"What do you mean?"

"A smart woman who's looking for more than just income to spend or a hunk of a body that will get flabby in a few years looks for more than she can see." He touched his chest. "It's in here. Develop your heart, and you'll be the right person when that special one comes along."

"How do you develop your heart?"

"You work on it like anything else. It takes time and effort. Your heart is like an unplowed field. Even if you have good soil, you have to work it up and see what's best to plant there. If you train your heart to see things, to lean toward others, to care about people rather than things, to always take advantage of an opportunity to reach out to strangers and sacrifice for your friends, you'll wind up with a good heart."

"Is that what Mama saw in you?"

He chuckled, one eye closed, one focused on a twinkling star a million miles away. "Your mother shattered all my theories about marriage and matters of the heart. It was like finding out the law of gravity sent apples flying up instead of down. I was in her spell the moment I met her."

"So there is love at first sight?"

"I suppose. Though I think for most people it's not 'falling in love' that happens; it's more of a slow drift. If you can drift one way, you can drift the other. That's why it's so important to have your heart right."

"Meaning . . . ?"

He turned on his side, an elbow crooked. "When you say 'I do' to someone—no, when you tell her you love her and ask her to marry you—you'd better be ready to commit yourself to that person for the rest of your life. And that means no matter what. You find someone you click with better, she turns out to be a slob, you strike it rich and want to go some other way—no matter what happens, you have to find a way to love her the rest of your life.

"Most marriages get tough. Sometimes it's right away, sometimes it takes a while, but usually you find out somewhere down the road that the things you wanted and the things you got were different. The trick is to hang in there long enough to let your hearts win out over everything else. If you pick a woman who's looking for a good heart in her husband, you'll make it."

He squinted at the fire as the embers grew hotter. Our extra potatoes steamed in their foil wrapping. "You got someone in mind already?"

I smiled at the memory and the way I'd tossed the question away, but I think he could tell even then there was someone. It would be years from that night before I could prove to Karin that my heart was something to fight for. That it was worth her devotion. It was to be a blood sacrifice neither of us could imagine.

I drifted off to sleep with the crackling fire and night noises. An owl flew overhead. Crickets chirped. There were no slamming doors, laughing guards, clinking keys, or flushing toilets.

Are you looking at this right now? I thought. *Is any part of you thinking of me tonight, Daddy?*

My father once told me that your first waking thought in the morning—the first thing that pops into your mind other than having to run to the bathroom—that's the thing your heart is turned toward. If you immediately think of work or a baseball game or something political, that's what holds you.

If he was right, my heart had been turned toward Karin a long time. Whether it was wrong to want her as my wife, whether someone would judge me because of her situation wasn't my concern. It was simply the truth. I loved her. I wanted her back. And as I closed my eyes and drifted off, I knew the first thing in my mind when I woke would be her.

I let my mind wander back to the concert—the last full night we spent together.

22

Will

July 1, 1980
Cincinnati, Ohio

Our lips had never touched until that night.

Karin and I had driven to school together for a few months before the concert. Her father had set up the ride, promising Karin would pay me a few dollars for gas each week. She had returned from a failed year away at college—she hadn't talked much about it—and was without a car. I assured her father that payment wasn't necessary. I was glad to give her a ride and it was right on my way, which wasn't true. It took a few extra minutes to get to her place, but I looked forward to time with her. On some days I waited three hours for her to finish class, but I spent my time in the library studying. Before her last class ended, I would make my way to the stairs and move outside, where I could catch her coming out the doors. She always seemed surprised to see me.

In all of our rides and talks, Karin hadn't come close to showing an interest in me romantically. She'd actually talked about her different boyfriends, pulling me into her inner world as a confidant. I was taking a summer school photography class and asked if she would be my subject in a black-and-white assignment.

I convinced her that she would be perfect because of her hair color and its contrast with her skin. After a few days of cajoling and a promise that I would buy her dinner afterward (which I had cunningly devised as a pretense—I would have taken her to dinner in a second), she agreed but on the condition I would take her photographs at a cemetery. It seemed odd at the time, but I didn't question it. I was just glad she had said yes to my proposal.

It was during the photo shoot that the subject of my birthday came up. Karin had begged me to turn off the makeshift cassette player I had hooked up and let her listen to the radio. I could not believe a person would listen to commercials and music others picked, but I let her flip stations until she found a song she liked.

"You like Jackson Browne, don't you?" she said, taking my camera and trying to make sense of the settings.

"I only have a couple of shots left—"

"He's coming to Cincinnati in a few weeks," Karin said, holding the camera to her eye, a slender finger dancing over the shutter release. "July 1."

"I heard about it, but I have to work the next morning."

"I got us tickets," she said, then laughed as she took my picture.

There's a line in one of Browne's songs about a man taking a picture of a lover turning—the camera captures a moment in time, a childish laugh, and that recorded moment secures a trace of sorrow. She perfectly captured my surprise at the invitation.

"How did you get tickets?" I said.

"The morning show I listen to was giving them away. I won two in the VIP section on the floor. We even got backstage passes."

My mouth dropped.

"You want to go, don't you?"

"Yeah, it's just that I don't—"

"Take a walk on the wild side. We can drive up in the afternoon, see the concert, then drive back on your birthday. That is your birthday, right?"

I nodded.

"Come on, Will. It'll be fun."

Over dinner we talked about the trip and the effect Browne's music had on me. "I was walking by the electronics section of a department store months ago. There was a record on the player spinning, the sound down, but there was something about the voice and the words that drew me. I listened to the entire side, flipped it over, and listened to the next. I stood there, mesmerized. It was incredible."

"Did you buy the album?"

"No, but I thought seriously about it."

"You are so cheap. Just like my dad."

I said little to my parents about the trip, just that I was going to be out late. I assumed Karin said little to hers.

After work, we drove the three and a half hours to Cincinnati. I found parking close to the Riverfront Coliseum, as it was called then, and we wandered around the city, looking at the buildings and stores. I took a picture of Karin at Fountain Square, the middle of the city, and an older man asked if I wanted one of both of us. I smiled beside her, as happy as I had ever been, not making much physical contact. Before the man snapped the photo, she grabbed me around the waist and hugged me tightly, burying her head in my chest. I reacted by wrapping my arms around her. The shutter snapped, and we had our first photograph together.

"You need to loosen up, big boy," she said.

We ate at a quaint restaurant she picked out because it served Italian food. I gasped at the prices but tried not to show my concern. Since the tickets were free, I figured we could splurge for the meal.

"Where do you want to be in ten years?" Karin said out of the blue.

The question took me by surprise, but I dabbed at my mouth with a stunningly white napkin and came up with an answer. "After tonight, I think I want to be somewhere with you."

She rolled her eyes. "Come on."

"Seriously, I think this is the most fun I've ever had."

"Good answer, but not good enough," Karin said. "*Where* do you want to be? Do you want to be like George Bailey and see the world? Or is Dogwood enough?"

"You say it like it's a hellhole."

"It is to some people."

"I guess it's all in your perspective. The way I look at it, the world is filled with lots of places, all of them different but basically the same. When you surround yourself with good people, it doesn't really matter *where* you are."

She poked at her shrimp and scallops in white sauce, finally snagging a swirl of pasta. "People are looking for more than just friends and a place to stay. They want passion. They want to *live*. They want to abandon their lives to something bigger than they are. Do you understand that?"

"I think people want their lives to mean something. That when you get to the end and look back, you'll be able to say it counted. If that's what you mean about finding something bigger, I agree."

Karin sat back, dropping her fork. "I don't think I could ever go for a guy like you, Will."

The way she said it was painful, so matter-of-fact. "And why's that?"

"You're too predictable. Your idea of passion is planting something and watching it grow or working at the same job for thirty years. The world's a lot bigger than Dogwood. There are places waiting to be discovered, waiting for the first person to set foot in the sand of some exotic beach."

"I could go for an exotic beach or two. But have you ever put a foot on the limestone on our hill?"

Karin gave a heavy sigh. "That's just what I expected. I'm talking about islands, places where the people have never seen a person with skin as white as ours."

"As pretty as yours."

"Stop trying to win me with compliments."

"Stop being so passionate."

"You're incorrigible," she said, stuffing a shrimp into her mouth.

"Does that mean you like me? They don't use big words like that in Dogwood."

She laughed and I knew I'd won at least some part of her heart.

We finished our meal and walked around the city some more. We ate ice cream at a Baskin-Robbins, and she threw most of hers in the trash, crunching the cone.

We walked to the Coliseum, taking pictures of Jackson's bus. Mostly we found 18-wheelers carrying equipment. We did get one shot of David Lindley, the long-haired lap guitar player who punctuated Browne's music with the searing lead riffs. He wore sunglasses and his hair flowed down his back, and he flashed us the peace sign.

Karin paused at the doors to the Coliseum. Six months earlier the Who had performed here, and in the confusion of fans storming these very doors, eleven were trampled to death. It was eerie walking inside the building. Standing on a spot where people had lost their lives seemed to unnerve her.

Our seats, assigned and numbered because of the tragedy, were on the floor, in the middle. The air filled with familiar concert smells, beer and an occasional waft of marijuana. The crowd began to sense something happening onstage when the lights went out. I heard drumsticks clicking through the whistles and cheers, and then the blasting beat of the guitar and the drums engulfed us.

23

Will

I awoke, cold as a stone, something sizzling in the fire behind me. My back stiff, I turned and saw ashes smoking as a man poured a yellow stream. It didn't take me long to figure out what the liquid was or that the person zipping up his brown pants was Eddie Buret.

He spat a stream of brown tobacco juice at the ground by my head. I could tell he had deadly accuracy, and I wondered if he was as good with his gun.

"Checked in with your parole officer yet?" Eddie said. He spoke around the chaw.

"Yesterday," I said.

"Good for you, Hatfield. Nice and prompt. Keep that up. Hate to see you get thrown back in over a technicality." He scanned the view and took a deep breath. "Real nice up here. Imagine you never thought you'd get back."

I let the statement hang in the reddening sky, remembering the old proverb my father used to quote: *Red sky at morning, sailors take warning.*

"It's a pretty piece of ground. Too bad your dad didn't have the gumption to sell it when he could."

"What do you mean?"

Eddie waved a hand. "What's done is done. Can't go back to the past, right?" He crouched like a catcher, his knees cracking, looking into my face to read something that wasn't there. "How'd those old boys treat you up in Clarkston? Probably a lot better than Moundsville, huh? I've heard stories of that place. But you don't look too much worse for the wear. Must've found somebody to protect you." He smiled and I saw bits of tobacco on his yellowing teeth. His star had the word *Chief* on it.

"Didn't know you decided to go into law enforcement," I said. "Last I heard, you were trying to break into NASCAR."

"When your father has lots of influence, you take what you're offered. He convinced me it might be a good career move, and I guess he was right."

Eddie didn't wear a wedding band, and I imagined a string of lonely apartments he had moved out of that would never look the same.

"Thanks for your concern," I said.

"You don't have to get smart about it." He stood, kicking a rock into the fire and sending a fresh wave of ashes over me. He surveyed the scene like a conqueror of a new world. "Everybody's asking about you. If you'd actually have the cojones to come back. I think they wanted to know if you were really that stupid, to tell you the truth."

I kept quiet, letting him grandstand. My father always said to let people talk who seemed to have the inclination. You could learn a lot more that way. He also said when a man talks to an empty theater, he's doing it for himself.

"That friend of yours Arron—you always called him Elvis. You hear from him?"

"I heard he was missing."

"Well, that's what his mother says. And his sister. Now there's a choice piece." Eddie shook his head. "I figured you and him being best friends and all, he might have said something to you."

"Elvis wasn't much of a writer. The last time I saw him was before Thanksgiving last year."

"Didn't mention any trips or plans he had?"

I shook my head. "What do you think happened?"

"Guy like that—in trouble most of his life, not too bright—probably just decided he needed to make a new start. Know what I mean?"

I knew what he meant, but he was wrong. Elvis wasn't some dim bulb. We used to pass notes to each other in school about various teachers and class members. Veiled and shaded meanings that often took me days to decipher. I couldn't wait to tell him about this meeting.

Eddie looked at me through his sunglasses, then crouched again. "I'm gonna be straight with you. This is a bad idea, you coming back here. There's family and kin of those dead kids not two miles from here. My daddy was the first one on the scene that morning, and he still can't shake what he saw. Those kids lying there in the mud and the blood. Gravel all over. Your license plate embedded in the guardrail. And all the radiator fluid. That's not an easy thing for a town to get over. You'd be a lot better off over in Poca or St. Albans—just about anywhere other than here. It's for your own good."

"So you're worried about what might happen to me? I didn't know you cared."

"I care about keeping things peaceful, just like they are. You stir some people up, they'll come here with a long rope and a noose on the end of it. Then I have to go throw some good people in jail."

I sat up and brushed the dew and ash from my sleeping bag. "That's real kind of you. I know people have bad feelings about me, but I can't help that. This is my home. I grew up here and I plan on staying."

"We'll see about that."

"I guess we will."

Eddie stood, and the leather belt and holster creaked like an old bedspring. "It's her, isn't it?"

I nodded. "Yes, I want to take care of my mother until—"

"You know who I'm talking about, and it's not your mother."

I yawned and stretched in the clothes I had worn on my trip from Clarkston, popping my neck and back. I felt something return, like some injured warrior or bruised lineman about to enter the field of battle. "I don't know that my personal life is anybody's business but mine."

He kicked another stone into the fire. "You're a marked man. There's not a person in this county who wouldn't hire me for life if I was to pull out my pistol right now and put a bullet between your eyes."

"Maybe, but you'd have some explaining about why you shot an unarmed man who was just trying to take care of his mother."

"Not a soul would care, not even your brother. He's so tired of hearing it from people around here that he'd probably write a thank-you letter to the editor." Eddie spat again, this time splattering the sleeping bag with brown juice. "You know what your problem is? You've got real bad timing. You realize if you'd been a minute earlier or later all those years ago, we wouldn't be having this conversation. You'd have finished school, probably married some cheerleader or professor's assistant, and moved on to the big time. Instead, you're sleeping out here on the ground in your prison issues with no future."

I crawled out and began rolling up my sleeping bag.

"You could have done something with your life. You and that girl you were so taken with."

My muscles tensed. In my mind, I was on him fast, driving him into the fire pit like a blindsided quarterback, then jumping on top of him and pummeling him. My heart beat wildly, the dormant juices of anger flowing. He said something else about Karin, and it was all I could do to hold back.

"I did a drive-by the other night for some people who thought they saw a prowler. She was standing next to a window with the shades up, undressing. And you know what? That girl still has it. I remember the taste of those lips. How about you?"

I stared at him, and this time I had his attention, his eyes trained on me, waiting to see how I'd react. "I'm not going to cause you any trouble. Last thing I want to do is draw attention."

"See to it, then." Eddie took a few steps down the hill and spoke over his shoulder as he walked. "Your mother told me to tell you she has your breakfast ready. Best not keep her waiting."

I scraped dirt onto the embers of the fire, but he wasn't finished. He took one more look from hill to hill. "Sure is a fine piece of land."

The lineaments of the mountain helped me settle into the task of daily living outside my prison. I called it *my* prison because each inmate seems to carry with him a singular impression of the steel and linoleum, the sounds, the smells. Ask any prisoner what it is like to lose his freedom and if he's honest or if he believes you really care, he will give a distinct answer. It may be the types of music you are forced to hear or not hear, or it could be the wafting fecal smell that permeates that world. Whatever it is, whatever the cost of freedom to the individual, it is impossible to shake that knowledge as you sit outside the scope and range of those interior walls. It continues every day of your life, every time you wake, every drifting moment of sleep, every time you sit down to a meal.

For me, it was the loss of an innate dignity I had experienced since childhood—the ability to watch nature's sublime work on the land. The planting and growing, the process of seeds dying and springing forth to harvest. I regimented my mind inside those

walls with reading, exercise, word jumbles, and crossword puz-
zles. If I couldn't finish the four words in the jumble in less than
thirty seconds, I considered my effort a failure. But no matter
how much I trained my mind to think of other things, I never
became used to the fact that nothing on the inside of prison ever
grew. Other than weeds through the concrete on the basketball
court, we didn't participate in growth. We were simply wasting
brain cells, flushing them from our bodies like toxins, never to be
used again.

The first few weeks after my release, I set my mind to several
tasks, including cleaning out the basement, dismantling what was
left of the barn, and taking inventory of all the farm supplies and
equipment worth salvaging. To my surprise, much of the wood I
pried loose from the barn was weathered but still usable.

The pile of boards was growing steadily when a younger man
turned in to the driveway and joined me. His name was Earl, a
cousin of someone who lived back in the hollow.

"You could make a fortune by selling this stuff," he drawled.

"That so?"

"Yeah, people are hungry for old things. Spinning wheels,
corncribs, that kinda stuff. If you can take it apart, I can help you
get it down to the flea market, and you could make some good
money."

"Why don't I just sell it to you?" I said. "I'll probably use some
of this for a shed later, but the rest you can have."

He shoved his hands in his pockets. "How much you want
for it?"

"Take the whole thing for five hundred dollars."

"I ain't got five hundred dollars."

I shrugged. "Okay. Just take what you think you can sell and
give me 20 percent."

Earl lifted his eyebrows. "How much is that?"

"You make a hundred dollars; you give me twenty."

His eyes lit up. "I can put some stuff in the back of my truck right now."

I helped him load an old loom and some rickety farm equipment, a seed planter, a few chairs, and some of my grandfather's old records.

"You're that fellow, aren't you?" Earl said as he closed the truck gate. "The guy who killed—"

"Yeah, I'm him." He just looked at me and I coughed. "I'll keep the stuff for a few more days, so if you want any more, just have at it."

In my quest for what I'd missed, what I'd lost, I rented every Academy Award–winning picture since I had been incarcerated, becoming conversant with the stars and subject matter. I also applied for a library card and printed the *New York Times* best-seller list for the past fifteen years. I vowed I would read each number one fiction and nonfiction book that I hadn't read in prison and round out my list with several classics.

My first trip to rent a video was a sensory experience I could hardly handle. The rows of movies left me helpless, and I gradually found myself retreating to the meager shelves of the library for less choice, more substance.

I went into town as little as I could, other than to take my mother for groceries, and my mission this day was a permit for a bonfire to rid the barn of every scrap Earl didn't take. I kept the car at or below the speed limit in town, but I nearly swerved into oncoming traffic when I spotted what was left of our high school.

I parked on the street and crossed, oblivious to traffic until someone honked. I waved, stepped back, and waited in front of the only familiar sight left, the F-86 Sabre that was displayed near the entrance to the school. It was now flanked by a defunct hot dog stand, peeling orange paint on the building, eaves hanging precariously.

The junior high had been built on a knoll with the high school directly behind it and much lower, which made it prone to flooding each year. But there was nothing on the knoll—it was just a vacant piece of land.

There is something about the loss of a school that tears at the soul. Memories of teachers and plays and music performances cannot be bulldozed from the mind, but the town had tried. How many times had I run up the front steps of that school in practice, toning my body, keeping in step with a coach's whistle? The cinder blocks holding up the school's name were gone, and a weathered sign was sunk deep into the ground in its place: "Future Home of First National Bank."

I climbed the diminished knoll, then walked down the other side toward the covered bridge. It had been restricted to foot traffic now, blocked by orange and white traffic horses. Even the river below had changed. It had eaten away at the bank, and several trees that had looked like pillars were gone, torn out by some flood. Most things in town seemed smaller to me, but this was one exception. The river had widened its path and seemed much deeper.

The new high school was another five miles west, and I wondered how early the kids at the other end of town had to awaken in order to make the bus trip. I shuffled to the edge of the river and up to the walkway. The murky water rushed past, deep and troubled beneath, as if I were somehow looking at my future in Dogwood.

I received the burn permit, promising not to use any accelerant, and went home to prepare the pile. I called Carson and Jenna, inviting them to the festivities, and in the cool of one evening, having dug a trench around the remnants of all my father held dear, we set the memories ablaze and watched the smoke and ash rise and float above the trees.

"It's almost pretty," Jenna said, taking my arm and drawing me close. Too close.

"A lot of history in that pile of junk," Carson said.

"A lot of your history you probably don't want to talk about," I said.

"You boys hush," my mother said.

"What history?" Jenna said.

"Just about every eligible girl in the county knew about this barn." I snickered.

Jenna loosened her grip long enough for me to get away. "What's he talking about, Carson?"

"Watch out now. I see a big copperhead coming out of there." Carson said it so convincingly and with such visible angst that my mother and Jenna jumped back and for a moment forgot about history.

I knew it was a ploy but a good one. Copperheads were the most feared snakes of our region, and a bite from one caused visions of horror and stories of relatives who had died or experienced unprecedented agony. Swelled and gangrenous limbs. Our father had protected a nest of blacksnakes around the barn to ward off the copperheads, which they were known to do, and now that nest was gone.

"Let's go inside," Jenna said, walking through a spent strawberry patch.

"Don't those copperheads like to eat strawberries?" I said.

Jenna hopped out of the patch, grabbing the hem of her dress and lifting it high. She looked at me and inched it farther. "Are you teasing me?"

I ignored her and turned back to the fire, the flames now reaching the tops of trees. They melted leaves and made them wither as the smoke and ash rose like prayers.

Carson called when he returned home and told me he could see the blaze from Route 60 and that people were pulling off and getting out to look. "I heard one old boy say you were back in town and burning the family home. They thought you'd gone crazy up in that prison. Thought you wanted to kill the rest of us."

"What did you say?"

"What was I supposed to say, that you're just fine? I wish I could, but I don't know what happened to the old you. If he's still out there, I wish you'd find him and tell him to come home."

I wanted to tell my brother that I was more myself than I had ever been, that I was finally understanding my place. I also knew no matter how loud I spoke, those without ears to hear can't.

He wasn't finished. "And this thing with Karin . . . you should give it up. It can go nowhere but bad. It's only going to lead to trouble."

"I've never counseled you in matters of love, and I'm not going to start now. Can you pay me the same courtesy?"

"Are you saying something against Jenna? You don't think I made a good choice?"

"I didn't say that. I just need you to give me some space."

"Space and time are all you have." Carson sighed as if he'd thought of something else that would put my life in perspective, that would solve all the mysteries and I'd snap my fingers and say, *Thanks. That solves everything. I'll be down to the hairdresser's shop at eight tomorrow to start so that tart of a wife of yours can seduce me.*

But I didn't say it. I didn't say anything. I just hung up.

Later that night, when I was sure the fire was under control and my mother was in her room, the strains of Christian music playing on her stereo, I eased outside and found solace in the darkness, the pitch-black anonymity of the country. Inside Clarkston, there was always a glow from something, even deep into the night, and voices of guards and inmates. Here there was silence, only the continual songs of crickets and frogs.

I slipped into the old Chevy Impala parked by the garage and drove the familiar route to Karin's house—the one I remembered so well. I passed the street three times before I got up the courage to drive down the cul-de-sac. Several students from our high school had lived here. Maybe they still did. The sidewalks were pristine, and the grass was finely manicured. Here and there my headlights illumined a Big Wheel or some other toy, but most of the yards were empty, cars inside garages. Upscale. Every bit of it said, *Don't live here unless you can afford it.*

Karin's parents had lived at the end of Summerdale Lane, and I turned off my lights and stopped at the first curb, parking between two mailboxes. When I'd arrive early in the morning, the outside light would be on, but it was dark now. No children to wait up for.

I don't know what I was looking for or hoping for—maybe a connection with the past that didn't hurt as much—but I got out of the car and walked the sidewalk under a new moon. The smells of lilacs and peonies and freshly mowed grass. An oily spot on the driveway. The stone bench where Karin used to wait for me on those late Tuesday and Thursday mornings. We took long walks on the campus together and sat on a bench and ate lunch outside Old Main or near the fountain dedicated to the plane crash victims of 1970.

Then I thought of the concert. The night that changed both our lives forever.

24

Will

July 1, 1980
Cincinnati, Ohio

We stayed until the last encore. Karin was like a vision beside me, standing and clapping, raising a cigarette lighter. It was a dream, even better than anything my subconscious could dredge up.

The crowd, frenzied during "Running on Empty," had relaxed into that long-tunneled view of life "The Pretender" offered and rounded out with "For Everyman." It struck me that though Browne's music had become popular, it was not the same as the Top 40, bubblegum, sticky sweet songs that pummeled the airwaves. It was thoughtful and transparent and revealing. His lyrics had depth, a self-confessional spirit that let you in just enough to identify but still kept a measured distance.

We walked backstage, showing our passes, and were ushered into a large room with Coke machines and tables where the band had eaten earlier. Jackson stood and spoke about the growing danger of a nuclear holocaust and what Ronald Reagan would do if we didn't stay the course with the current president.

When the line formed for a picture and a personal word, I told Karin I wanted to leave. She wouldn't and pushed her way closer until she stood next to the singer, winking at me. "He's so short," she mouthed.

We walked through the empty auditorium. The only people left were roadies in their white T-shirts with the names of every stop printed on the back.

"Wouldn't you just die to have that job?" Karin said, looking over her shoulder. "Getting to go to all those places, see all those people. And listen to great music every night."

"It's probably kind of boring," I said. "Plus, the pay isn't good. Probably minimum—"

"Who cares about how much they pay?" she interrupted. "You'd be rubbing shoulders with musicians. Poets. It would be such an experience. Haven't you ever wanted to do something just for the experience?"

"I'm here tonight," I said, smiling.

Karin turned and walked ahead toward the car. She huddled close to me as we passed a homeless man begging. If I'd been alone, I probably would have walked right past him, but I handed him the rest of the change in my pocket.

"That's nice of you, sir," he said. "You have a real pretty date with you. You deserve something pretty like that."

I gave him a look, as if I were going to take my seventy-eight cents back.

He held up a hand and moved back.

Karin huddled even closer to me. "He gives me the creeps. He smells terrible and looks worse."

I opened the door, and she slid in and glanced at her watch. "It'll be the witching hour soon."

"What do you mean?"

"Your birthday. You said you were born early in the morning, right?"

"Yeah, somewhere between four and five o'clock."

Karin reached under the seat and pulled out a paper bag. "I figured we could celebrate."

It was a bottle of wine, and she hadn't thought to bring a corkscrew. I had one on my knife, but I was leery about using it. "That's all I need is to come home drunk with you."

"My parents think I'm staying at Vicki's house. Come on." She hounded me for the first few miles, then began to pout. "I thought you'd appreciate it. I even brought two glasses. It doesn't taste good unless you use real glass."

I shook my head. "If the police pull us over with that open, you know what they'll do?"

"You worry too much. You never do anything without thinking about the worst thing that can happen." She looked out the window as I found a station tracking Jackson's *Hold Out* album.

When they reached "That Girl Could Sing," Karin looked at me. "How about something . . . for your birthday?" The way she said it was breathy and out of character.

I felt my face flush.

"You agree to open this and share a glass with me, and I'll give you a little present. Our first kiss." She raised an eyebrow and pursed her lips. "Ready to pucker up, farm boy?"

Blood raced through my body, and I felt a sense of urgency. *Just breathe,* I thought. The car was suddenly hot, and I rolled down my window. I had no idea where we were going, but I knew I had to keep driving. "All right, we'll have one glass each, but that's it. And not while we're on the road."

"Fine," Karin said. "Pull off at the next exit."

A few miles later we snaked up a winding off-ramp. Mosquitoes and other bugs splattered the windshield. I hit the windshield washer fluid to erase the stains, but it just smeared. We reached a light at the top of the hill, and the county road was deserted. I didn't know if we were in Kentucky or Ohio. "Right or left?"

"Surprise me," she said.

I turned left and we quickly escaped the harsh lights of the interstate. The road rose above the homes that lay below us on the ridge. It reminded me of our own area—newer homes with long driveways and ivy-covered brick walls mixed in with trailers and run-down homes. Cars propped on cinder blocks. We passed a Kroger and a gas station, and I started to turn into a wide spot in the road sporting a picnic table.

Karin touched my arm, pointing at a blue sign that said Swimming Pool. "Keep going."

We drove another mile and the hills dropped on one side, revealing a flat plain bathed in moonlight.

"Turn here," she said.

It was the entrance to a high school. The brick building was older, and the grass needed mowing. Four dilapidated tennis courts, laid out east to west, stood at the end of a long parking lot, a high chain-link fence around it. A baseball field and a cinder track in the distance. I didn't see a football field, but I knew there had to be one.

"Go over there," Karin said, motioning to a small building with another fence connected to it.

I drove slowly, as if someone from the school might jump out, but the place was deserted. The trash can near the building was full of soda cans and paper plates. The familiar smell of chlorine wafted through the area, but the temperature remained hot and muggy.

"I've got an idea." Karin grabbed the bottle and the glasses and opened the door. "Park at the tennis courts and meet me back here."

I tried to stop her, but she had made up her mind. I left the windows rolled down and parked, then followed her to the small building. The front had turnstiles and a large window covered with plywood. Above it was a sign listing the prices of hot dogs, sodas, and candy.

"Hey, where are you?" I said.

Karin was on the other side of the building, trying to scale the fence.

"There's barbed wire at the top," I said. "You'll cut yourself."

She stepped down, and I saw she had pushed the bottle and glasses through the bottom of the fence. There was no way we were getting in that way.

"You have an old blanket in the backseat, don't you?"

"It's full of dust," I said.

"Get it."

Her eyes twinkled a fluorescent reflection of the security light above us, and her hair glistened. I thought myself the luckiest person on earth to be alone with her. And then she smiled and I thought of the Eagles song "Witchy Woman."

"Look, the cops probably patrol this place," I said. "You try to get over that and the people in those houses up there will call."

Karin cocked an eyebrow and put a hand on her hip. She was about to speak when she spotted something on the ground and picked it up. A good-size rock. Looked like it could do some damage.

She hurled it with a speed and accuracy that surprised me, and the flickering light smashed and sparked. A shower of glass fell onto the roof. Instead of snapping us into darkness, the light faded, the filament going from white to orange to nothing.

"Won't be able to see us now." She grinned.

"If they catch us out here . . ."

Karin ran toward the car in the moonlight, darting like a cat through the parking lot. She returned a few moments later with the old quilt I kept in case I had a flat tire. It was several inches thick, and I imagined it laden with European diseases and used to wipe out tribes of Native Americans. I'd found it in my grandfather's trunk along with several 78 rpm records of some singer named Caruso. I had thrown the albums into the woods just to see how far they would fly.

She folded the quilt lengthwise and almost threw it over the fence, but it stuck on the barbed wire perfectly. "Don't want you catching anything on those barbs up there." She laughed. She pulled herself up on the eight-foot fence and got her foot stuck between the post and the building. "Little help."

"I'm not coming in there," I said, reaching up and pushing her higher.

She turned and grinned at me like we had just shared something forbidden. Her foot came out easily. "Yes you are."

"You can try to charm the cops if you want to, but they'll throw my butt in jail."

Karin leaned again and tipped forward, taking my breath away. It looked like a cheerleader move and she dropped to the ground, landing squarely, but she let out a squeal as she touched down and melted to the ground. "My ankle," she said, her back to me, bent forward at an awkward angle.

"Stay right there." I scaled the fence and used the quilt to help. I wasn't as graceful, but I hit the ground beside her and knelt as she slipped off her sandals.

"Told you I'd get you over here," she said, laughing and pushing me over.

I fell back, and when I regained my balance, I watched her trot across the edge of the freshly mowed grass. Tiny pieces stuck to the bottom of her feet as she dipped a toe into the edge of the pool.

"It's warm," Karin said.

"You can't be serious. Let's get out of here before . . ."

She put the bottle on the concrete and both glasses beside it. If her forward flip on the fence had taken my breath away, what she did next stopped my heart. Turned away from me, she pulled her shirt over her head in one motion and unclasped her jeans and stepped out of them. Her dive into the water was perfect. She swam to the other end of the pool before I realized I hadn't moved.

"Come on!" she said, waving. "It feels great."

The moon rippled in the disturbed water, and she went under. The lights at the side of the pool were off, and soon the pool calmed. I edged forward in the grass, remembering the songs I had heard tonight. "That Girl Could Sing" became "That Girl Could Drown."

Karin was waiting at the edge, and she burst from the water and grabbed my leg like in some horror movie.

I fell back, catching myself with my hands.

"Come in!" she said. "Right now or I'll scream. I'll say that you got me drunk and attacked me. How would that look?" She floated into a backstroke and turned into Scarlett O'Hara. "A big old country boy taking advantage of a poor little girl like me."

I stared, thinking that she wasn't little or poor or in the least bit unhealthy, and why wasn't I in the pool?

"I mean it, Will. If you don't come in here, you won't like what happens."

I gathered her clothes, snagged the quilt from the top of the fence, and stashed them in the darkened exit from the showers. I kicked off my shoes, then peeled off my shirt and socks and added them to the pile.

"Whatcha doin' in the dark over there?"

"Keep your voice down," I whispered.

When I emerged from the shadows, she protested. "Uh-uh, no way are you swimming in your jeans."

"I never agreed—"

"Plus, it'll be a wet ride home. Take them off. I promise I won't look."

I hesitated, then returned to the dark, throwing my jeans into the corner and running back in my briefs. She giggled and shook her head as I dived in, the warm water welcoming me like some maternal spring, pulling me down and surrounding me. I burst through the surface and shook the water from my hair and found her at the far corner.

"You're a chicken—you know that?"

"I don't like swimming with strange women," I said, my voice carrying across the water and slapping the brick building.

"Is that what I am? A strange woman?"

"You're strange and you're beautiful."

"Is that a come-on?"

"Nope. Just the truth."

Karin leaned back in the water, wetting her hair and pushing it from her face like an Olympic diver emerging from the pool. "Any other guy would be all over me right now. And he wouldn't have jumped in with his briefs."

"Guess I'm not any other guy."

"Ask yourself what Jackson Browne would do."

"He's shorter than me. I could beat him up."

She laughed.

"*You* could probably beat him up. He'd have to reach up to hit you."

"Are you scared, Will Hatfield?"

"I don't know if you could characterize what I feel as fear," I heard myself say. "It's kind of like jumping into a pool of cold water. You like to get used to the idea before you do it."

Karin swam with her head slightly above the surface, like some elegant animal paddling for the shallow end. The clouds were gone and the moon shone on us. She looked up. "Pretty, isn't it?"

"Like the star over Bethlehem."

She kept swimming away from me. "That's pretty close to blasphemy—don't you think?" She made it to the pool stairs, next to the silver railing the little kids play on, splashing and jumping with their inflatable rings. "Why don't you open the bottle and bring me a glass?"

I swam to the edge and retrieved the bottle. The corkscrew was in the pocket of my jeans, so I had to get out and drip through the grass, enduring her taunts and whoops as I did. I jumped back in and worked on the cork. I'd never touched a drop of wine, not because I didn't like it but because Carson had never supplied any. We'd had his beer at our campouts, but we'd never moved past that.

"Where'd you get this stuff, anyway?" I said.

"My dad has a cabinet downstairs. There's another bottle under the seat in case we finish this one."

I laughed and shook my head, part of the cork stripping from the top.

When the cork finally popped, Karin gave a mock cheer and watched me pour a glass. She came close and leaned toward me, gripping the wine bottle and pouring a full glass. "What's the matter?" she said coyly, taking a long drink. "Aren't you glad you came into the pool?"

I coughed and that made her smile. I was in the water now, totally immersed, baptized in her beauty and leaning against the poolside.

She set the glass down behind my head and floated for a moment in front of me, the moon reflecting on her back.

It happened like a gentle breeze, a cloud floating by, a calf nuzzling its mother, or the lifting of a child's hand to embrace its father's. Her lips met mine, and I tasted the sweetness of the wine. With savage tenderness I pulled her to me, and for a moment there was no earth or sky, no air or water, just the two of us, suspended in that womblike pool, floating, mingling.

Karin turned away and laughed. She took the wineglass and floated on her back, a white figure in the moonlight. "That wasn't so bad, was it? You acted like coming in here was the last thing you wanted to do."

"I didn't know *that's* what you wanted to do."

She took another long drink. "Happy birthday, Will Hatfield."

We embraced, and with our mouths searching, it felt like I

was drinking an ocean. Like a man who had just crawled across a desert, I was parched and thirsty. I kissed the water from her face and her forehead. I kissed her eyes and pushed a dangling strand of hair back to join the others.

Karin seemed just as interested, holding my face with her hand. When she kissed my ear and whispered, "Make love to me," I caught my breath, never envisioning this scene or set of events.

"At some point in your life," my father had said when we were alone by the campfire one night, "a woman will offer herself to you. And if you haven't made the decision before then what you'll do, if you haven't run through your mind what you'll say and how you'll act, I can guarantee you that your body will make that decision for you."

I was quickly understanding what my father meant and how right he was. I probably would have given in to her invitation had we not heard tires on gravel. Lights scampered down the hill as they wound toward us, and we pulled from our embrace.

I snatched the bottle and the other glass and steered Karin to the deep end of the pool. "I told you somebody was going to find us," I whispered.

She laughed. "Does that mean you're not going to make love to me?"

"Stop. We're in big trouble."

"Maybe it's your mother."

We held each other, the bottle floating next to us, wine mingling with the chlorine, our heads just below the edge of the pool.

"Or maybe it's my father."

"Would you be quiet?" I hissed.

The car drove toward the tennis courts, where my car was parked, and I heard the unmistakable squawk of a police radio.

"We are seriously in trouble," I whispered.

"I was led here under false pretenses," she purred. "You overpowered me and threw me in. You are a wicked young man."

"Stop moving. You're making waves."

The car parked near the pool, and we stayed as still as we could, hoping the officer wouldn't see us. He stopped, got out, and slowly walked toward the fence. A flashlight beam pierced the night, and the chain-link fence rattled. "I know you're in there. Come on out."

"Don't move," I mouthed.

"Don't make me climb this fence and come in there."

The beam of light searched the grounds, but I had hidden the quilt and our clothes well. Karin's eyes were wide with a mixture of anticipation and delight.

The radio squawked again, and the officer returned to the car. He stepped back and yelled, "I'm goin' on down the road a piece, and when I get back, you two better be out of there and gone or I'm gonna throw you in jail. You hear? We don't allow that stuff around here."

Karin stifled a laugh, and I put a hand over her mouth.

He drove away, swirling lights casting an eerie glow as he gunned the engine and sped up the hill.

I jumped out of the pool and reached for Karin.

"Where do you think you're going?" she said.

"You heard what he said. Let's go."

She swam the length of the pool with perfect breaststrokes.

I shook the quilt out and dried myself, pulling on my jeans. I met her at the other end of the pool, throwing the quilt around her and retrieving her clothes. I turned as she got dressed, then helped her over the fence.

She left the bottle in the pool but opened the second one under her seat as I spun out of the parking lot and made my way back to the interstate. There was no sign of the officer. The car smelled of chlorine and wine, and though we'd both dried off, our clothes stuck to our bodies. I avoided her eyes, somehow overcome with what had happened, and turned on the radio, settling in for the long drive.

Karin poured another full glass and drank deeply. "Well," she said, not as a question but as a statement. She drew her feet up under her and turned, smiling at me, flicking off the radio. "Are we going to talk about what happened back there, farm boy?"

"I really wish you'd stop calling me that."

"What would you prefer?"

I checked the rearview mirror, then noticed dust on the dashboard and swiped at it.

"Will, look at me."

I did.

"You want to say anything? do anything?"

I couldn't tell if *she* was talking or if it was the wine. "I'm not *shore* I know what to say, missy. Other than that was about the purtiest swimmin' hole I ever seen."

The farm boy routine worked and lightened the mood. She put a hand on my shoulder and twirled at the back of my hair, her eyes twinkling in the oncoming traffic. "We need to work on your wooing. I made the moves on you back there, and it looked like you were one of the frozen chosen."

"You don't know how much I wanted to . . . and how much I've wanted to just kiss you. I don't know if you can tell, but I really like you. More than just a friend. But I like to take things kinda slow. Plus, you wouldn't have respected me in the morning if we'd have . . ."

Karin snorted—one of the little laughs I'd become accustomed to.

I wanted to tell her it was all I could do to hold back, that the ache in my body felt like I'd been shot with a cannonball through the chest.

Maybe our story would be different if I had made love to her that night. Maybe the story of our town would be different. My life.

She offered me a sip of wine and I refused until she pouted;

then I drank some. The wine burned my throat and stomach and felt right, the perfect cap on the night.

"Where do you want to be in ten years?" Karin said, repeating her question from dinner. She curled like a cat beside me, putting her head on my shoulder.

I lifted my arm and she snuggled close, as if we were made to fit this way. The first pieces of a puzzle. "I'm still not sure about where, but I am pretty sure about who."

"Missed your chance. You could've had your way with me."

"Maybe you'll appreciate that in a few years."

Karin yawned and took another long drink, then settled beside me. In a few moments she was asleep.

I turned the radio on and rolled down my window so the rushing wind and music mixed. I wanted to taste and smell and feel this moment and know I was alive, truly alive and not dreaming.

25

Bobby Ray

I went to see Karin on Sunday after church. Lynda wasn't feeling up to much of anything but a nap, so I drove over and found my sister in good spirits. She asked about my new job as she served tea. I told her it was different being in a small town police department, being the new guy, lowest on the ladder, and about the challenges.

"I don't suppose you've stopped any bank robberies yet." She chuckled.

"It's been a lot like Mayberry," I said. "Cats up trees and kids joyriding. We do have a missing person, but the chief thinks he might have come into some money and headed to Vegas or Atlantic City. Maybe he robbed those gentlemen's clubs up toward Charleston."

"Who is it?"

"Guy named Arron Spurlock. Worked over at—"

"The Exxon station!" Karin said. "I saw him not long ago. He made a point of saying hello."

I took a sip of the bitter tea. I didn't have the heart to tell her it needed sugar. "How did he seem?"

"He was okay," she said. "He helped us get rid of our trash."

"Us?"

"Ruthie and I. We were . . . we had a little trip."

I sighed and nodded. "I suppose he'll turn up one of these days."

"Sudden money can change people. You heard about the couple in church who won the lottery?"

"Really?"

"Mr. Lundy was waiting for the coffee to brew one morning at the Fast Mart, and he just picked some numbers like they were blueberries and put the ticket in his shirt pocket. The next day he sees the numbers in the paper and pulls out the card—he still had the same shirt on—and they matched. Perfectly. Can you believe it?"

"What happened?"

"The Fast Mart got a percentage of the winnings, and Mr. Lundy and his wife sold their place and moved to Florida. Sounds nice, doesn't it? Moving someplace where it's warm all the time and you don't have to worry about shoveling snow or falling down."

"You can fall and break a hip in Florida just like you can here, sugarplum."

"I know. I'm just saying it would be nice. I suppose we're planted here for a while with the kids growing so much. Have you seen how big Darin is getting?"

I nodded and smiled.

"And little Tarin has so much energy that I run myself ragged trying to keep up with her."

I sipped my tea and watched my sister flit about the room in her Mary/Martha mode, trying to keep my cup full. "You remember Ernie from my unit in the army, don't you? Big muscular guy from Louisiana?"

"Head like a bowling ball?"

"You got him. Well, he's coming through this summer. Said he wants to stop and see the family."

"Well, you should invite him to church. If he needs a place to stay while you fix up your place, we have extra room here." Karin's eyes lit up. "I'd love to see him. Is he married?"

"At the moment." I laughed. "We'll see how long it lasts."

"Tell him I said hello. I remember how much you two liked each other."

"Wouldn't have lasted long without him. Have you spoken with Mom and Dad?"

"They came over to play with the kids last week. I'm hoping I can convince Dad to go with us to Camden Park. You and Lynda should come."

"I think her ankles would swell up bigger than the Cloud 9 if she tried walking around there."

Karin laughed, and it was good to hear that genuine belly laugh. She hugged and kissed me as I left and held on to my hand as I walked out. "We sure had some fun times as kids, didn't we?"

I looked into her eyes and saw something of the old Karin there. But not much. "Other than that hornet's nest."

"Take care of yourself, Bobby Ray."

26

Karin

"Tell me more about him," Ruthie said one day, turning down the country music station she listened to.

I was trying to forget about Will and move on with my life, but for some reason she wouldn't let go, so I launched into a spiel about Richard, how I'd met him after some horrible relationships, how he accepted me as I was. She noticed my hesitation, which was always the wrong thing to do with Ruthie. She had an innate sense of when you were giving her your heart, lying through your teeth, or just plain holding back.

She probed again, and to spite her, I guess, I told her of boy-friends past and the vagaries of my dating life. I felt nothing but shame about those years, but Ruthie didn't seem shocked. It was the first time I had regurgitated the past without someone trying to clean it up or make it pretty. But the more the story gushed, the better it felt, stumbling through piles of my own dirty laundry.

I thought of Ruthie's belief that women, especially young ones, don't listen to their gut, that inner voice that tells them something is wrong and needs to change. I suppose I've done that a thousand times in little ways, pushing my feelings aside.

"Do you know where those gentlemen are now? Have you ever talked with any of them?"

I laughed. "They've probably all moved on to executive positions or jobs with the government. The funny thing is that my parents thought a lot of those guys were knights in shining armor. They couldn't understand why I married a preacher."

"They don't like him?" Ruthie said.

"I guess they're happy for me, though they don't understand how we'll possibly make it on his salary. I tell them that love conquers all, but my mother doesn't believe it can conquer the mortgage *and* the MasterCard bill."

Ruthie bent over Tarin and smiled, as if giving a blessing. Ruthie's skin looked even more wrinkled next to that baby face. She was such a kind woman, and I wondered if I could ever be thoughtful like her.

"I moved in with my parents after a particularly bad relationship and let them think what they wanted . . . that I needed some direction. I looked at my mother's cabinet full of pills more than once. But something kept me going."

"He knew," Ruthie said. "He was there with you."

"God?" I said, laughing. "I don't know if I've ever felt as far away from God as during those months. It felt like, 'You abandoned me. I'll abandon you.' I didn't put much stock in him during that time. Then the preacher came along, and my ship stopped listing. At least for a while. Now I still think God might have abandoned me."

"There's something you're not telling me," Ruthie said. "Maybe it's *someone* you're not telling me about."

I excused myself to her bathroom, a quaint, quiet escape. A bouquet of flowers sat haphazardly in front of the mirror. The sink was tiny but elegant, the wallpaper festooned with eagles soaring above the mountains. It would have looked kitsch in any other bathroom in the universe, but it spoke to me of Ruthie here.

She had stitched a quote and framed it with a beautiful, weather-beaten piece of wood. It hung at sight line of the toilet, unavoidable. I wondered if it was there for me or another of her disciples who happened to find themselves sitting there. Words penned by Mark Twain, perfectly positioned.

> *Twenty years from now you will be more disappointed by the things that you didn't do than by the ones you did do. So throw off the bowlines. Sail away from the safe harbor. Catch the trade winds in your sails. Explore. Dream. Discover.*

The words sank deep, like an injection of adrenaline. I had been afraid so long. After all the empty and broken dreams, I had come to a place where safety was the prize. Could God restore the dream? Could he patch the torn sails of my life, fill them, and push me into deep water?

27

Will

I had been home a few weeks, searching the want ads each day and going through the process of reclaiming the room of my youth, when I came upon an envelope at the bottom of a dresser. My name was on the front, nothing else. I opened it carefully, finding a baseball card that had survived our bikes—we used to tape them to the spokes to make it sound like we were riding motorcycles.

The card was a Pete Rose rookie, 1963. I examined it and figured it would bring a lot of money to some collector. Rose stared just to the right of the camera, as if he couldn't bring himself to look at it squarely. Or his attention had been drawn away, or perhaps someone had suggested he look away. He played second base that year and wore the white Reds cap only seen on retro days. He had the boyish look of a man following a dream, unaware that he would garner the most hits in the history of the game, 4,256, and that he would be banned from the Hall of Fame.

Along with the card was a note. My father's handwriting. A little shaky and slanted to one side, but it was his. I closed the door quickly and sat on the bed.

Will, my son,

I think I managed to keep this from your mother's eyes, and if you find it in your room, congratulations. She moves my stuff around. My gut tells me she won't come into your room. She likes to keep things as they were, not as they are, and I can't say I blame her.

I didn't want to send this to you because I knew you would need to hear from me when you're out, and I'm confident that day will come. I'm just not confident I'll be around. So here goes.

I was never able to give you what you needed when you were young. I'm talking about the words—speaking into your life. They've never really been my thing. I don't know why, but it wasn't because of you. I guess I didn't have much for you or Carson, but I've learned a lot since you've been gone. In fact, I've probably learned more through your experience than all the good combined, so I should start by thanking you. You've helped change our lives.

You're probably wondering why I put the Pete Rose card here. It's because I want you to remember that character counts. You can be the best there ever was at something, but if you have no character, what do you have? On the other hand, if you have very little as far as accomplishments but you have character, well, then you're all right in my book.

If you're unsure of where to go and what to do now that Clarkston is behind you, don't worry. It will come to you. Give yourself time. Good things come to those who wait, as they say. You need a place to heal the broken parts, and I'm hoping home will serve as that place.

If I had to describe what I've learned these past few years, and you would probably echo this, I'd call it "a death to illusions." We all have our preconceived notions of what the world is about and what will make us happy.

At some point, everybody glimpses how hard life really is, and they either go into depression or they throw themselves into the illusion. Despair is what some call it. My guess is, you've looked this full in the face and lived with it for a while.

As a young man I chased things that appeared to fulfill or excite me. It took a few years, but life beat the expectation out of me. For some people it never happens. They hang on to what they think life ought to give them. I lost that the day of your sentencing. It was a brutal feeling. I don't bring it up to punish you but to learn from it.

To be honest, some deaths are good. Some deaths teach that chasing a mirage is useless. The mirage that a job or a car or a house or a person can make you happy. When everything good is taken and you're left with a fading hope that the world was fashioned by someone who cares and loves you, you begin to understand how much you've hung on to what isn't because you can't stand the thought of what truly is. I'm not sure I'm making much sense, but I think what I'm saying is true.

You've died to the illusion that life is fair and that every story ends happily ever after. That's why they call them fairy tales. You've died to the illusion that you can understand why. None of us knows the answer to that, and those who think they do are the saddest lot of all because they've never come to the end of their own understanding. It's not faith to say that when something painful happens, when you lose and lose again and the hurt goes so deep that you don't think you can take another breath, it's all going to work out for good. Faith doesn't explain. It doesn't even need to know or expect a happy ending. That's not what we're promised. Faith is abandoning illusions. It rests in something bigger, something beyond us and our ability. And I suspect you know that now.

There are only a few things I know for sure. One is that I believe in you. That may sound shallow, and to anyone else it would be, but I think you know what I mean. I believe there is another explanation for the awful thing that happened. When you walked away from us and into that courtroom, it seemed to me there was something we didn't know. One day I'll find out, but I don't have to know the truth to say I believe in you. I'm proud to call you my son. I can say that with my head high and my chest out. I'm proud of you.

The other thing I know is that I won't be here when you return, and that breaks my heart. Some people probably think I dread that day, and we're ashamed. I won't lie to you and say it's easy to feel the stares and hear people whisper, telling their kids who they're walking by. But I could not care less what those people think about me or you or anything else. They just know us from a picture in the paper and what some newshound printed. The only thing that matters to me after you clean out the barn of life, after you strip away all the illusion, is that I love you. That's it.

I can't imagine what you're thinking as you read this rambling letter. I suppose you're in your room or on the hill by the trees, and if some developer hasn't gotten to it, there's woods that will explode with color come fall. I wish I could be there right now. Maybe I am somehow. It eases the pain a little bit to think that I am.

I do have one prayer for you, Son. One thing in my heart I want to give that I hope you'll remember. I pray you will let go of what isn't and hold on to what is. It's going to be a big adjustment coming back, and there may be part of you that just wants to move on, move away, and start over. If so, I'll understand. You deserve a fresh start. But no matter where you go, no matter how far away from these hills your path takes you, I hope you'll let go of the dead things, the illusions, and hang on to the hope you know is true and good and real.

I am so happy to call you my son. I wish we could go to a game together and share a hot dog or two. Possibly a beer if you promised not to tell your mother. Maybe you can take Carson to a game and talk about me and laugh a little.

Never underestimate your heart, Will. Never under-estimate the things you can accomplish. You have given a lot, but there are no limits on what love can do through a man with a good heart.

I love you with all of mine.

Daddy

28

Karin

The spring luncheon came and went without Ruthie. I tried to talk her into sitting on the periphery of the room, but she said her bones ached and she couldn't "abide" being there. I honestly thought she was trying hard not to disappoint me, but in the end she couldn't bring herself to face all those people.

"There will be another spring and more luncheons," she said. "I'll eventually work up the nerve."

For someone who could push me into a penitentiary and face a notorious citizen, I was surprised she couldn't sit and chew on a rubbery piece of chicken, but I guess there are stranger things in the world.

During my waking hours, I poured myself into caring for my family, trying new recipes and dishes, and staying busy. But in the quiet hours, when I was left with my own thoughts and nothing else, I thought of *him.* These were guilty times. I was responsible for my own thoughts, and if they kept going to *him,* if my mind kept wandering, something was wrong.

The speaker at the luncheon had shared her story of being depressed and how God had helped her through desperate times when she felt like she was losing her mind. A nice story, but I wanted to ask so many questions. *How* had God rescued her? What was the process? Did she feel as stifled as I felt in our church? Was there hope? And what if you're plagued by thoughts of other lovers? Does that make you bad or just normal?

There were nights when I'd drift off, only to wake up in a sweat, having dreamed of Will's face. I was under his spell, even though I didn't know what that spell was.

God, I prayed, *deliver me. Protect me from myself.*

29

Will

I cleaned everything I could find at home, mowed the hillside and yard, planted some corn and beans in the upper garden, and took my mother for midnight grocery runs to avoid people. After a few weeks I decided I needed something more constructive, something that would pay and keep my parole officer happy.

I had received a modest check from Earl, the man who took away the part of the barn I hadn't burned. It was enough to begin buying materials for my project. Using my father's tractor, I graded a road from the barn to the hilltop, winding through the junipers and dogwoods as best I could without taking too many out. Now I needed enough gravel to fill the road, which would take more truckloads than I wanted to think about.

"What are you doing up there all day?" my mother asked after I came home sweaty and hungry and sat down to dinner. She had begun the long decline of widows, making dinners that were supposed to be for others but eating them herself. She cooked fried chicken livers twice a week, and the smell lingered long after.

"Just staying busy," I said.

"Why don't you talk with your brother about that job? He said he could find something for you."

The distance between Carson and me had widened. We both knew it, both felt it. He rarely called to check on her, and when he found out I was doing something on the hill, he called even less frequently.

My mother had long been the safe one of the family. What my father gave me in an adventurous spirit, taking chances and grabbing life by the horns, she had wrestled from me with all her might. She had more reasons not to do things than "Carter's has pills," as she would say. Still, I figured if she'd lived this long, unable to change, there was something to be said for that lifestyle. I attributed it to a tenacity of spirit, only in a different, inward direction.

"I was thinking of applying at the radio station," I said, avoiding her question about Carson. "Is old Seeb still around?"

"Are you sure that's what you want to do? Be out there in front of the public?"

"You can be pretty anonymous on the radio. Change my name. My voice is different since I worked there as a kid. And Seeb did say some nice things about me at the trial."

"He did. Didn't seem to help much, though. Everybody wanted blood, as if enough hadn't already been spilled."

We clinked our silverware a few minutes.

"Mrs. Spurlock called earlier and asked about you."

"She heard anything from Elvis?"

"Not a thing. It doesn't look good, Will. I think he might be gone."

"As in gone away or dead?"

She shook her head.

"Didn't he have a steady job at the Exxon station? He wouldn't have just left that, would he?"

"That boy was scarred inside and out."

❧

The Spurlock house sat on a postage-stamp-size lot near the interstate. Shingles hung off the roof. The same cinder blocks I climbed as a kid were used as steps into the house. Attached to the back of the house was Mr. Spurlock's workshop. Claude had been a perpetual welfare check recipient ever since his accident with a coal company. He coughed like he didn't want to and drank like he did. He'd fix shoes or carve figurines or do almost anything to pick up extra cash, but black lung got him a few years ago.

Elvis's truck sat near the house, parked as if it waited for his return. The tires and wheel wells were caked with dried mud. I opened the door and looked inside. It was full of Coke bottles and cans and candy wrappers. Elvis once told me the blast had burned everything but his taste buds. I found a *Hustler* magazine under the seat. There was nothing else of interest, so I reached to close the door and noticed something on the back of the seat. Little flakes of dark red, dried, like a watery pizza sauce or something worse.

"Can I help you?" a woman drawled behind me.

I heard the familiar click of a shotgun and turned.

Doris Jean stood in the doorway, propping it open with a shoeless foot. Her hair looked like something had nested in it overnight. She wore a man's T-shirt with a pocket over the left breast. I immediately recognized her, though she was thinner and older, but she had more trouble with me.

When I spoke her name, she pointed the gun at the ground. "Will? Is that you? Mama, it's Will Hatfield."

My mother had told me that Doris Jean was working as a waitress in a bar near Charleston. It was widely believed, she said, that she did more than wait tables, and from the circles under her eyes and deep lines in her face, I believed it. Her eyes looked vacant, and next to her mother she looked skeletal. Of course, next to her mother most people would look skeletal.

"Will, it's so good of you to come over here," Mrs. Spurlock said. A cigarette dangled from her mouth, and she waddled out to hug me and kiss me on the cheek. She smelled like a tobacco factory, and I was glad when she pulled away for a better look, her eyes shining. "How long have you been home?"

I knew that my mother had answered every one of her questions about me, so I just smiled and asked if we could go inside.

"Goodness, I haven't been able to clean up in so long, but come on in. I can get you something to drink if you'd like."

"I'm fine. Did the police go over Arron's truck? take a close look at it?"

"I had to go get it from the Exxon station a couple of days after he disappeared," Doris Jean said. She nodded toward an old Toyota, the bumper nearly rusted off. "Mama won't let me drive it till we find out what happened."

Flies seemed to be trying to get out of the house rather than in as we walked through the screen door.

"What happened to your dogs?" I said.

"Oh, after Claude died, the only one who kept up with them was Arron, and since he's been gone, they've been runnin' the hills. You might see them over yonder at your place before long."

"Want a beer?" Doris Jean said.

I politely declined without pointing out that it wasn't even 9:30 a.m. Once a server, always a server, I guess.

"Doris Jean has a real good job up in Charleston," Mrs. Spurlock said. "She's a dancer."

"Oh?"

"I'm just fillin' in for a couple of the girls who are sick. That drafty old place, it's a wonder they all don't get pneumonia." She handed me a blue business card that said "One Free Entry" on the back. On the front was a silhouette of a nude woman standing by a pole. "I'm usually just a waitress, but the owner said I could fill in if there wasn't nobody else who could dance. I've seen your brother up there a couple of times. You wouldn't want to bring your mama, but you're always welcome."

I nodded, thanking her for the card, and turned to her mother.

"About Elvis. Did the police say anything about leads? where they thought he might have gone? tracking a credit card?"

She laughed. "Arron didn't have no credit cards. I cut 'em up for him when he racked up a big bill. He paid it off, though, before he left. Every penny."

"How much are we talking about?"

"It was something like fifteen thousand dollars."

"Where'd he get the money to pay it off?"

"Saved it, I guess. I don't know. Heck, Will, you're askin' more questions than the police."

"I don't mean to pry. I'm just concerned. I figured he'd be waiting for me with a fishing rod when I got out. Or a hunting dog or two."

"Well, that's what I figured," Mrs. Spurlock said. "He was always talking about when you came back and all the stuff you two were going to do."

Doris Jean moved into the kitchen but was still listening. I noticed her mother glancing her way a few times.

"Mind if I have a look in his room?" I said.

"If you think it might help," Mrs. Spurlock said. The fat on her arms hung down over her elbows as she wobbled toward the back of the house. The floor creaked, and the house smelled of mold. She opened the door, stepped in, then closed it behind us.

She whispered quickly, as if someone was following us. "I didn't want to say anything Doris Jean could hear. I think she may know more than she's letting on."

"Like what?"

"She's mixed up with more than those people up near the capital. There were some rough characters nosing around after her a few weeks ago, just before Arron took off."

"So you think those guys are why he ran?"

"I don't know what happened, but I can tell you they were rough. That's why I keep a loaded shotgun at the door. I don't think Arron would have come back with them nosing around. There was a bust up at the end of the hollow of an old farmhouse. They were making some drugs there."

"Meth?"

She nodded. "I think so. It was in all the papers, but I don't think they caught the fellows who were actually making the stuff."

"Sounds complicated."

The floor creaked outside the door. "Mama, you two all right in there?"

Mrs. Spurlock clouded up, scrunching her face and getting emotional. "Oh, honey, it's just that being in here brings it all back up."

"I know, Mama," Doris Jean said through the door. "He'll be back."

"I hope so. We'll be out in a minute."

"You missed your calling," I whispered. "Should have been an actress."

She put a meaty hand on mine and gave a knowing look. "With hips like these, I would have knocked 'em dead." Then she turned to her son's bed. That he still lived at home at his age was troublesome, but who was I to talk? "Arron is a good boy. He's just a trouble magnet. Everything he touches or that touches him goes wrong."

"Why don't you talk to Doris Jean? ask her what she knows?"

"I'm scared, Will. If those people have anything to do with this, they'll hurt Arron and maybe Doris Jean too."

"Or you."

"I don't care about me." She glanced at the floor.

"Maybe if we find those guys who run the lab, we'll find Arron. Maybe he got hooked."

"I don't think he would have touched the stuff, but I can't say for sure."

The phone rang and Doris Jean answered. "Mama, it's for you!"

"Be right there." Then, to me, "There's something else. I haven't told a soul this since Arron left. He left something here for you." She bent over and reached under his mattress. "When he went missing, I opened it. I hope you don't mind. It's a will, but it also looks like there's some kind of message for you. I don't know what it means."

I stuffed the envelope in my pocket and followed her out.

She talked on the phone, laughing loudly, as Doris Jean walked outside with me. "You find anything in there?"

I shook my head. "I can't figure it out. Why would he just leave?"

"I don't know. Any more than I know about why you killed those kids." Doris Jean leaned against the house, bending a knee and putting a foot behind her, puffing on a cigarette. A car passed and she stretched to see who it was, exposing more of her body. I had to get out of there.

She watched me drive away, then moved back into the house.

I pulled to the side of the road and opened the envelope. It had nothing on the front, but on the page inside was my name and the date, one day before Arron went missing.

I don't know if anything's going to happen, but if it does, I want my mother to get all my worldly goods. If she wants to give them away to somebody else, that's fine, but she gets first choice. That goes for the truck too.

I have only one other thing of value, and it should all go to Will Hatfield because he's probably as tired of the police around here as I am. He'll know where it's at, and I think he'll know what to do with it.

Sincerely,

Arron P. (Elvis) Spurlock

I read the note again. It was Elvis's handwriting, no doubt. It was written just like he talked, just like his thought process. There was something here, but what? I knew nothing about a thing of value Elvis owned nor where to look.

∾◯

Naseeb S. Tweel chose his call letters to reflect the town's name, WDGW. He had wanted to use WMUD because the building overlooked the banks of the Mud River, but those call letters had already been taken. The river overflowed each spring and fall and flooded homes built near the riverbank. Why the people didn't move was a mystery, especially since the *Farmers' Almanac* could predict the rains with great accuracy.

A new Lincoln sat at the back of the building, a monument to the power of spot announcements. Seeb did a trade-out with the local dealer and for as long as I could remember had been driving a new Lincoln with all the bells and whistles.

The morning announcer, Tom, who also served as chief engineer, head of sales, and maintenance man, had gotten up at 4 a.m. for twenty-three straight years, and not a day went by that he didn't remind listeners that he was doing this for them.

The secretary looked just out of high school and stared at the ringing phone as she watched her nails dry. She was in midchomp of a sizable wad of Bubblicious gum (I saw the rest of the pack on the desktop), her fingers stained yellow, when she finally glanced at me. "Who you want to see?"

"I'm looking for Seeb."

She reached for the phone, looked at her nails again, and lifted her head. "You can just go on back." She said "go on" as one word: *goewn.*

Seeb was in a familiar pose, the way I'd remembered him. Hands behind his head. Feet up on the desk. Eyes closed. A fat cigar twitching in his mouth.

He still had the first microphone he'd ever used in radio on his desk, the framed one dollar bill—also the first—along with a *Playboy* desk calendar. He had learned the hard way to tip it over when someone came in. The hard way was a local Boy Scout troop taking a tour that lingered behind his desk. It was even worse when a local pastor had reached for a pen to sign a contract for more airtime.

The only difference in the new and old Seeb was the absence of a cloud of smoke in the room. Somewhere between the time I was sentenced and got out, he had stopped smoking and started chewing his cigars. Perhaps a doctor's order?

I sat in the faux leather chair across from his desk, and it creaked just enough for him to raise an eyelid, then shut it. Without warning and with only the smallest intake of air, his voice rang out in the office. "Virginia!"

"Yeah?" she yelled back.

He did not open his eyes. "How many times do I have to tell you not to send people back here when I'm working?"

It was meant as a rhetorical question, but Virginia tried to answer, which sent Seeb's feet banging to the floor, and his eyes bored a hole in me. "You want to shut the door?" he said, the stogie hanging out of his mouth.

I stood, kicked the hollow door closed, and turned back to him. "Nice to see you again too."

His face fell and I could see the blank spots in his corneas, white and unseeing. "Do I know you?" Then he squinted and moved closer, his hands like spiders, skin hanging from his arms. "Will? Is that you?"

I smiled. "I survived."

He sat back and laughed. "It's the eyes. They're going on me, with the diabetes and all." He shook his head, pursed his lips around the stogie, and smacked the desk. "Will Hatfield," he whispered, looking me over as if he were passing by a casket. "Never thought I'd see you again." He grabbed my hand and shook it.

"I never thought I'd be back here asking for a job," I said.

"Sit down. Sit down. How long you been out?"

I told him.

"You okay?"

I nodded. "I feel kinda marked. Branded."

He looked at his desk calendar. "Yeah, I suppose you do."

We sat for a long time, just staring.

Finally Seeb said, "It was a real shame what happened. This town . . ."

"I don't know that you ever get over something like that."

He thought a long time. "I don't know what people would say or think if I . . ."

"Mark Joseph," I said. "I was thinking that might be a good name. Or you don't even have to put me on the air. I could write copy. Fetch Tom's morning coffee."

"You hear he has cancer?"

I shook my head. "I'm surprised he's still alive. I see the hole's still in the wall where his wife threw that hatchet at him."

"No, he patched that a few years ago. That's another one."

"What was it this time?"

"Same thing. She caught him with the secretary and threw a Coke bottle. Couldn't keep his hands off the help."

"And Virginia's safe?"

"That's his daughter."

"You're kidding."

"Hard to believe a girl who looks like that could come from those two, isn't it?"

We talked about others who had worked at the station. I had always felt it was one of Seeb's secret ambitions to hire the next Howard Stern or Rick Dees and pay him as little as possible so one day he could put his picture on the wall and tell prospective employees, "I made this guy what he is, and I can help you too."

There had been modest success for a couple of DJs. One was

working in Cincinnati, another in Louisville, but most had been content to stay in a small market world and eke out a living.

A few who had come through the doors of the station had been on a long spiral down. Drugs. Alcohol. Trouble with the law. Or all three. Several people had been taken off the air in Huntington or Charleston for some indiscretion and had fallen all the way down to Dogwood. It was truly the bottom of the radio barrel, but it was a job and it paid the bills. At least some of them.

"You introduced me to a bunch of characters, Seeb. The underbelly of the business."

"We did have some strange birds. Remember the guy who did afternoons—always rode his motorcycle to work in those leather chaps?"

"Steve," I said. "He's the one who trained me to do news and not laugh. Wrestled with that big six-foot Easter bunny just outside the window while I tried to make it through a story about the Jonestown massacre."

Seeb smiled, biting his cigar. "I found out later that bike was the only thing he owned. Slept in the park most nights or down by the river. Found him a trailer to rent for a hundred dollars a month, and he was happy as a clam." He looked straight at me. "But I never hired anyone I didn't believe in."

"You always told me that once radio was in my blood, I'd never get it out."

He nodded. "It's genetic to the species. A little taste is all it takes. When was the last time you were on-air?"

"I guess it was the morning before the accident. Didn't come back before the trial. The warden let us do a talent show every year, and he heard about my experience, so he let me emcee the thing. Don't suppose that would look too good on a résumé."

"Sure it would," Seeb said, flipping to the next picture on his calendar and squinting. "You've got to be a little rusty on the board—hasn't changed too much."

"I could use a refresher."

"Come in Saturday afternoon. Clay is on the board. You can run it for him and let him do all the breaks. We'll go from there."

I told him how much I appreciated it.

"Whatever happened to that girl you brought in here? Anything ever come of that? Carrie or Carleigh or . . . ?"

"Karin," I said.

"Yeah, what happened to her?"

"I've kind of been out of the dating scene, if you know what I mean."

"She get married?"

I stood and walked to the door. A spider crawled up the side of the wall until it reached a grainy black-and-white picture of a radio antenna, the original one that stood in the field behind the station. Three workers stood on the antenna, their faces as fixed as the guy wires, waving, smiling. A few minutes after the shutter snapped, so did the guy wires and all three were killed. The one at the top from the fall, the two on the ground from the tumbling steel. It had been the most publicity the station ever received. Until news reports came out about the accident, naming me as a part-time announcer at the station.

"She's the reason I came back here," I said.

❧

I walked into the station on Saturday afternoon, an unusually hot day for that time of year, my stomach churning like I was sixteen again. The announcer who had trained me almost two decades earlier called himself Chip Stevens and spent the first hour showing me the incomprehensible display of buttons and knobs and how they worked. He taught me the best way to cue a record on the turntable without scratching it. When I tried, the needle jumped and bounced because my hands were shaking so much.

Then he sent me to a fast-food restaurant for ham sandwiches.

It was his pattern for the next two weeks—an hour of teaching, then a food run. It was part of the reason he weighed close to three hundred pounds and wore out just about every chair in the building.

There were two cars in the parking lot when I arrived, a late model Chevy and an older Suburban. The monitors were turned up to earsplitting levels as I walked through the front door, but no one was at the board.

Weird sounds came from the production room. Like someone was doing some heavy lifting. The song playing was a Kenny Rogers tune, and I figured Clay was in the middle of a set of five songs in a row, which was probably more than enough time for him to finish whatever it was he was doing.

I stepped back outside and rang the bell, moseying around the front of the building.

A young kid came to door, buckling up, his shoes off. He reminded me of myself at that age. He had curly hair and pimply skin, thin but not muscular. His handshake was firm. "Clay Woodman," he said, smiling. He had lipstick on his cheek and earlobe.

"I'm Will. Nice to meet you."

"I wasn't expecting you until later."

"Well, Seeb never told me a time, and I flipped on the station and heard you and thought I'd just come by."

Virginia came out of the production room—an apt name for it now that I thought about it—straightening her shorts, pulling at her bra strap, and slipping into flip-flops. She had pale, long legs, but her toenails were a bright red to match her fingernails. She still worked at her gum. Sunglasses were propped above her forehead to hold back her blonde-streaked hair.

When she saw me, her jaw dropped. "You're him, aren't you?" She clenched her teeth and glared at Clay. "Why didn't you tell me he was coming?"

"Come on, Ginny," he begged.

In the background a stinger sounded—a computerized series of blips and splashes overcome by a deep-voiced announcer saying, "Classic Country"—and Willie Nelson began a scratchy-voiced tune.

Virginia grabbed her keys, slung her tiny purse over her shoulder, and sashayed out the door.

Clay cursed as he watched her hips. She skipped down the stairs and he followed. "I'm sorry! We still on for dinner?"

She floored the accelerator and spun a truckload of gravel out of the parking lot.

Clay returned and walked past me. "Sorry 'bout that."

"I met her yesterday and she didn't say a thing. What's up?"

"She didn't know who you were yesterday."

"Oh."

He put a dollar in the soda machine and pulled out a Mountain Dew. "She went to kindergarten with one of the kids you killed. Used to play over at her house."

"I guess she has a right to be upset."

"Yeah. I don't know what Seeb was thinkin'." Clay took a long draw from the bottle and burped. "People around here are gonna be hacked off when they find out."

"I was hoping to use a different name. Listeners don't have to know."

He gave me one of those slack-jawed teenager looks, as if I had no idea what I was saying. "People who listen to this station know who works here. I won't say nothin' if that's what you want, but it's only a matter of time."

Clay showed me the automated playlist on reel-to-reel and walked me through the board. It was a lot more complicated, a lot more computerized than I remembered, but in a way a lot easier. I knew other stations were even more advanced and that WDGW was trailing the competition by about ten years.

There was still a wall full of 33 rpm records stacked on shelves in the control room. Most of the 45s were gone, except for a few strays here and there. The carpet was worn thin under the control room chair, and there was a new table in front of the window housing the transmitter with a microphone and headphone amp.

"Seeb said I should sit over there and do breaks and let you get the hang of the board," Clay said.

"You don't record your stuff and play it in between?"

He shrugged. "We can, but Seeb likes to hear stuff live. He says it's cheating and unprofessional to record the stuff and not try to do it live."

I had first "flown solo" that summer long ago under the teaching of Vern Jackson, one of the best DJs on the air. His full-time job was with the wastewater treatment plant, but his first love was country music. He was our music director and did a board shift Saturday and Sunday. He produced the Country Countdown, a two-hour song-by-song countdown to number one. The station didn't have half the records on the Billboard chart, so Vern threw some in just because he liked them. He seemed strange, somehow out of place, but I couldn't put a finger on what was so different.

He came in Saturday afternoon with bloodshot eyes, turned up the speaker in the back room, and told me he'd listen from there. "Knock 'em dead, Hatfield."

I had a question about ten minutes into my solo flight and found him asleep on the couch in Seeb's office. Those first six hours were the longest of my life, and I felt worse than a new driver navigating rush-hour traffic. There were so many things to do at once. Things to say, not to say, when to start the music, the time, the temperature, promoting the next songs and on and on.

"You've got real talent." Vern yawned after my shift was over. "Good voice. Personality. Humor. You're teachable, which is unusual. You probably can't stand the music, but I wouldn't know that listening to you. That's good."

He told me some things to work on, like pronouncing my *w*'s correctly. "It's not *dubba-you*. It's *double-you*." He wrote it out on a three-by-five card, *Double-you DGW*.

After a month of working with him and after receiving my official license, which meant that I could really fly solo, I was deemed ready for on-air work alone.

Vern came by after sign-off to get his show for Sunday ready, telling me what he liked and didn't about my shift. He carried his own set of headphones instead of using the community pair in the control room. He sat on the secretary's desk, the logbook propped against his leg. "I want to tell you something important because I think you should know."

I squinted at the book. "I did a legal ID at the top of every hour."

"It's not that." Vern smiled. He had a mustache that was the most neatly trimmed I had ever seen and jeans that were always pressed and crisp. "A few years ago I realized something and it scared me. Something about myself. And then I tried to talk myself out of it, but it kept coming back."

He paused—whether for effect or searching for a thought, I didn't know—but I wasn't about to interrupt.

"Will . . ." Another long pause, then he looked straight at me, locking eyes. "I'm gay."

Vern let the news sink in. Looking back, it took a minute for me to even realize the ramifications of what he was saying.

"Okay," I said as nonchalantly as I could.

"That doesn't bother you?" he said.

"Why should it? You can still teach me radio, can't you?"

Vern smiled again. "I thought you'd freak out or something. Most people around here do. Seeb took me off the Sunday morning shift when he found out because there are some groups who come in and do live shows. Guess that's your domain now." He put a hand on my shoulder. "I'm glad we can still be friends."

Two weeks later Vern tried to massage my neck without my

consent, and I jumped up from the control room chair so fast the needle popped off a Merle Haggard tune. He ran from the room with his hands in the air, like someone had held him up at gunpoint. He never tried to get physical again, but the teaching ended with that episode. I was on my own.

"Eighty-one beautiful degrees at Classic Country 16, WDGW," Clay said. He rolled his *w*'s like a pro and I felt intimidated. He named the last five songs that had played from memory, read a Red Cross liner about blood donation that sounded like he was making it up on the spot, and pointed at me.

I hesitated, then remembered the button I needed to push. A series of commercials began highlighting the latest specials at Foodland and Mohr's Tire Farm.

"So you really think you'll be able to work here and not have people know it?" Clay said.

"I stopped caring what people think about me a long time ago. I know seeing me or hearing my name brings back the hurt, and I'm sorry. Believe me, if I could turn back the clock and change what happened, I'd do it. Or if I could take the place of those kids, I'd do it in a heartbeat. But I can't. I guess I'm choosing to live rather than retreat."

He waved a hand at me and I turned on his microphone. "Classic Country 16, WDGW. Coming up, the Cash man, Barbara Mandrell, Waylon, Willie, and to get started in this superset, here's Ronnie Milsap."

Clay hit the post, Ronnie sang, and I turned off the mic.

"Guess you're right to go on with your life, but a lot of folks wish you'd do it someplace else." He walked into the sales office and closed the door, and I saw the first phone line light up.

I began my career with weekends and returned doing the same. The same couple who had done a live service each Sunday still showed up at 6 a.m., the wife strumming a guitar and singing, the husband preaching. They went for a half hour and at the end gave the same invitation I remembered from high school.

"And if you're listening in radioland, anywhere within the sound of my voice, and you do not know Jesus as your personal Lord and Savior, we invite you now to ask him to forgive your sins and wash you clean."

Behind him, his wife began strumming lightly and singing, "Softly and Tenderly."

"I don't care if you've been running from God for years. You may be listening now from this very radio station, wondering if God loves you. Well, friend, he does and he's calling to you. Reach out and receive his mercy and grace, and I promise you on the authority of the Word of God that he will save you and sanctify you."

I segued an appropriate song out of some spot announcements, figuring the preacher and his wife wouldn't appreciate "Whiskey River" coming on the heels of his message. After I had everything set, I walked them to the door.

"Were you touched by the Lord this morning, Will?" he said.

I was surprised he remembered my name. "Yes, sir. I remember when I used to engineer for you. Brings it all back."

His wife gazed at me, steely eyed.

"Brings back things for a lot of people," the preacher said. "And we said a prayer for you when you went away."

"I appreciate that. There were probably a few praying I'd get more time."

"Did you find the Lord inside Clarkston, son?" he said, maneuvering the guitar out of the way of the swinging door his wife had just exited.

"I found a lot of things, Pastor."

Work is a gift for body and soul, if you choose to look at it that way, and I slipped into the easy habit of overnights, sleeping after breakfast and waking midafternoon, ready to tackle the roadwork that consumed me. By the end of July I had made enough money to buy seventeen truckloads of gravel, and I borrowed our nearest neighbor's skid loader to more easily distribute it. He had his reservations about lending it to me, but my mother convinced him.

The woman I replaced overnight moved to evenings as Seeb situated the on-air talent. Shirley had moved from Roanoke, Virginia, and had landed in the middle of Dogwood without a job or much of a radio pedigree, but she was another of Seeb's misfits who turned out to be surprisingly good. I made sure she got safely to her car each night at midnight and also made sure I was gone in the morning before Virginia strolled into the office.

The knowledge of my identity escaped listeners, probably because there were few at those hours of the night. I found the work comforting. Instead of lying awake all night, I could work myself to exhaustion and fall asleep during the light, then do it again, a routine that felt natural and eased the ache I carried.

Plus, and this will sound strange, I felt closer to Karin. On those starry nights when I had a twenty-minute set of Classic Country ready, I'd prop the back door open, take a fresh cup of coffee outside, and sit under the blinking red light of the tower and look at the moon's reflection in the river as it curved below. There weren't many streetlights in this part of town; it was mostly pasture, wilderness, and housing developments.

There were a few motion sensor lights that came on with the skittering of dogs and raccoons across driveways. A few lights in people's houses burned through windows and dotted the undulating landscape. A cool, swampy breeze blew through, and the night was filled with chirping insects and the *garuump* of frogs. It was peaceful, and the steaming coffee helped keep me awake.

I wondered what Karin might be doing at 2 or 3 a.m. Did she know I was on the radio? Each time I spoke, I pictured her listening, the way she had done in high school. She would call and help keep me awake or ask for a song, even though she couldn't stand country music any more than I could. I thought about sending her veiled messages. The urge to speak to her, to give her a message only she would understand, was too strong. With her current situation, I couldn't call her up and ask her to listen, so I resorted to the request line, cajoling her into responding, hoping and pleading for her call.

After a set of six songs, I would backsell them, telling the listeners whom they'd heard, as if they didn't know these artists better than I did. Then I'd launch into something more personal, a chance at a connection. "Hope you're doing well this Tuesday morning, wherever you are. If you're listening at work, I hope I can help you stay awake. Or maybe you're passing through on your way east or west—welcome to wild, wonderful West Virginia. Or maybe you're just having a little trouble sleeping tonight. I understand that—it's one of the reasons I took this job. So no matter what state you're in, you're welcome here, and thanks for making us a part of your night."

I'd usually throw in the phone number and say, "And if I can play something special for you this morning, let me know what you'd like to hear."

There were the requisite number of lonely women with smokers' voices who called to tell me how much they loved my soothing tones and ask what I was doing after I finished. One woman gave me her phone number and address and said her friends tell her she looks an awful lot like Heather Locklear. By the way she coughed, I figured the "awful" part was closest to the truth. She sent a picture of herself in a skimpy outfit near the entrance to a bar, and though she wasn't ugly, she looked to be on the wrong side of fifty.

There were nights when I'd sit outside and a car would pass slowly on Route 60, or I'd hear the gravel crunch in the parking lot at the front of the building. I kept the front locked, but I wondered if some night the woman or someone like her might knock on the window seeking more than a favorite song. Or if someone who knew about my past would burst through and try to end my life.

30

Bobby Ray

A week before I was hired, there had been a raid on a meth lab. A couple of months later the chief told me to check out a report of some new activity—someone who lived nearby had seen strange lights over there, and the place was boarded up. The house was at the end of Benedict Road, a winding, paved road that turned into dirt and ruts, and was so secluded that the cruiser was covered in dust and needed a new muffler by the time I made it back there.

An old Chevy Impala sat along the road, and at first I thought it might have broken down. When I saw a man moving at the back of the house, past the yellow tape strung around the place, I jumped out and pulled my gun. Other than cleaning it, this was the first time I'd taken it out. My heart accelerated, and I thought about the Kevlar vest I'd mentioned a few times to Chief Buret. He still scoffed at the idea. "Too expensive and do you know how hot those things will be in summertime?" I kept after him but I don't know why. Lots of studies have shown that the vests save lives, even in small towns, but he was as closed to that as paying a decent wage to his new officers.

"Stop right there and put your hands in the air!" I yelled.

The man immediately raised his hands and came toward me.

"I said stop!"

He did; then he got down on the ground like I asked. "Officer, I live down the road. I was just up here looking for a friend of mine."

I hopped over some scrub brush and asked if he had a weapon. He shook his head and I asked for his wallet, but I recognized him before he handed it to me. "You're Will Hatfield, aren't you?"

"In the flesh."

"Who were you looking for?"

"It's kind of a long story. There's this guy Arron Spurlock and—"

"Elvis?" I said. "There's a missing person's report out on him."

"Right. I thought he might have been mixed up with these meth people in some way, so I came out here to have a look."

I put my gun away. "What makes you so interested in this?"

"I told you, he was a friend. And I need all the friends I can get."

"You thought it would be different coming back here?" I told him he could get up and gave him his wallet. "I heard you were back."

Will shoved his wallet in his pocket and studied me. "I know you, don't I?"

"Bobby Ray. Karin's brother."

"Oh yeah." He reached out and shook my hand. "I didn't know. I still remember when you were this high. Looks like you did all right for yourself. How are your parents?"

I stepped toward the cruiser. "The less I say to you, the better as far as they're concerned. As far as anybody's concerned. Why don't you get back home? Leave this place alone."

"All right. But would you look into this Elvis thing? He wasn't the most upstanding citizen in the county, but he didn't make a habit of running off and scaring his mother half to death."

"I have looked into it. Talked with the Exxon station owner. Talked with his mother and sister."

"What about the people running this place?"

"Can't talk to what you can't catch. My guess is they cleared out and Elvis went with them."

He pursed his lips. "Doesn't sound like him. It feels wrong."

"Well, now, I guess you'd know about that, wouldn't you?"

Will nodded and returned to his car. The dust from him driving away lingered in the air a long time and settled on the trees and plants below. I waited until then to head back to town.

31

Will

August came — the dog days when the heat and humidity make you long for a swimming pool. I slept until afternoon underneath the hum of the window air conditioner I'd bought at Sam's Club. After I ate, I worked on the hill, digging the foundation and laying the pipe. Hooking up water and electricity back there was going to be a stretch. I'd talked with a contractor who told me it could be done, but it was going to take some cash I didn't have.

Pouring the concrete was another problem. I'd done some flat work with a man who owned a mixing truck over in Wayne County. He finally came by and looked at what I'd done. "Driveway won't support my truck, and it'd cost a fortune to snake a line back there. The pump I have wouldn't be strong enough for what you need. Probably best to get a portable mixer and do it by hand. Just frame up the sides like normal and pour it yourself. It's going to take a while, but that's the only way I can see it working."

"I've got the time," I said.

I rented his portable mixer and pulled it back on the hill. Seeb let me have two days off, and I hauled the concrete by wheelbarrow. It was backbreaking, sweaty work, and I labored until after midnight, when I collapsed. At the end of the second day I had the whole thing poured, but I looked as white as a concrete ghost.

After that, every day brought progress as the house took shape. When darkness came, I would sit on the porch slab and study the valley and wonder what it would look like finished. Sipping a cool drink from my deck. Visualizing the whole area covered with a blanket of new snow, the only tracks made by a passing deer or a fox. Or what it would look like in a few months when the trees blazed with color only God himself could paint.

I was excited at the end of August to put in a large order at 84 Lumber for most of the flooring and joists. The money I didn't spend on food, gas, and a used 4x4 pickup went to materials. Every week I would lose a few hours repairing the truck or running Mama to the doctor or to see her two siblings who were still living, a brother and a sister.

"We should have some sort of get-together," Carson said one Sunday afternoon when he and Jenna came for supper. "These relatives of ours are dropping like flies trapped in an old refrigerator."

There were a few of my father's relatives in the area, but most had moved to other states, too old to travel or too ill. Mama quickly put the idea to rest by saying she wasn't holding any reunion at our place.

Jenna put a hand on my leg under the table, and I glanced at her. She smiled, eating her potato salad, and I asked her to pass a dinner roll. While her hands were occupied, I grabbed the greasiest chicken breast I could find and slid it under the table, holding it just above my leg. I thanked her for the roll and she smiled sweetly, then returned her right hand to the chicken breast and jumped a little in her chair.

"What's wrong, darlin'?" Carson said.

She wiped her hands on a napkin and excused herself.

Carson rolled his eyes and looked at me.

I just shrugged.

"Mama tells me you're spending more time on that project on the hill. You really building a shack up there?"

"Come see it after dinner. We'll hop in the truck and I'll take you back."

He looked at his watch. "No, Jenna has a couple of shows she likes to watch. Some other time."

"I don't know what he would want with a big old house on top of that hill when we have this one right here," Mama said. "I probably won't be around much longer, and you could have the whole place to yourself."

"You're gonna outlive us all," Carson said.

"Plus, Will's gonna start a family back there, aren't you?" Jenna said as she walked into the room. "You've been here long enough to check out the merchandise. Anyone strike your fancy at church?"

"I can't get him to go with me," Mama said. "But there are several women who I'm sure would be interested—don't you think?"

"I could think of several at the shop who would jump at the chance to go out with an ex-convict. Just to add some spice to their lives."

I put my fork down and walked away from the table.

"Aw, now, Will, she didn't mean anything by it," Carson said. "You come back here and tell us who's gonna move in with you in that hillbilly palace."

But I wasn't listening. I'd been gone since the two arrived. Sunday was my night off, and I grabbed a sleeping bag and a toss-up tent, the kind you throw on the ground, anchor, and crawl inside. I slept by my house that night with a small fire and thought about all the things Carson and I had done as kids and things we wished we hadn't done.

I still had woodsmoke in my clothes the next night when I

went to work, and Shirley noticed. I told her I'd been camping and she smiled.

As I walked her to her car, she said, "Oh, I almost forgot. There was somebody who called on the request line for you." She dug in the pocket of her denim shirt and handed me a pink slip.

I figured it was my secret admirer, the Heather Locklear look-alike. But the message said, *Karen said to tell you she'd be listening tonight.*

"When did you get this?" I said.

"A little after ten, I think," she said.

"How did she sound?"

Shirley raised her eyebrows. "Like any normal love-starved country music fan, I suppose. Is there something special about this one?"

"Maybe." I thanked Shirley for the message and watched her drive away. The leaves were turning up in the wind like a storm was brewing. The tree branches waved a warning.

I took the steps two at a time and hurried inside, the light above the door blinking, letting me know the request line was ringing. "WDGW," I said, out of breath.

Click.

It had to be her. She'd let it ring as many times as she dared. I glanced at the list of upcoming songs. The music director had programmed the station so we wouldn't replay a tune in any twenty-four-hour period except for current hits. Since I knew Karin would be listening, I wanted to pick something she'd remember, something we had shared.

That's when it came to me, and I ran into the production room to a stack of albums I had gone through during a long stretch in the summer. I found what I was looking for, stuck it on the turntable, and cued it up. It was all coming back to me. That night. The music. The wind. The smell of the wine on her breath. The taste of her lips.

"Welcome to another set of solid Classic Country. I'm Mark Joseph with you again and happy to be back, ready to take you through the early-morning hours and hopefully see you through to the other side. If you have a request, a memory this next song brings, or you just want to suggest something, call the request line and I'd be glad to hear what you have in mind. This is Jackson Browne from a long time ago—not necessarily classic country, but it's close enough."

I flipped the remote switch to the production console, and "These Days," a simple ballad that spoke of things forgotten and the chances missed by lovers, began. The needle was ancient, and Jackson's voice muffled but no less powerful. It had been so many years since I had heard this song, and I couldn't help but think Karin and I were hearing it together. If the program director was listening, I'd be in trouble, but compared with everything else, it was the least of my worries.

I watched the request line, the phone mounted near the desk, praying for Line 1 to flash. There were four lines, and the station used them for contests in the morning and afternoon drive. Caller number five. Caller number ten. We usually just picked up the first line and said they had won.

About a minute into the song, Line 1 rang. I let it blink three times and picked it up. "Classic Country 16."

Nothing on the other end. Just someone breathing heavily.

Line 2 rang. I put the first on hold. "Hello? Can I help you?"

Nothing.

"Okay, hang on. I'll be right back."

"Wait," a raspy voice said. "Don't hang up."

"Do you have a request?" I said. "Because I have someone holding on the other line."

"Whoever it is can't be as important as what I'm about to say."

The voice sounded vaguely familiar, but I couldn't place it. Something about the way the guy talked rang a bell.

"All right, go," I said.

"Turn around."

The hair on the back of my neck stood up, not because there was a draft behind me or I could sense someone else in the building, and not because I was hearing the voice on the phone and in the room, or because I noticed Virginia's line was lit up on the phone tree, but because in my haste to get back inside the building, I had forgotten to lock the front door.

Instead of turning, I punched down Line 3 and dialed 9 and 1. That's as far as I got before something hit me in the back of the head and I slumped to the spider-infested floor.

32

Will

"How many were there?" Eddie Buret said.

My head was on fire and my jaw felt loose. I had cuts on my face and a knot the size of a mouse on the back of my head. "I only know about the one who cracked me in the head. Guess there could have been more."

"Could you identify them?"

"After I hit the floor, I remember seeing cowboy boots. And the guy wore a mask. That's about it."

"You're lucky somebody noticed the station was off the air," he said. "You could've been out the whole night."

"We have loyal listeners," I said, glancing at the phone. "Who called?"

"Female, I think. Didn't give her name. Said something was wrong over here and for us to look into it."

I wanted it to be Karin.

Tom, our morning guy, entered groggily as Eddie finished taking my statement. "They roughed you up pretty good," Tom said. "You should get that looked at."

I waved him off. "Just let me finish my shift."

"No," Tom said. He didn't sound mad—actually it sounded a

lot like compassion. "You were attacked and I'm here. I just talked with Seeb. He said he wants you to go to the hospital."

I turned to Eddie. "There's no way to trace the number of the person who called, is there? I want to thank her."

He shook his head. "Came up unavailable."

I shook off the rain and climbed into my truck. Eddie followed, leaning down and pecking on my window until I rolled it down. I could hear the rain-swollen river and the rising tide that seemed to envelop me.

"You know this is not going to stop, Will. This is not going to be the last time somebody tries to hurt you. Or worse."

"I'm surprised it took them so long."

"You should have been prepared."

"You know I can't carry a gun. You suggesting I should?"

"Wouldn't want you to break your parole. Just be more careful. And you might think about relocating. No secret where you live. Your mother too."

I nodded and rolled up the window as he walked to his cruiser. The whole thing felt like a setup. If it was someone looking for justice, they could have just killed me. And Eddie's warning seemed almost as ominous as the attack at the station.

I started my truck and raced home.

PART THREE

33

Danny Boyd

I told my counselor everything I'd found out about Will Hatfield, his mother, his friend who was missing, the house on the hill, and the woman Karin. Everything except my dad and what he'd done.

There were conversations with my mother I wasn't supposed to hear. Conversations with people who came by the house. Talk in secret in quiet voices.

I don't know what they expect a man to do whose children have been wiped from the face of the earth like june bugs on a windshield, my dad had said to a neighbor. The law says the boy's paid his debt to society and that we've taken enough from him. Locked him away for a few years to teach him a lesson. But every day he wakes up and takes a breath of air is another day my kids are never coming back.

I hear you, the neighbor said, spitting a line of tobacco juice on the ground.

He's out, free as a bird. If you ask me, he didn't get anything compared to what he did to us.

My father's calendar at work had red Xs on it, all the way up to the day Will Hatfield was released. There was a string of letters and numbers written on the calendar, and after checking,

I discovered it was for a Greyhound bus that came to Huntington. My dad loaded his shotgun that night and sat in the dark after Mama went to bed. Just sat there almost all night in the living room, staring out the window.

We're a Christian family, good Christian people who believe in the power of God to forgive and to change people, Daddy said when the preacher came over the next day. The preacher said he was there to talk, but I think Mama called him. I don't have no reservation in believing that God can forgive somebody. That's his business. But I figure if God can forgive a man for what Will Hatfield did, then God can forgive me too.

The preacher read some verses, something about vengeance being mine and all that.

Daddy said he would think on it, wait for the right time, but that in his heart he knew what was right. I can't stand the thought of that man sleeping soft and warm in his bed while my babies are cold in the ground. I'm never gonna walk in their room and watch the sun warm their faces. I've lived all these years hearing their voices echo through this house. Do you know what that's like?

You know that the Lord has them safe in his hands. You know that you will see them again.

Now that is a comfort; I'll admit. I want to see my babies again. But the Lord has told me he's going to use me to get justice—mete it out.

I guess that's what my daddy was aimin' to do the night he took his gun to his car. He had kissed my mama good night and sat there in the dark again, something welling up inside him. He kept mumbling something as he drank the stuff he'd poured for himself. I couldn't understand, and when he went to the gun cabinet, I snuck out and got in the back of the car. It was as dark as pitch and I hunkered down. I should have known he wouldn't see me because his mind was someplace else. Maybe he was thinking about the funeral and the little caskets. Or listening to the pitiful way the women were bawlin' and you couldn't stop 'em. Little kids with their bunches of flowers getting ready for the cemetery.

My daddy always said he used to be fast when he was a kid. That he could run like the wind. Well, as old as he was, he sure ran up that driveway that night, hightailin' it away from his car parked by the road. He was kind of snorting as he ran and frothing at the mouth like some rabid dog, panting and wheezing like it was the last race of his life. He didn't slow up till he got near their yard. He stood by a persimmon tree and listened.

He had his hands on his knees, doubled over, the crickets and frogs trying to see who could make more noise. He saw something in the moonlight—a stepladder by the garage—and he put his gun down and went to it.

I wanted to pick up the gun and run back to the car or throw it in the creek that ran past their property. I wanted to ask my dad if he would like to give Mrs. Hatfield the same heartache he had known.

He'd seen her at the Kroger in Barboursville, and he told Mama that it liked to kill the woman just to look at him. I tried to pretend I hadn't seen her, but she knowed. She could see the hurt in my eyes all the way from the bakery.

My dad moved the stepladder to a window that was lit. The ground was soft over there, and the stepladder sunk a few inches. They had planted bushes under the window that didn't do very well, and I figured there was just too much water in the soil for the roots to get a good hold. He climbed up a step at a time till he reached the windowsill, then put the gun in his left hand and steadied himself with his right.

He looked inside, the light shining on his face, and he had to lean closer to see what it was he was looking for. His mouth dropped open, and he studied it for a few seconds. He put his lips together in kind of a defiant look—or maybe he was resigned to do what he'd come to do. I was about to reach out and grab him when he started back down the ladder. He didn't put it back or anything. He just took off down the driveway toward the car.

I knew I was dead because there was no way I could catch him, so I watched him drive off. I got up on the ladder myself and took a few steps. I had to get to the third one from the top before I could see inside. Will Hatfield was on the bed, a hand behind his head, every stitch of clothes on, even his shoes, staring at something. It took me a moment to see it was a newspaper clipping. I could tell by the picture it was the one that talked about my sisters. I wondered what had happened to make my daddy not want to go through with his plan. Surely Will looking over the newspaper clipping would have set him off.

Then I noticed Will's stomach. It was moving up and down and his chest was heaving and his shoulders shaking like people at the funeral. Will was crying. He dropped the article and reached up and put his arm over his eyes, and I could tell by the spittle in his mouth that he'd been at it for a while. Just bawlin' his eyes out like some grieving mother.

I wondered what Daddy had thought, if maybe letting him suffer for what he did would be better than killing him. At least right then.

I walked down to the road and headed back for the house in the dark.

34

Will

Two days after the attack at the station, while I was taking my mother to a doctor's appointment, our house was ransacked. We came home to a tidal wave of dust and debris. Whoever had done it didn't seem to discriminate. They'd gone through every room upstairs.

"They must want you out of here really bad," Mama said.

I sat on the dust-covered couch. "Maybe they're right."

She got that steely-eyed look I remembered seeing as a kid. "You can't let them win. *We* won't let them win. You understand?"

I waited for Karin's call that never came. I threw out hints for her that were only picked up by a few older women lying in their beds with nothing better to do than call some stranger at 3 a.m. I didn't have much else to do, so I listened.

I had kept my injuries from my mother for a couple of days, but there was a blurb in the *Cabell Record* mixed in with a few car break-ins and a domestic dispute. She looked at the back of my head and gasped, saying I needed stitches. I told her I was fine; I poured a gallon of Betadine on it, then repositioned my father's John Deere hat and kept working.

It took me several weeks to get up the nerve to go to the

Ashworth house in the daytime. It was the early fall when the weather turns cold one day and gives you a taste of what's to come, then switches back to the heat and humidity and makes you plunk your jacket in the corner a few more weeks.

I'd settled into that routine of working life where each day had a certain ebb and flow that felt right. I was getting my voice back, feeling the strength and power return, and I wasn't as tentative on air. It felt good to have calloused hands *and* work at a job that was so nonphysical.

I hadn't planned on going to the Ashworths', but driving back from 84 Lumber, I turned toward Summerdale, passed over Interstate 64, and found myself in the neighborhood. It looked a lot different in the daylight. The lawns were still nice and green, but I noticed some neglect to the houses with younger families. Maybe they didn't have the money to live in such a neighborhood. Mailboxes were missing letters and flags, and a few homes had cars parked on the street.

The Ashworth house sat at the end of the cul-de-sac, and I parked in the roundabout, the truck knocking a few seconds after I turned off the ignition. I made sure there was no one outside the surrounding houses, no one who might recognize me.

I was out of the truck and to the driveway when a kid on a Big Wheel raced out of the shadows of an open garage next door. He wore a NASCAR shirt and a #3 Dale Earnhardt hat. He stopped a few feet from me, and I squinted into the setting sun.

"You here to see Mr. and Mrs. Ashworth?" he said. He held a half-eaten peanut butter and jelly sandwich in one hand. It looked like a gun.

"Sure am. They still live here?"

"Right yonder," he said. "Nice people."

"What's your name?"

"Little Wendell. My daddy's name is Wendell too, so they call me Little Wendell so they won't get us mixed up."

"Well, Little Wendell, I'm glad to meet you."

"What's your name?"

I hesitated, and it was in that split second that I glimpsed movement in my peripheral vision. Someone had come onto the porch and stared at us.

"My name's Will. Now if you'll excuse me, I have some talking to do."

"Okay," Little Wendell said, taking a bite out of the barrel.

It was Mrs. Ashworth on the porch, her hand on one of the pillars holding up the portico. The columns always looked like the entrance to some Southern mansion that seemed out of place here. It might fit on a Georgia plantation or maybe in Montgomery but not in Dogwood. There was always something forbidden and uninviting about the place, and I couldn't put my finger on it.

"Robert?" Mrs. Ashworth called to the open door, not taking her eyes off me. "You'd better get out here."

I slowed, getting only halfway up the walk before Mr. Ashworth came through the door. He looked the same, a little weathered perhaps, like a creek that widened while you were on vacation. He'd always had a little paunch in front, and it didn't seem to have grown much. His hair had receded, revealing brown spots commensurate with his age, and he seemed a bit slower to focus. He had always seemed sharp to me, like having a conversation with him was a challenge of wits.

Mrs. Ashworth, though she was heavier and had added lines of worry around her face, showed a hint of the beauty I recalled. Her strawberry blonde hair had flecks of gray that sparkled in the fading sunlight. I thought about telling her she was as pretty as a picture or, as Atticus did to Mrs. Dubose in *To Kill a Mockingbird*, flattering her about her flowers, but I didn't.

Uncle Luther had once given me good advice on a fishing trip we took to East Lynn Lake, Kentucky. He said that a person picking a wife should be careful to examine the girl's mother because that's generally what his wife would wind up like. It was strange advice coming from someone who had never married, but when I tested the theory out on old photographs and yearbooks, I found he was right.

I had seen my share of ugly mothers in our hometown, ones who attended their children's school plays and recitals, but I had never seen a more beautiful mother than Mrs. Ashworth. She had an almost regal look, as if she could pass as a sister to some European countess.

Her eyes seemed more tired now, though, and her skin a bit pale, but she did not look as ravaged by the years as most ladies of the town. Her ankles were puffy and I noticed some varicose veins, but those were her only flaws. That and the look of worry that had come over her face when I stepped into their yard.

"Will?" she said, almost as a statement of horror rather than a question.

"It's me, Mrs. Ashworth." I touched my John Deere hat and nodded to her husband. I still bore some marks of the attack, but at this distance I figured they wouldn't be able to tell.

"You can stay right there," he said. "We don't want you coming here."

I stopped a few feet from the porch stairs, below these two who stood ramrod straight, like sentries guarding the castle of the wicked witch. I noticed peeling paint over the doorway and on the porch railing. The eaves sagged in several places, and it looked like the roof near the chimney had sustained some water damage. The house wasn't falling apart, but it was certainly showing its age.

"I don't mean to cause trouble," I said, my voice soft and even, though my heart was beating wildly. Why hadn't I called and gauged their feelings? This was more of an ambush than a visit. "I saw Bobby Ray not long ago—"

"He told us," Mr. Ashworth said.

"Well, I was just driving by from the lumber yard and took the turn—it was kind of familiar. I wanted to ask about Karin. Is she doing well?"

Mrs. Ashworth put a hand to the railing for support and shook her head like an umpire calling a ball too far outside the strike zone. "Haven't you caused us enough pain? Haven't you done enough to this community without coming back here and torturing us?"

Mr. Ashworth put an arm around his wife, and I caught a glimmer of the past. I remembered them standing on the porch as Karin and I drove to school, looking every bit the doting mother and father.

"The letters I sent," I said. "When I saw her at the prison a few months ago, she said she never received them."

"We never should have let her do that," Mr. Ashworth snapped. "They said it might help, but they were wrong. It put her into a downward spiral."

"She seemed fine when I saw her."

Mrs. Ashworth moved to her right, to the top of the stairs. "If you have any love for our daughter and an ounce of decency left, I suggest you get in that truck and drive as far away from here as you can. And stop harassing people. How you can drive up and down these roads after what you did I'll never understand." She put a hand to her mouth and leaned into her husband.

"It's beyond me," he said. "I don't get it."

"It's beyond any of us," she added into his chest.

It was like unloading a wagon full of hay for them. Once they started tossing the bales from the top, the whole thing had to come down.

"Those poor people have stayed in this town after losing everything they loved," Mr. Ashworth said. "Why can't you have more respect for the dead? Why don't you just leave?"

I had taken their most potent artillery fire to the heart. Part of me wanted to retreat to the safety of the world I'd created, but the longer they looked at me, the more it felt like they were waiting for some kind of response.

"I understand. Believe me, I've thought about packing up and going where people don't know about my past. But the truth is, I love your daughter. I've loved her since the first day I met her. And I suppose I'll love her till I die."

"Which won't be much longer if you stay here," Mr. Ashworth said.

I put up a hand. "I've heard the talk. If it were me in their shoes, I might think the same thing. But I've paid my debt, and I can't let people push me around because they don't like the way the law treated me. If they can do that, we don't live in America. My dad fought along with you, Mr. Ashworth. He talked about what a fine soldier you were—"

"Leave your father out of this," he said. "You'll never be half the man he was."

"Well, at least we agree about that."

Mrs. Ashworth put an arm around a column. "You're too late. You know about Karin. Ruthie Bowles said she talked to you. I figured you'd understand and leave instead of coming back and upsetting her."

"I don't want to hurt her in any way. But you also know—"

"Then leave," Mr. Ashworth said.

"—that I still feel the same. I love her with everything in me. I think of her every day. I pray for her every night."

"You pray?" Mr. Ashworth said, incredulous. "You should ask the Lord to forgive you for what you've done and leave us in peace. Leave *her* in peace. You don't know what you're doing, son."

"I have asked God to forgive my mistakes. And I believe he has." I looked at Mrs. Ashworth, and the emotion caught in my throat. "Why didn't you give her my letters?"

"The worst decision she ever made was being your friend.

We don't control her life now, but we'll do everything we can to keep you away from her. We've already talked with the police about a restraining order. You will not harass our daughter. You will not have contact with her of any kind, Will Hatfield. Do you understand?"

"The very thing that might help the most—"

"Is you leaving this town, this county, and this state for good," Mr. Ashworth said. "Now do not come back here. And do not make contact with our daughter."

The two retreated behind their white door and slammed it. Mrs. Ashworth broke into muffled sobs.

I stood a few moments, taking in the feeling, then turned for my truck.

Several neighbors had come out of their houses. A mother whispered, "That's him" to a middle school–age girl. Little Wendell had finished his sandwich, and his mother chased him back up their driveway and into the garage, glancing behind her as if I might follow.

A man in khakis and a collared shirt approached. "Those are good people. Why don't you leave them alone?"

"Amen to that," someone said.

I stared at him a few seconds, not trying to be mean but just trying to take in the hatred and not give it back. I wanted to say something. Everything in me wanted to defend myself. But I held back and just got into the truck.

The neighbors returned to their houses, looking at me as if I were some loose circus animal they wanted to see but couldn't stand to look at.

In my rearview mirror I saw a curtain part in the front window of the Ashworth house. A face appeared but I couldn't tell who it was.

Sometimes when you follow your gut, good things happen. I had a feeling this one would come back to haunt me.

35

Karin

Ruthie talked about what I should do with my time in the closet, which was becoming more frequent. I couldn't sleep next to my husband, so I withdrew to the safety of soft lights, books and journals, and a small radio Ruthie gave me. It was my one contact with the outside world. I couldn't stand the noise and news of the TV. People throwing chairs at each other or revealing the most personal things to complete strangers.

When I was in high school, Will worked at the local country music radio station. My parents listened, but I hated it. Will invited me there on several occasions, and some nights I would sit in the production room and read magazines or write mock news stories about my family. He even recorded some of them and threatened to play them on the air.

During songs we talked. I always thought I was helping him with the boredom, but I suppose he was helping me as well. When he worked overnight, I'd tune in to hear his voice. He always sounded older and somehow wiser. Will had an incredible vocabulary. I guess it was from reading all his mother's books. He always seemed to be a bit further ahead than me, than our whole class, except for the social part. He was a social misfit, and I could tell he was self-conscious about his clothes and his hair. But he was always genuine, and even on the radio he would give little pieces of himself.

One night it was unbearably hot in the closet, so I turned off the light and just lay on my cover, fanning myself with a magazine. I plugged the earpiece in and turned down the radio. It felt soothing to listen to voices coming from so far away. Traffic news in Chicago. A thunderstorm in Des Moines. Someone being executed in Texas.

There were strange call-in shows that dealt with space aliens. Those creeped me out, and I couldn't listen for long. One station rebroadcast Rush Limbaugh, played for the truckers who didn't catch his show during the day, but that wasn't what I needed. Something in his voice made me sad. Like there was a lot of pain amid all that opinion.

I flipped to the FM band and scanned past the classic and alternative rock stations and about fifteen different varieties of country. There were a few Christian stations as well on either side of the dial, some playing music, but most featuring preaching programs. There were so many answers to questions I'd never considered but none to the ones that burned within.

At the right of the dial, past the station in Charleston that always played the most obscure rock songs, was the little country station in our town. It sounded the same, had the same music I remembered as a teenager, the same tired lyrics about cheatin' hearts and women doing men wrong and men doing women wrong and drinkin' and fightin' and being proud to be an American. I still couldn't stand the music, but there was something comforting to it, something familiar, and I lingered there, the twang and the steel guitar bringing back good memories.

When the announcer came on—he called himself Mark Joseph—something fluttered in my chest. At first I thought it was just the heat in the room, but as I listened to his voice, warmth spread through my body.

I listened closely, and a phrase that rolled off his tongue reminded me of someone. And then I put it together.

"Will," I whispered.

It was really him. The next set confirmed it when he made some joke about all the troubles the singers had been going through in the past few songs.

I sat up, knees tight against my chest, sweat rolling from my underarms, and it was the best feeling I'd had in ages. Not even talking with Ruthie got me this excited.

I listened throughout the night, drifting in and out of sleep, and cursed when I woke up to the morning man giving the farm report and prices of hog futures, pork bellies, barrows, and gilts. I'd missed Will's good-bye — the sign-off.

There was something thrilling and forbidden about listening to a former boyfriend in my closet, alone, my husband and children in the same house. Will had touched my life in so many ways when I was younger, yet he was the one man I had been reluctant with.

I spoke with Ruthie later that day, and she was glad that I'd heard him. "What kind of feelings did it stir up?"

"It felt so good I feel kind of guilty."

"Why would it be wrong?"

"I'm betraying my husband for thinking about something that can't be. And my children. What would they think if they knew their mother was locked in a closet thinking about an old flame?"

"Old flames don't die easily, especially the really hot ones. Not even time extinguishes those."

"Ruthie, you know I trust you more than anyone. But what should I do? I know nothing can come from it. Nothing good, except something to occupy my time and keep me company at night."

"You're worried about the illusion."

"What?"

"We talked about this. Life is filled with illusions. That the grass is greener on the other side of the fence. That you'd be happy with some man who doesn't snore or have love handles. A lot of women idealize their past relationships and think, *What if? What if I'd married that guy who made it big in computers? What if I hadn't chosen the loser I'm married to now?* You ride that rail long enough and you'll convince yourself the illusion is real, that someone you knew twenty years ago is the real thing and what you have now isn't worth saving."

"I don't understand. I thought you wanted me to listen to Will. You went with me to see him."

Ruthie grasped my shoulder as tightly as she could. She touched her head to mine and just stayed there a moment. Then she pulled away, and it was as if she didn't have to say anything. She was speaking with her eyes. But, of course, she was Ruthie. She spoke anyway. "My point is that in all of this, you have to see what's real. You have to be able to distinguish what *is* from what isn't."

"I'm trying so hard."

She hugged me. "I know, girl, and you're really close. You've come a long way, but there's still a bit more road to travel."

"I'm glad I have you."

Ruthie nodded. "I'll treasure this time always. But there are some things you have to do alone."

"I don't understand."

"It's time, Karin. It's time for me to back away and let you go."

I pulled away in horror. "What do you mean? You're the one who has gotten me through this. You're the one—"

"No, it's been you all along. And it's time to stop leaning on this old buzzard and fly."

"Are you leaving? Where will you go?"

She looked at me through misty eyes. "I've tried to be a good friend to you. But Richard has helped me see that you're leaning on me rather than going forward, and though it pains me, I need to step back a little."

"Richard told you to do this? But why?"

"Think about the things we've talked about. Think hard about the past. So much of it carries the key to your future. And know that I will always love you."

36

Will

It was one of those dingy, dark days of rain and wet leaves familiar to our area of the world. Low-hanging clouds and mist over the road. The same kind of weather I remember when, as a child, I heard the Marshall University football team's plane had gone down.

As I walked into the station, the rain seemed to intensify. The river was up and rising and had covered the field below, a brown monster growing outside its banks. I was glad to see cows moving to higher ground.

I passed Virginia's desk but she didn't look up. She had her purse at the ready for a quick getaway as soon as the clock reached five.

Seeb was in his office and it was past his regular quitting time, but he'd called me in for an emergency meeting. I should have guessed what this was about, but I had faith in him as a friend that it wouldn't end this way.

My wounds had healed—except for an oozing scab on the back of my head that I kept covered with my hat. My face was still discolored, but the blackness was gone and I no longer got stares from people, except the normal stares from those who recognized me.

Seeb rose from his desk as I closed the door. "You okay?" he said.

"I'll tell you after our meeting. What's up?"

He looked at his desk and an envelope sitting there. My name was on the front. For some reason I thought of the Johnny Paycheck song "Take This Job and Shove It."

"I'm sorry, Will. I truly wish there was something else I could do, but I just can't make it work anymore. I hope you'll understand."

"Understand what? I haven't missed a shift since you gave me a second chance."

"You've done everything I've asked and then some." To my surprise Seeb admitted, "With the little we pay you people, I couldn't ask for more. But listeners are calling. Maybe the police blotter started it; then the *Dispatch* ran a story. You've probably seen it."

I nodded. "Yeah. Nice to know I'm still a news item."

"Once listeners start calling the advertisers, it's all over. I tried to head that off, but we're losing money now."

"I've noticed the spot load is down."

"It's not down. They've stopped. I'm just running those for good faith."

"The dealership threaten to take your car?"

Seeb pursed his lips around the cigar and held his long-fingernailed hands out, palms up, like he was pleading for his life. "What am I supposed to do? Tell me. Give me another option than letting you go and I'll take it."

A spider crawled up the wall behind his desk and disappeared in a small hole in the ceiling tile. "I understand. I can't say I'd do anything different if I were in your shoes. I really appreciate what you did for me."

He handed me the envelope, pulling his dress slacks high. "Your check's in there for the last two weeks. I went ahead and paid you for the rest of this week." He turned to the safe in the corner and rolled the tumblers. In all my years I'd never seen him open it, but he pulled out a crisp stack of bills, leafed through them, and came up with four hundred dollars. "I didn't add any more to the check, but this is sort of a bonus. You won't even have to claim it on your taxes. It's a gift." He plopped the bills on the desk in front of me.

I just looked at it. "I can't accept that."

Seeb pushed the money closer. "I want you to have it. Go on. Use it to buy a grill for that new house. Or some shingles. Whatever."

A better man would have thanked him and walked away, but I took the money. I had already calculated how many electrical sockets and how much wiring it would buy.

"Maybe if things settle down a bit we can rethink this," Seeb said.

We both knew things wouldn't settle down. The best you could hope for was the passage of time and the eventual closing of the open wound that was our town. I got the feeling that this wasn't the last time I might be fired for being Will Hatfield.

"This has been coming for a while," I said. "I hoped it wouldn't, but I just have to deal with it."

"If there's anything else I can do for you or your mother, let me know. I'm real sorry, son."

I nodded and shook his hand.

He smiled sadly, the cigar still jutting out, and I couldn't help but think how much he looked like some character from a Dr. Seuss book. Yertle the station manager.

"I'll never forget your kindness, Seeb."

He nodded once, then rubbed a finger underneath his nose.

When I left the station, I waved at Clay, who was on the air, but he didn't see me. Virginia's desk was bare, and I saw her taillights blink red as she sped away. I took one final look at the production room and the years of memories. Just one more thing to say good-bye to.

37

Danny Boyd

The police report from the accident was written in a slanting cursive that looked a lot like my fourth-grade teacher's handwriting. Mrs. Munroe was my first real love. She smelled like a fresh bouquet of flowers, and when she walked into the cafeteria, it was hard to eat she was so pretty. She'd sit with kids from our class, even after we'd played basketball and had that fourth-grade boy smell to us. She used to write notes on our papers, and once she wrote on mine that she thought I would go really far someday.

The report said that a hit-and-run accident had occurred at approximately 7:43 a.m., and then it gave the location on Route 60, right where I had led my sisters. I couldn't look at their names or the description of their injuries, but I already knew what they looked like. I'd been there. Jumped the guardrail and let them die.

The officer described the scene, said there were no visible skid marks but that the car had veered off the road and into the gravel and lost control and spun into the guardrail, killing the children.

There was talk around town that the sight had torn up the chief who was first on the scene, and the other officer who showed up had to take a week off from work, then didn't return. I don't know if that's true or not, but I believe it could happen. That kind of thing's like glue and not water. It sticks.

There was something strange in the report. It said, The driver of the vehicle, Will Hatfield, left the scene of the accident, only to return after police and rescue personnel had responded.

Do you find it strange that you don't remember that part of the accident? my counselor said after I told him some stuff I'd discovered. That you don't remember seeing Will pull away from the scene?

Can't people get kinda spacey and go off and not know what's happening? I've heard about that before.

It's called shock, he said.

Yeah. Maybe that's what happened. I jumped over the guardrail and was down there a long time. I don't remember the hospital or even very much about the funeral.

After looking at the police report, you still hold yourself responsible? You still think you killed your sisters?

I was in charge of them and I blew it. I didn't even have the guts to hang on to their hands. I just let go like.

You should have held on?

I should have tried to help them. That's all I'm saying.

What about Will? What responsibility does he have?

I shrugged. At least he called the police. I gotta give him that. But he drove away and left them there.

But he came back. Why do you think he did that?

Guess he felt guilty.

Should he have?

Yeah, he killed my sisters.

I thought you killed your sisters.

The room felt a little hotter than when I'd arrived. Well, I guess we both did. It's like leaving a loaded gun lying around and having a kid pick it up and pull the trigger, you know? The kid did

266

it, but it was the fault of the person who left the gun there. Like a double fault, if you know what I mean.

So you don't think you're totally to blame for the accident?

They're totally dead, so it doesn't really matter. I still should have held on. Maybe if I had, they wouldn't both be gone.

38

Will

A week later I awoke to a knock at the front door and a deep voice trying to explain something to my mother. At first, I thought it was the Jehovah's Witnesses back for another talk with my mother. There seemed to be no end to the visits they paid to her and other people in the community.

I lay there, watching a cloud pass the window, one of those slow-moving ones that would probably stay the entire day. A hole opened in the middle of it as if some astronaut would appear soon and drop through.

The conversation in the next room was not theological but legal in nature, and the man's voice grew more strained.

My mother, who had tried to keep things as quiet as possible while I slept during the day (I had not broken the habit of sleeping days and working nights), was uncharacteristically loud. "I don't understand," she said, her voice turning to a whine. "This is impossible. I've paid taxes on this land for longer than you've been born."

"I'm sure you have. But the fair market value will be paid—"

"How do you calculate fair market value of all I've invested in this place? or Will's work back on the hill?"

I walked into the room scratching my head, picking at the scab. Splotches of blood marked my pillow each morning. "What's going on?"

The man at the door wore a bad suit, and his hair was slicked from one side to the other, hiding a bald spot. He had a high forehead and beady eyes like some little animal kicked out of the nest to fly when it wasn't quite ready.

My mother held out a piece of paper with a shaky hand. "Will, he says they're going to take our land. Just up and take it with a court order."

The man looked at me with those small eyes, as if I were supposed to help him explain things to my mother. "Eminent domain," he finally said. "The town passed an ordinance last night saying this land was to be condemned and taken in the public interest."

I read the document. "What public interest?"

"I won't go into all the legalese, but there's really nothing you can do at this point. The decision's been made."

"What possible good could this land be to Dogwood?" my mother snapped. "What's the compelling interest?"

He looked at me instead of my mother, as if someone had told him this might not be the easiest job he would have today. At the end of the driveway was a police cruiser, and I recognized Bobby Ray. He'd been sent as backup, I guessed.

"I'm very sorry this has come as a surprise, ma'am. I was just told to deliver this and explain it as best I could so you could make other arrangements as quickly as possible."

"Make other arrangements?" my mother squealed. "How dare you say—?"

I put a hand on her shoulder. "Keep your cool, Mama." Then I said to the man, "Thanks for coming by. We'll take it from here."

The relief that spread over his face was immediate and complete. "Yes, well, have a good day."

I closed the door before he could say anything more trite.

"But, Will, could there be oil here? a coal seam? What? Why would they want this property?"

"It's not about this property or what's under the ground. They don't want me here, and I can't say I blame them."

"What are you going to do?"

"Something I should have done a long time ago."

39

Karin

The first night I didn't hear Will, I'll admit I was disappointed. The next night came and no Will. I figured he was on vacation. Maybe some kind of minor surgery. People take time off from work in every profession, right? But the longer he was gone, the more worried I became.

I was at the church for a meeting one afternoon when I got the nerve to call the station. A young, talkative woman answered, and I asked what happened to Mark Joseph, the guy overnight.

She groaned. "He's gone and none too soon if you ask me. People were complaining and the station lost business."

"But why? Did he do something wrong?"

"It was because of that accident years ago—he killed some kids walking by the road. One was my friend. I can't believe he came back here, but everybody's glad he's gone."

I hung up even though she was still chattering. My thoughts swirled, and I knew I had to get to Ruthie.

Lucille saw me in the hall. "Karin, are you all right? You look flushed. Here, sit down."

I tried to make it to my husband's office; then I turned around and headed for the front door. There was no way I could talk to him about this. No way I could tell him what was going on in my heart. The pain and the heartache and the past were all catching up faster than I could think.

I hurried through the atrium of the church, a sunny room with lots of tables where people congregate and talk and have coffee. At any time of the day you'll find a hum of activity.

A few of the women gathered around me, asking what was wrong and why I looked so upset.

I checked my watch and gave a nervous sigh. "The kids will be home from school soon and I need to be there. I almost forgot."

That seemed to satisfy them, but when Richard came around the corner and saw me, my face flushed again.

"Is everything all right?" he said.

"I don't know. I feel . . . something's not right."

He took me by the arm and walked me to his office.

"I have to get home and meet the kids," I protested. "I like to be there at the driveway and make sure they're okay."

"Shh, they're going to be fine. Now what's troubling you?"

The emotions came when I looked into his face. I could not bear the thought of letting this good man down, and neither could I bear the thought of losing Will, illusion or not. So much of what Ruthie had said to me kept coming back, but I was drawn to Will again and I felt my heart being led astray.

"I'm just so mixed up," I cried.

"It's all right. There's nothing you could say to me that would shock me or make me care any less. You can be sure of that."

"That's what I can't stand to think about. Hurting you. Making you feel less of me."

Richard smiled that wide, toothy smile that I remembered from when I first met him. How could I break the heart of this good man? If I told him what was really going on inside, what would happen to him? to the church? to the ladies who looked to me for guidance?

"I've been having awful thoughts," I said. "Terrible thoughts about a man."

"It's okay. Just calm down and tell me. What man? Someone here?"

"No, someone I knew a long time ago. Someone who's come back."

"That's good. Tell me what you remember. Tell me everything."

"But I have to get home. The children will expect me. I need to pick Tarin up at the preschool in a bit, but Darin and Kallie will be home on the bus soon."

He raised his voice and spoke through the slightly open door. "Nancy, the children will be coming home on the school bus in a few minutes. Would you mind having someone meet them at the house?"

"Sure," she said. "I'll call one of the neighbors."

"There," Richard said. "All cared for. They'll be fine. Now, who is this mystery man?"

I gave him a deer-in-the-headlights look and again he smiled. I had held this in so long—I even felt guilty for that.

"His name is Will Hatfield," I blurted. "I met him in high school, and we rode to college together for a while, before he moved away."

"He moved away?"

"Yes. I mean, no. He had some kind of accident before he moved. I just heard about it today from a girl at the radio station. He worked there in high school and college. I used to go over and visit him and we'd talk. Nothing romantic, we'd just talk."

"Did you date him?"

"Not that I remember. No, wait, we went to a play once, I think. Or a concert. Yes, I remember that. And I think we saw a movie or two. But nothing happened. At least, nothing physical happened between us. That I can remember."

"You don't need to be anxious. I can take this. Really."

That brought the tears again.

"Isn't this the man you visited in prison with Ruthie?" he said. "Will Hatfield?"

"Yes. Yes, I went with her and we had such a good talk, but everything . . . it hasn't been the same between us since then. She abandoned me. She won't talk." My chin crumpled and gave way. "Oh, but you don't know, do you? You don't know."

"I don't know *what*?"

"You don't know what's happened."

Richard handed me a box of tissues. "What's happened, dear? What's upset you so much?"

Like a kaleidoscope that swirls the colors of the rainbow in shapes so vivid and then stops in a perfect stained glass picture, my life came into focus and I stared into the eyes of my husband. "I think I'm in love. I think I've always been in love with him."

He nodded and kept his eyes trained on me. "I understand."

"How *could* you? How could *I*? Why did you ever let me go see him in prison? Why would you do that?"

"I thought it might help you."

"Help? How? It's made me more confused. I hadn't thought of him in years, and now I'm thinking about breaking every vow I've made to you. And our children." I stood and grabbed him by the shoulders. "Tell me I'm infatuated! Tell me it's just a schoolgirl crush! Scream at me! Yell at me! Do something!"

Richard looked at me with such . . . love—that's the only way to describe it—and pity and concern in one expression. "I think there's more to Will than you've realized. There's more to your history together, isn't there?"

"What do you mean?"

He gently pushed me back into my chair and sat on his desk, his arms folded. "I spoke with him."

"Will? He came here? To the church?"

"He's a gentle and kind man. I can see why you were taken

with him all those years ago. He told me some things about you—
the two of you."

"What did he say? What did *you* say?"

"That's where it kind of gets tricky. You know, in my position,
I can't talk freely about what everyone says in this office. But he
did tell me how much he enjoyed being with you. He told me of
the letters he wrote you from Clarkston."

"Letters?"

"I suppose you haven't seen them."

"No, of course not. Is that all he said?"

Richard took a moment, as if trying to frame a picture just
right. "He said that he's been waiting for you."

"Waiting?" I almost couldn't breathe.

"And he told me about *that night.*"

"What night? What are you talking about?"

"There was a concert in Cincinnati. He told me you went
together. It was—"

"—his birthday. Yes." The sound and the lights and the smoke
came back to me. "We saw Jackson Browne." I stood and walked
to the window, the floor rushing under me like so many summer fields. "I do remember. We stopped at a park—no, it was a
pool."

"What happened there?"

I reached out for the window treatment. I had hung a set of
flowered curtains to liven up the place when he first moved in. But
the curtains were gone. Only shades now, the off-white ones that
swung back and forth as soon as the air-conditioning engaged.
"Where are the curtains? The ones I put up here?"

"Karin, let's talk about that night. What happened?"

I turned and faced him, a hand to my forehead, scratching,
trying to remember. "We stayed for the concert and it was late. He
had asked me to go with him and I wasn't sure I wanted to, but
. . . No, that's not right. I think I asked him. I got the tickets from

some radio . . . We were good friends, not lovers. He was always very kind to me, and he didn't take advantage in any way."

Richard nodded. "Go on."

I walked behind the desk and ran my hand along Richard's chair—the high-backed leather one had been replaced by a wooden one, Spartan. "He bought a bottle of wine or two, I think. And . . . no, I had it with me. Yes, from my father's cabinet. I hid it under the seat so Will wouldn't see. To celebrate. It was his birthday and we were going to drive back, but we stopped to go swimming. It was dark and a police car came. And he was arrested? Oh, I can't remember."

"Don't give up. You're doing well. Just stay with me. Stay with the story."

"I don't understand. Why are you doing this? It's like you're trying to convince me to leave you. Or to turn my heart to him. I really have to make sure the kids are okay."

Richard intercepted me and went to the door to speak with his secretary.

"Yes," Nancy said, "they went to the bus stop to get them. They're all fine."

"But Tarin is still at preschool."

"Nancy, would you mind going over and picking up Tarin for us?"

"That'll be no problem," Nancy said.

"Now," Richard said, "don't you think another thing about them." He shut the door and sat in a chair beside me, putting a hand to his chin. "I know this seems strange, but I want you to keep going. Let's stay on this track and think about that night."

"But why?"

"Humor me," Richard said.

Closing my eyes, I saw us in the moonlight together. "Will and I were at this pool in Ohio, I think, or Kentucky. It was after midnight. We kind of celebrated when it went past midnight, I guess, because it was officially his birthday."

"So it was a happy time. You didn't feel threatened or under duress."

"With Will?" I laughed. "No, it was good. I mean, he wasn't the most exciting guy I ever went out with, and we didn't do all the things—well, I've told you about some of those things and you said they were all forgiven."

"Surely."

"But Will was so nice. The whole thing was comfortable with him, and I never once thought of myself as . . . vulnerable, you know? In danger, like with some of the others."

"And then what happened?"

"We drove home. He had to work the midmorning shift at the radio station, so we decided to stay up the whole night."

Richard took a breath. "Are you sure?"

"What do you mean, am I sure? Yes, I'm sure. I came home and . . ." Something flickered in my mind. The car pulling over. Will saying he was tired and saying I should get in the backseat and sleep. I'd had too much wine. I stayed in the passenger side, curled up.

"What is it?"

I sat up. "I just remembered something. He pulled over. We slept in the car. Both of us were so tired and it was still dark."

"Do you remember waking up? going home?"

The image in my mind was blurry, like someone shooting a video through Saran wrap. "Will must have dropped me off on his way home. I remember we swerved, and I woke up fast . . . and then . . ."

A panic swept over me more intense than anything I'd experienced in my closet. A wave of nausea and horror. "When were those kids killed? The girl at the radio station said her friend died and that Will killed her."

"The accident was in 1980. The morning of July 2."

"His birthday," I gasped.

"That was the same morning."

My stomach tightened, and I felt like I was losing control of everything inside me. "No, no, no," I whispered again and again. "It can't be."

My face must have turned pale because Richard was there with a wastebasket, holding it out to me. "What's wrong? What are you thinking? Tell me."

"I was there. I was in the car when he killed the children."

40

Will

I walked into the small police station and asked for Eddie.

The woman at the front just stared at me.

"Chief Buret. Tell him Will Hatfield is here."

A haggard officer going through the mail put a hand on his gun and looked squarely at me.

"Tell him I need to see him outside," I said.

I walked out and waited under the gray, overcast skies. It was on this street that I did my first remote broadcast for Seeb, describing the town parade when I was seventeen or so. Seeb parked a pickup near the route, then hooked a microphone to a long cord and attached the alligator clips to a telephone inside one of the stores. As soon as I climbed onto the back of that truck, I knew it would be a long day. Kind of like the *Hindenburg*'s crash. Nothing of that magnitude went wrong, but Seeb had the driver park near the guardrail, and I couldn't see over it to read the signs of the dignitaries or different bands marching by. Karin laughed at the broadcast, especially the part when I said the majorettes looked cold. It was the only thing I could think of to say. I had felt naked and exposed, just like I did as Eddie, Bobby Ray, and the other officer emerged from the station.

"Will," Eddie said, acting genial, as if he were my best friend, "what brings you to town? Didn't think you came out in the daytime. The Vampire of Dogwood, that's what some call you."

"You really need this much protection?" I said, nodding at the others.

He turned and smiled at his friends. "These are just concerned coworkers making sure the threats you made inside aren't followed through."

"Threats?"

"You used a threatening tone of voice to our secretary," the other officer said, talking through his nose. I recognized his voice from the phone on the night of the attack.

Eddie looked up and down the street, then moved closer. "To be honest, they'd rather gun you down right here and be done with you, but that wouldn't be legal, would it?"

"My mother got served today. Eminent domain."

"Yeah, schools are getting crowded around here. See, while you were in the pokey, the rest of us have been doing the hokey, and there's a bunch of kids needing desk space."

Bobby Ray didn't laugh, but the other officer did, then pulled out a nightstick. The back of my head throbbed just looking at it.

"What do you want, Eddie? You don't have to kick my mother out of the only house she's lived in for forty years."

He was so close I could smell the sausage pizza on his breath. He had a smudge of red sauce on his cheek and mustache. "If you'd have listened to me when you first came back, she wouldn't have to move. But your kind doesn't learn. Wasn't enough you had to wipe out some kids on the side of the road, you had to bring your stink back to this town and remind us."

"What if I leave?" I said softly.

"Well, did you hear that, boys? Will here says he's thinking about moving on. Starting a new life."

"It's about time," the officer said.

"Looks like you'll be leaving whether you want to or not," Eddie said.

"I know you and your father have a lot of pull on the town council," I said. "Call them off and leave my mother and her place alone."

Eddie scratched his head. "Problem is, it's not just the town that wants you gone. We notified your family about this, and there wasn't an objection."

"My mother never heard anything—"

"It wasn't your mother we talked to. It was the executor. You knew that because of her fragile state, your brother was assigned legal guardian for the estate. He didn't have a problem with the eminent domain."

I let the truth sink in. Carson had given them the okay.

"You gonna take that woman with you, Casanova?" the officer said. "The one Eddie said you were in love with?"

I made a move toward him, and Eddie pulled his gun and pointed it at my chest. "Not so fast, killer."

I put my hands at shoulder height. "I'm not armed." I looked at Bobby Ray. "You can see I'm not armed."

Bobby Ray came toward me. "Just turn around, get in your truck, and get out of here."

I kept my hands in the air.

Eddie glared at Bobby Ray, but by the time he had turned around, I was in my truck kicking the engine to life.

The knot in my chest was tighter than my serpentine belt. I clattered over the streets, passing old couples headed for dinner specials. I had avoided Carson's office, but I knew exactly where it was. I didn't worry about parking. I let the truck roll to a stop in front of the entrance, blocking two handicapped spots, and jumped out. I saw him at a window on the second floor, a phone to his ear. He didn't wave.

A winding staircase led to the top, and an aquarium filled the whole wall. A sign beside the aquarium read, C & E Weapons Analysis. I wasn't sure who the E was, but I knew the C.

A nicely dressed woman at the front desk peeked up from her paperwork. She gasped and picked up the phone.

"Don't bother. I know where he is," I said.

"Mr. Hatfield, I think it's him," she said.

A door led to a hallway but it was locked. I turned to her, and she backed against a cabinet. I was familiar enough with buzzing doors after being in prison that I easily found the button under her desk and pushed it. As soon as I let go, it locked again.

"You want to hold this for me or do I have to get some tape?"

Her eyes were wild. Finally she stepped over and pushed it until I opened the door. So much for company loyalty. The door led to a hallway and three more doors to my right.

"Carson!" I yelled.

"Don't do this!" he said.

"You want me to kick it down or are you coming out here?"

The lock clicked and I walked through.

He held a small pistol in his right hand. "Don't make me use this."

"Why did you do it?" I said. "Why did you give our land away?"

"They offered enough to take care of Mama the rest of her life. That's all I'm concerned about."

"What if she doesn't want to live somewhere else the rest of her life? You ever thought about what *she* wants?"

"I've called the police. They'll be here any minute. You'd better just go."

"You called them or they called you?" I spat. I turned a chair over and moved toward him, pointing a finger at his chest and ignoring the pistol. "I took the fall for you. That drunk driving charge would have kept you from the scholarship."

"Don't bring that up. I never asked you to do that."

"You never thanked me, either. And it was that prior that worked against me and you never said—"

"I was in D.C., little brother. Trying to get ready for Armageddon or whatever next war's coming our way. What was I *supposed* to do?"

"What you ought to do right now. What would Daddy say about this? You know it'd break his heart."

Carson laughed. "You're accusing *me* of breaking his heart? After what *you* did?"

I wanted to hit him. I wanted to hurt him as much as he had hurt me. Instead, I walked into the hallway and muttered, "Judas."

I left before Eddie got there and followed a back road toward the next county. I needed time to think and cool down. There had to be some way to keep our land, some way to keep my dream alive.

I bought a sandwich and something to drink at a gas station and drove to the park in Hurricane where Carson and I had played tennis and Little League. Just sitting there in the stands, watching the empty field, made me long for the days when the rest of our lives stretched out in front of us with so much promise.

Good luck. Bad luck. Sometimes the worst things that happen to us can lead to some of the best things. It hadn't happened for me, but I figured it couldn't get much worse.

I was wrong.

41

Bobby Ray

The baby had a mind of his own, like a lot of kids, but this one was a tiger even in the womb. He moved around like a linebacker in search of a quarterback, and Lynda was up with the sun scrubbing and shining anything she could get her hands on. My mother said it was a "nesting phase," and I needed to give her space. She was right. A little comment, just some offhanded thing that didn't mean anything before, now set Lynda off and sent her on a downward spiral, so I tried to be careful with my words.

We'd moved into our house the week before, and that night my old army buddy Ernie was due. He showed up with his third wife, and they didn't seem to mind the boxes and furniture. The two of them even rolled up their sleeves and helped unpack.

Outside I broke out a bottle of white wine—Lynda looked like she was dying to try some but didn't dare with the baby only a month away—to go with our Pizza Hut order. We laughed and talked until it was almost dark, and Lynda went inside to freshen up.

An old Camaro I'd never seen before passed, and I didn't think much about it. Probably some kids horsing around at the end of the road. It was either that or going to Dairy Queen. My beeper went off and I called the station. It was Eddie, asking if I would come in for a couple of hours. He had something going on. I told him I had guests from out of town, but he said in his Eddie way that I should get my rear downtown now or I'd be sorry.

I told Ernie I had to go to work. I changed back into my uniform, which wasn't clean, but I wasn't going to tell anybody.

"Hang on," Ernie said as I was heading out. "Got something for you in the trunk. Almost forgot."

42

Will

There was no "back way" home, but I waited until dark to return. I figured Mama would be worried and that Carson had called and spun things his way. It didn't matter anymore. I'd made up my mind to leave and stop fighting it. I was still committed to Karin, but there had to be a better way to reach her. Maybe it would take leaving and giving her space. I didn't know. But what I was doing wasn't working; that was for sure.

I had rounded the corner and could see our house when a gray blur zoomed out of a driveway straight at me. I instinctively swerved left off the road into a row of rosebushes so thick the truck rolled onto its side, then bounced back far enough for me to crawl out the window. I was in a tangle of briars and sticks as the car pulled beside me.

"Get in the car, Hatfield!" someone shouted. I didn't recognize the voice.

I continued climbing through the thorns and was trying to get my shirt and pants free when I heard the gun click. It was the deputy. "Get back here now or your mama's gonna see your brains all over that field."

43

Karin

I fell into Richard's arms, weeping. He's not the type uncomfortable with a woman's tears, and for that I'm grateful. You can do a lot worse than that in a husband.

I rested in his office and tried to pull memories from the accident. My mind was like a quilt with missing patches. I heard a commotion outside.

My mother walked in. "Karin?"

That started the tears again and we embraced. She looked into my eyes, repeating my name. "Oh, Karin."

My father was at the door, his hands shoved into his pockets, watching from the sidelines.

"I can't remember some things," I managed. "The morning of the accident. Do you remember?"

Her face turned stern, and she looked at Richard. "Has *he* been here?"

"Not today," Richard said. "I talked with him earlier, though, and that seems to have brought up some things with Karin that she can't remember."

"It's fuzzy," I said. "I know that Will brought me home that morning. He must have."

There was an awkward silence.

"Mother, tell me," I pleaded.

Richard gave her a look I had never seen before, and it seemed to compel her.

"I wasn't up yet," my mother whispered. "Your father was about to go to work."

"Dad?" I said.

My father whispered something to Richard.

"Dad, talk to me!"

"He parked in front of the house and carried you inside," my father said.

"Carried me? Why?"

"You were sleeping. Unconscious, I guess. You'd had a lot to drink."

"The wine," I said, my heart racing, the room spinning. "I took it from your cabinet. I'm so sorry. If I hadn't done that, this whole thing—"

"Don't," he said, patting me on the shoulder. "It's all right now. That was a long time ago."

Something stung my arm. *A bee,* I thought. I tried to pull away, but my mother's arms were around me. "The onion, Mom," I said, already groggy. "Get the onion. It takes all the poison out."

"It was our fault," my mother said. "We never should have let you go with him."

Something felt off-kilter, as if the floor had tilted and the lights were strangely close to my head. "Ruthie. I need to talk with Ruthie."

Then the lights went out.

44

Will

The lyrics to "Take Me Home, Country Roads" were on my mind, but these had become less familiar and weren't leading home to the place where I belonged. I'd been pushed inside an old Camaro, slamming the back of my head into the doorjamb. Something wet and sticky, like hot motor oil, ran down my neck.

They drove me to the bend at the top of Benedict Road, one of them with a gun pointed at my head from the front seat. I reached back and grabbed a handful of blood, then wiped it on the seat. Maybe a crime scene investigator would find my DNA someday and put the case together. But the way things were going, I wasn't hopeful.

"What do you guys want?" I said.

"Shut up, Hatfield," the driver said. I recognized the voice of the deputy, Wes. The guy with the gun was wearing a mullet.

A mullet, I thought. *I just got out of prison and even I know better than to wear a mullet.*

The passenger clicked a two-way radio.

Someone said, "Go ahead."

The guy laughed like Elmer Fudd. "We got him. His truck is off in the bushes. You can say he came home drunk or something."

293

"Just go the back way like we planned," someone said. "I'll meet you up there."

"All right, we'll be there in a few. Out."

Benedict Road snakes up the hill at a serious angle; then the road curves right and keeps going all the way to the meth house at the end. Instead of bearing right, Wes turned left onto an old, rutted logging path. Decades ago gas drillers had left a trail surprisingly smooth. There was still mud from the rains, and we slid sideways into the hill a few times but finally made it to the top of the ridge.

"Know where you are?" Wes said.

I kept quiet but I knew exactly. My father and I had walked every square inch of this place when I was a kid. I knew it like I knew my cell at Clarkston. The cracks in the wall. The leaky toilet.

A barbed wire fence cut across a field, and beyond the tree line was our property. Once we hit the ridge we simply went through a thicket and we were at the top of the hill where my new house stood. What there was of it.

Not my house anymore, I thought.

The two got out, both holding guns. I waited for a chance to run, but they looked like they wanted me to. Looking for a reason to shoot.

"What do you want with me?" I said.

"You'll see," Elmer Fudd said. "Just walk. Thataway."

They never got close enough for me to make a move on them. They pointed toward the ridge and we walked for twenty minutes, finally reaching my handiwork. Wood was piled high by the side of the house, and the framing made me proud. It looked professional.

A haze hung over the two mounds and extended to the valley, but I could make out the lights of cars as they zigzagged their way through town.

"Right pretty up here," Elmer said. "Shame you'll never get to finish this house." He pulled out his two-way. "Okay, we're at the house. And bring some of them zip things."

"10-4."

A plan began to gel in my mind as I sat. I had hidden tools in a loose pile of sawdust in case someone came along. It had been more the product of my time in Clarkston than anything else. I started picking briars from my hands as if I was uninterested in getting away, willing to let whatever happened happen. But I was searching with my toe, digging in the sawdust for something I knew was there.

"Who you guys hooked up with?" I said. "My brother?"

Elmer lit up a smoke. "Didn't know you had one."

They both turned their backs, and I reached down and pulled out the box cutter and put it behind me.

"Don't make us shoot you to shut you up," Elmer said. "We'll do it too."

I lifted my hands. "Just trying to make conversation."

I opened the box cutter with my thumbnail, working the screw out behind my back, and pulled out one of the razor blades. It wasn't much, but it would be a weapon if I could get close. There was no question these people weren't going to let me get off this hill alive.

Two sets of headlights rounded the curve on Benedict Road and drove to the lower house. After a few minutes, one car headed up the gravel driveway I'd built and parked near us. I thought about running; then I saw the lights on top of the cruiser and Eddie stepped out. He cursed at them for not at least tying my hands or feet together.

"He's no dummy," Elmer said. "If he'd have taken off, I'd have emptied this in his back quick as a wink."

Eddie gave Elmer a pair of plastic cuffs.

I fiddled with the razor blade in my back pocket, wondering

if this was the best time to use it. When Eddie turned his full attention to me, I shoved it far enough into the pocket that Elmer wouldn't see it.

I kept my hands as far apart as I could as Elmer put the strips around my wrists and I heard the familiar zip.

"Put another one around the post and hook him to it," Eddie said.

Elmer did, and it gave me what I hoped was enough room to get the blade out.

"Guess you're wondering why we brought you here," Eddie said.

"We?" I said. "This your undercover team?"

Eddie nodded to Elmer, and he kicked me in the stomach. I would have dropped the razor blade, and I was glad I hadn't retrieved it.

"Heard from a friend that you went to talk to Mrs. Spurlock a while back. You have a nice chat?"

I groaned, unable to breathe.

"What did you two talk about?"

When I regained my breath, I said, "Elvis was my friend. Wanted to see if she needed help finding him."

Eddie bobbed his head. "Good. I also heard she gave you a letter from him. Addressed to you."

I tried not to, but I froze and they could tell.

Elmer leaned close, pork rinds on his breath. "Doris Jean said you took it with you, but we can't find it anywhere."

The ransacked house.

When I didn't answer, Wes took a turn at kicking me, and I thought I heard something crack above my stomach.

"Should have put a bullet in your head a long time ago, Hatfield," Eddie said. "Would have saved this town a lot of misery." He slid a pack of Marlboros from his pocket and lit one. He blew the smoke in my direction. Secondhand smoke was the least of my worries.

As a child I had always fancied myself as the hero. I had watched enough episodes of *The Wild Wild West* to know that at the most impossible moment James West could get out of anything, save the beautiful woman, the president, and the shipment of gold. Carson and I pretended we were James West and Artemus Gordon, but he never let me be James.

On Sunday nights during church I had stared at the ceiling, wondering what would happen if robbers broke in to steal the offering (as if robbers would want the measly tithes we were able to offer). Or my fourth-grade class—when armed men took my teacher hostage, what would I do? I went through a thousand scenarios, always coming out the hero. But now I was in the most remote place on our farm without a prayer, or much of one.

"All right, let's try it again," Eddie said. "What was in the letter?"

I stared at him. "Is that what this is about? Elvis?"

Eddie exhaled more smoke and walked back to his car. A radio clicked, and he paused for effect. "Yeah, we're having some problems up here getting the info we need. Go ahead in the house and wake her up."

"Wait," I said.

"Wup, hold on," Eddie said into the radio. "We might have a breakthrough."

I shifted against the pole. "It wasn't a letter to me. It was a will. Mrs. Spurlock thought it was to me because it had 'Will' on the envelope, but it was basically him giving stuff away if anything happened to him."

"What did it say about the money?" Eddie said.

"What money? I don't know what you're talking about."

He picked up the microphone again and clicked. "False alarm, Randy. Go on in."

"I'm telling you the truth!" I said. "It didn't say anything about money."

"Hey, Randy," Eddie said, "make her scream real loud so we can hear it back here."

"Okay!" I yelled. "Call him off. My mother doesn't know anything about this."

"Sorry, Will. She's in it as thick as you are. Poor old thing down there. She'll be bawlin' and tied to a chair before you know it. Randy will keep her company, but he gets an itchy trigger finger." Eddie straddled the pile of lumber. "We did find something the other day though. Looked like a 20-gauge shotgun. Probably used it with your daddy up in these woods."

I struggled against the plastic strips, making it look good.

"Here's the way I figure it," Eddie continued, spitting into the sawdust near me. "The pressure of coming back here, having people hate your guts, your mother always on your back to get a job. Then you finally land some gainful employment and they take it away. All your hard work here means nothing when the land's gone. And then you find out your brother betrayed you and let 'em take it without a fight." He looked at Elmer. "Bring me the sack in the backseat."

Elmer obeyed and handed Eddie a bottle of Jack Daniels. He opened it, took a swig, then held it out over my head. "Open up, now."

I shook my head, but he poured it down my shirt. The other two held my head back and forced my mouth open with a stick while Eddie poured some in. I spit most of it out, but when I started choking, I swallowed some.

"Never seen anybody so anxious not to get drunk," Elmer mused.

"You see what happens when you drink and drive?" Eddie said. "That truck of yours is down there in the rosebushes. They'll find it in the morning, along with your mother's body, a victim of circumstance." He broke the stick in half. "Wait a minute. *We'll* find it. Your mama just happened to be there when you snapped."

"A real shame," Wes said.

"I'll bet the TV truck will be out here and everything," Elmer said.

"So you eased your mother's suffering, you came up here and made a little bonfire out of your project, and then you stuck the gun in your mouth and pulled the trigger."

"Nobody who knows me will believe that."

Eddie laughed. "Nobody knows you, Will. The people who did don't want you around here. You don't have any friends. Elvis was the last of the bunch committed to you. Plus, Randy down there writes a great suicide note."

Wes and Elmer laughed.

"You royally trashed your life, Will—you know that? You got nothing left. Only makes sense you'd come back here, get upset, and finish what you started."

"Okay, so if you're going to kill me, why should I tell you what was in the letter?"

"Friends, we have had a breakthrough," Eddie said, sounding like an old-time preacher. He slapped me on the back and sat close. "That Jack Daniels must have done the trick. Old Will here has finally figured out we mean business. And that's a good question. Shows your mind is still working, even under duress. You must have learned a thing or two in Clarkston."

"What do you want?" I said.

"I figure you're the only person on this planet who knows the location of Elvis's stash. He was your friend. He must have told you something."

"I haven't seen him in years."

"Not true. He visited you up in Clarkston. Don't lie to me."

"You know they monitor everything we say up there. I meant back here. How do you know he's not hiding out somewhere with this stash you're talking about?"

The others laughed and Eddie looked at the stars. Elmer started a fire in the pit behind us, and I heard something clink on the rocks that surrounded it. Eddie worked with whatever it was, kicking up sparks. "Oh, we know he's not out there. We actually know exactly where Elvis is right now, and he's gonna stay there. A long time."

"What did you do?"

"Let's just say he became intimately acquainted with the Mud River and a couple of cinder blocks."

My heart fell, and I was overcome not with fear but with grief for my friend. Things began to clear in my mind, and I steeled myself against the evil surrounding me. "Why didn't you get the information about his stash before this all happened? That would have saved a lot of trouble, wouldn't it?"

"He wouldn't talk. We tried being nice to him, promising him things, but when it came down to it, it was his high tolerance for pain that got him. I guess it was all that scar tissue. He made it hard on us."

I was struck with what a small and twisted world Eddie had constructed for himself. He had taken one of God's most beautiful creations—innocent and guileless—and he was thinking of how hard Elvis had made it on him. "Where'd it happen?"

"We shouldn't get too specific," Eddie said. "You know, in case you want to take my offer."

"Go ahead."

"You tell us where he put it, and we let you and your mama live. You pack your stuff up tonight and never set foot in town again."

I knew Eddie would never keep his promise. He had told me too much. I tried to make him think I believed him. "What about the money for the farm? Fair market value is what it said on the notice."

"The town will make out a check in your brother's name. He's the executor. You can work it out with him. I'll make sure you get it."

I could only imagine what my mother was going through at this moment. She was frightened by the slightest possibility of danger, and if I was right, Randy had a black mask on and was ordering her to stop whimpering. "All right, but I want to make sure my mother is okay. I want to talk with her."

"He wants to talk with his mommy," Eddie said to the others. "Isn't that sweet?" He got in my face. "You don't make demands here. You tell us or it's over. Got it? And it's over for the . . ." He paused. "Mommy won't see the sunshine either if you don't cooperate."

I looked at them as I worked the blade out of my pants. I didn't know how long it would take to cut through the plastic, but I had to get started.

"Tell us," Elmer said, "or we'll tie these cinder blocks around you and drive to the covered bridge."

Eddie whirled on him and cursed. "Just shut up!"

Crickets and insects were out in full force. The fire crackled and warmed my back. A rage was building and I tried to fight it, to keep my head clear, to stay focused on survival and one step ahead of the enemies encompassing me.

"My mom can stay with my brother," I said. "He was trying to get her to move in with him before I came back anyway, after my dad died."

"That's a real nice family story, but where's the letter?"

"Tell Randy to take her to my brother's place, and I'll give you what you want."

Eddie stood. "Boys, looks like we have a communication problem. What was it that guy said in *Cool Hand Luke*? A failure to communicate?"

They laughed as Eddie moved to the fire and pulled something out of it. At first it looked like a stick, but when he got closer, I recognized the metal rod I used to set the concrete. The end glowed red, and the other guys whooped and hollered when they saw it.

"I've tried to tell you I mean what I say. Maybe this will convince you." Eddie stuck the metal rod to my neck and flesh sizzled.

I finally knew a little of what Elvis had gone through. The smell of the burned skin was nauseating, and he held it there a good ten seconds before he pulled away, taking a section of my neck with it.

"That's a mighty good brand, Eddie," Elmer said.

I slumped over and nearly passed out, the pain unbearable. But I managed to hang on to the blade as I fought. My hands were getting numb as I worked the blade back and forth on the plastic, and I'd cut the meaty flesh of my palms several times. Maybe I'd bleed to death before these guys could toss me in the river. But as the searing heat pressed against my neck and my arms tensed, I felt something move, something crackle, and I shoved the blade with all my might through the plastic—like a man biting a silver bullet.

"Now I'll give you one more chance," Eddie said, leaning close to me. "Where's that will?"

"I don't need it," I said, writhing, shaking my head. It must have looked like a reaction to the pain, but it was actually a cover for freeing my hands. I saw the ceiling of the church, the cloakroom of my fourth-grade classroom—a way out. "The old tree. I almost shot my foot off down there. A big hole in the trunk."

"That's where he stashed it?" Eddie stood. "That's how you've been paying for the construction. I knew it! Which tree you talking about?"

I threw my head back. "Past that pine grove—go to the fence and follow it about a hundred yards. At the end of the fence, where it turns and runs down the hill, you'll see it. It's in the shape of an L."

"I noticed it when we came by," Wes said.

"Grab a flashlight," Eddie said. He looked at Elmer. "Stay with him."

The car door slammed and the two men hurried into the night, the beam of the flashlight flitting on the landscape of my youth.

Fudd rubbed his hands together and laughed. "We're gonna be set now."

"Where'd you guys come up with all that cash, anyway?" I said, struggling at the last edge of the plastic.

"Had it all worked out till that lunkhead got involved."

"Elvis?"

"Yeah. Eddie didn't even know he was the one who took it until . . . Aw, why am I telling you this? Just sit back and shut up or I'll give you another brand."

I chuckled.

"What are you laughing at?"

"You really think Eddie's gonna let you have any of that money?" I said. "You're crazy."

"We got us a deal—gonna split it even."

I laughed. "You don't see it, do you?"

"Just shut up."

"You're dumb as a stump. You know why he picked Randy and Wes? Because they're stupid. You watch. We'll hear a shot and Eddie'll come back up the hill alone."

"I said, shut up!" he yelled, and as he did, he moved to kick me in the face. It was a move I had seen a thousand times at Clarkston. Someone gets the upper hand and closes in for the killing blow, a kick that snaps the head back and renders the victim unconscious.

But I had worked through the plastic and felt freedom's snap. I kept my hands behind me until I saw my chance. With the kick coming at my head, I caught his foot in both hands and twisted it, the knee cartilage stretching and snapping like a watermelon rind.

His face, shocked and unbelieving at first, now screwed up in pain as he focused energy on his leg. Unable to cry out or suck in breath, he went down hard on his back. By the time he reached for his gun, it was too late. I gave him a swift blow to the temple with it, and his body relaxed against the side of the house.

I spotted the flashlight beam that was now in the midst of the trees. I didn't have much time before they found the tree and climbed up to see there was nothing in that hole. I checked the car for keys, but they weren't in the ignition or over the visor.

I checked Elmer again. He had a pulse, but his head was lolled back, his mouth open, totally gone. I found his keys but his car was too far back in the woods, so I jammed the gun in my belt and ran.

There is a feeling of weightlessness running down a hill, like a child windmilling his arms as he heads into the unknown. My neck burned and my wrists ached from the biting of the plastic cuffs and the slicing of the razor, and the back of my head was on fire, but I was free and the feeling was even better than my release from Clarkston. My Sunday school teacher would have been horrified had she known I had lied my way to freedom, but I have come to believe there are some things you simply can't explain to Sunday school teachers.

I glanced back but couldn't see the flashlight in the woods. I figured I had at least five minutes. Instead of running for the driveway, I ran through the trees, leaning on my knowledge of the hill, the dips and swells, the rotted and decaying trees and the healthy ones. I hit my share of saplings, stinging me in the face as I rushed by, and tripped over a couple of rocks and went down hard, but I managed to regain my balance and keep going.

The house sits at the bottom of the hill in a small valley surrounded by a creek that cuts its way lazily through a meadow. I could see only the end of the house as I came out of the clearing, crossed the driveway I had built, and peered into the inky darkness. No lights on inside. I slowed to catch my breath, scanning the yard and driveway for a vehicle.

It wasn't until I moved past the remains of the barn that I saw the orange glow of a cigarette in front of the persimmon tree. A man stood there watching the house. Was this Randy? Was there someone else in the house? The second cruiser was behind him in the driveway. I had to believe they hadn't harmed my mother.

I moved as quietly as I could to the hill, skirting the ashes of the barn and heading toward the creek. I reached behind and felt for the gun, but it wasn't there. I had lost it in one of my falls.

I whispered a curse, wondering if they had really found the shotgun inside our house.

A radio squawk nearly sent me to my knees.

The man at the tree keyed the mic. "Yeah?"

I knew I only had seconds. I sprinted toward him through the grass, avoiding the gravel of the road I had built.

"He lied to us," Eddie said, out of breath. "Bring the old bat up here and we'll give him one more chance to tell us." I slowed and crouched in a catlike pose, the way I had seen the barn cats hunt birds on the hillside. I was nearly to the tree. I could smell the smoke from his Marlboro.

"Got it. Be there in a few."

As he replaced the mic and headed for the house, I hit him with a crushing body block. Carson had been all-state in his senior year, and when I came along, the coach was expecting someone a little heavier. He would have smiled if he'd have seen the hit I put on this guy. The first one knocked the air out of him with an "oof," and I followed him to the ground, smashing his lungs flat as I drove my weight into his chest. I thought I heard a crack, but it could have been the clattering on our concrete walkway. He reached for his gun, and I punched him hard in the face. It took two hits in the back of the head with the butt of his gun to put him out.

The radio squawked again, and I could tell that Eddie was not in a good mood. I'd learned to imitate voices as a kid watching Rich Little and Frank Gorshin. I hadn't heard this guy talk much, but I figured I didn't have to. "Yeah?" I said, keying the mic.

"He got away. He's probably headed toward you."

"I don't believe this," I said. "What do I do with the mother?"

"Just keep her there. Look, we gotta find this guy. Don't waste time trying to grab him. Shoot to kill."

I figured I had done okay, that in the confusion on the hill Eddie hadn't recognized my voice, but I couldn't be sure. I raced inside and found my mother in her room, the stereo softly playing—a trombone and strings. She had a night-light on the wall, the same one I remembered growing up with, the face of the clown on the front. The thing had scared me rather than comforted me. I could make out her lumpy form under the covers.

I touched her shoulder and squeezed it gently. "Mama?"

She sat up groggily, squinting and looking into my face. "Will? What in the world?"

"I need you to get up and come with me."

"Are you drunk? You stink of Jack Daniels."

I wondered how she knew the smell.

"What time is it, anyway?"

"Mama, this is important. We don't have time to discuss it."

"Well, I'll need to get dressed."

"No, you don't. There are some men looking for me. They'll be here any minute."

"What have you done?"

"Nothing. Now come on."

"Will, running won't help—"

I threw back the covers and picked her up. She was heavier than I thought, and the way she slapped at my arm didn't help, but as soon as I got in the kitchen, she could tell I meant business.

"All right, I'll go. Just put me down."

I grabbed the car keys from the mantel and we hurried downstairs. A .22 caliber rifle sat on the stairs, a remnant of my father, who always kept a loaded gun there just in case. I grabbed it and flew into the dust and musty smells and cracking concrete of the garage.

"Who is it?" she said behind me. "Who's after you?"

"Quiet," I said. "It's Eddie and some guys—"

"Buret? The new chief?"

"He's the one responsible for Elvis disappearing."

"No."

"It's a long story. Let's just get out of here."

She flipped the garage light on, and I quickly clicked it off and helped her through the maze of old lawn mowers, bikes, electric saws, and boxes filled with nuts, bolts, and tools. I tossed the rifle in the backseat, and instead of using the garage opener, I opened the door by hand to keep the noise down. I thought I might find Eddie standing there, grinning, but there was no one. I glanced around the corner and saw an unmoving lump of humanity near the persimmon tree.

"I'm worried about you carrying that gun," she said as I got in and started the car. "That's a violation of your parole and if—"

"I'd rather violate my parole than wind up dead."

"Is it really that bad?"

I backed the old car out of the garage, keeping the lights off, and drove through the yard and over the septic tank buried a few feet below. "They told me they had you handcuffed to a chair and were going to use a shotgun on you."

"Well, see, that wasn't true."

I turned my head and showed her my neck using the dashboard light. "This was."

She gasped at the wound.

We headed down the long driveway and crossed the creek. Behind us, a car roared down the road I had built, its headlights piercing the night. I didn't touch the brake but rolled straight onto Benedict Road and floored the accelerator. My mother had rolled a 1968 Impala into the rosebushes here when I was in grade school, so I had to be careful not to get too distracted, but I couldn't help looking back at the police cruiser barreling toward our front yard.

We passed my abandoned truck and neared the corner. I let up on the accelerator and glanced behind us.

"They must have seen the guy on the ground and the open garage. They're headed for the road. Hang on, Mama."

45

Karin

I awoke after dark in a fog and Richard was there. My parents had gone home after he assured them I was okay. I just needed some rest. He sat with me and talked awhile, mostly about Will, my feelings for him, and what had happened long ago, though most of it was still blurry. I had known Richard as a kind and generous man, forgiving to a fault, but I could not understand why my revelation hadn't brought up his own feelings. If *he* had been harboring an old flame, nurturing it and teasing it along, I would have been heartbroken. But he seemed unconcerned by the whole ordeal.

Maybe that's what happened, I thought. *Maybe he has his own feelings for someone. Maybe my revelation makes it okay for him to indulge in his own secret sin.*

I tried to chase the thought away but it stayed. No matter what happened, our marriage and the church were in big trouble. I couldn't imagine sitting in the atrium and talking with the ladies of the group again.

I called Ruthie but there was no answer. It had been my experience that once she drifted off to sleep, nothing would wake her till morning. So I was left alone with my thoughts and what little praying I could do in my closet.

I knew from different sermons, preachers on the radio, and my own study that God had a problem with a wayward bride. His chosen people had continually run from him, then pleaded for his help. One crisis after another brought them back, begging forgiveness. They would receive it and then make the same mistakes again. I was not trying to fall in love with another suitor. I was not trying to leave the love of my life. But the events of the past few months had brought Will back with a vengeance.

Was I falling in love with the *idea* of him? Except for seeing him at the prison, I'd had no contact other than on the radio and through my memory. What would life with an ex-con be like? How could I even be thinking like this?

No matter where my scattered brain went, I knew something was drastically changing in my life. Something big. And Ruthie's absence only accelerated the pain. It felt like the tide had been pulled out, and a tsunami of thoughts and emotions was about to crash down—or had already crashed and I was just rising with the tide, searching for a lifeboat, clawing for anything that would keep my head above water.

Ruthie had suggested my recurring dream could be about God and my soul. That he was interested in it fascinated me. How does he hear all those prayers at once without getting stacked up in a waiting queue?

"Your prayer will be answered in the order in which it was received," I imagined. *"Estimated wait time is . . . eternity."*

I couldn't look at my quote books or poetry or even Scripture. I couldn't pray. Didn't have the heart. But I did manage to scribble a few lines in my notebook that night.

God, I wrote, *I don't know if you care about my heart or my life, but if you do, I desperately need you. Or maybe you're already doing something and I'm oblivious. I don't know how this works. I'm at the end. Break through. I don't want to hurt my kids. I don't want to hurt my husband. I don't want to hurt the church. And I don't want to hurt you. Please help me.*

46

Will

During the early 1970s, my one foray into the outside world had been through the CB radio. I had a base station in my room and installed a radio in our car. My father, not wanting to waste anything, had transferred it to this vehicle. I flipped it on and cycled through the channels as my mother and I hit Route 60, choosing to drive west rather than east. I'd heard from a friend in Clarkston that people fleeing police have a better chance at escape by going straight rather than weaving through back streets and alleys. There aren't that many in Dogwood anyway.

My old haunt was channel 4. I could only imagine what those people thought when they discovered the kid they had talked with all those years ago was in prison.

". . . was supposed to be back last night, but he got his rig hung up in Missouri and he probably won't make it until late tonight."

I waited until the drawling lady stopped and keyed the mic. "Hey, I'm sorry to interrupt, but I need some help. This is Will Hatfield, and I'm being chased by the Dogwood police chief and some of his thugs." I let go and listened to the static, my mind swirling.

"Will, they're behind us," Mama said.

We hit a straight stretch that ran past the radio station and got the car up to eighty. The left front tire began to wobble, and I had to back off the accelerator. "I need somebody to call the sheriff. Or the state police."

My mother unbuckled and tipped her seat, struggling to roll into the back.

"You ought to pull over, Will," a man said. I recognized the voice of Coyote, one of the grizzled crew that made channel 4 so much fun to join. I didn't know the identities of these people. They were just voices on the radio.

"Coyote, I need your help. Eddie Buret killed Elvis—Arron Spurlock. He knew something about some stolen money. Eddie and his crew kidnapped me but I got away. I need somebody to help me."

"Hit the window lock," Mama said from the backseat.

I released the microphone and hit the lock.

"Who is that?" Coyote said.

"My mother. I couldn't leave her there. This guy is catching up with me in a cruiser. If you're gonna help me, I need you to do it now."

Another long pause. Then a woman's voice. "I hope he does catch up with you, you murdering jerk."

A bullet crashed through the back window, shattering the glass, and I ducked.

"You all right, Mama?"

"These people are playing for keeps," she said.

Through the rearview mirror I watched her pound the rifle barrel against the window, making a small hole through the glass. She took aim and fired, missing badly.

"You'd better get down," I yelled.

Mama fired twice, and the left headlight on the cruiser went dark. She whooped. "I got one!"

"Aim a little higher," I said.

Another shot pinged off our roof, and the side mirror shattered. I swerved into the oncoming lane, then back to the right.

"Hold it still." She fired five shots with the .22, one right
after another. The fourth one hit the windshield. Immediately the
cruiser slowed.

"You did it!" I shouted, approaching the corner and the flea
market that lay below us. I slowed enough to make the corner and
keyed the mic again. "Coyote, he's shooting at us. He's trying to
get rid of the evidence, which is me."

"You know who that is, don't you?" Mama said. "Coyote is
Judge Henderson."

He came back on the radio. "I talked with dispatch. They're
saying you're armed and dangerous. That shots are being fired
from your automobile."

"Sir, my mother and I are defending ourselves. Please. You
have to help us."

"Let him rot," somebody else said. Then a flurry of voices
echoed the same sentiment.

Finally, Coyote spoke. "You need to pull over now. There's
a sheriff's deputy dispatched, but you have to surrender to the
authorities."

"If I surrender, we're dead," I said.

"Son, you're in violation of your parole if you have a firearm.
Don't make it worse."

I tossed the mic away and mashed the accelerator to the
floor.

All my life my mother had been the one to play things safely.
When my father had a chance to buy more land for next to nothing, she had said they had enough. When he wanted to quit his job
and farm full-time, she had said they needed a steady income and
health insurance. Now, faced with the most dire circumstances of
our lives, she was rising to the occasion and becoming a lot less
safe than I had ever imagined.

"Daddy would love to see you like this," I shouted through the noise and wind.

We passed the Family Dollar and Pizza Hut doing seventy-five, and the funeral home came up on the right. There was only one stoplight in town, and just as we approached, it turned yellow, then red.

"Hang on," I said. "We're not stopping."

I slowed to about forty, and when I saw no cars nearing the intersection, I sped up, heading straight for the site of our old school. The Sabre was all lit up, waiting like an old friend. "We make it past here and we might meet that deputy coming the other way," I said.

I saw the Dogwood police cruiser too late to react. It was behind the plane, and when it flashed its lights, I was distracted and didn't see the spike strip.

All four tires blew and we swerved left. Our momentum kept us going, but I smelled burning rubber and felt the clunk of the rims on pavement. Sparks flew, showering up beside us, and my mother threw her hands over her head. Swirling lights lit the darkened field ahead, and instead of braking, I pushed the accelerator to the floor.

It took both hands to control the wheel even though we had slowed now to about thirty-five. The grinding worsened, and over the grating and groaning of the wheels came the warbling siren. I drove in the middle of the narrow road so the cruiser couldn't pull beside me and approached the Bridge Closed sign and the orange and yellow horses.

"That bridge will never hold this car," Mama yelled from the back.

"You bring your swimsuit?" I said.

"No, just my gun."

I would have laughed, but the situation was just too bleak.

The car crawled up the incline to the bridge and pushed the

horses away. One of them stuck underneath the right wheel, and we clattered onto the bridge and over the ancient boards that had been meant for horse-drawn carriages. The car lunged left, then came to a violent halt as it plunged through the rotted wood. All I could hear was the hiss of the engine and the rushing water beneath us.

"You okay?" I said.

Mama mumbled something.

"Put your hands up and get out of the vehicle!" the officer shouted behind us.

Mama put something in her nightgown and struggled to sit up, looking out the back window and squinting. "Is that you, Bobby Ray?"

The officer held his gun in front of him, partially blocked by the open door. I couldn't see his face, but I did see the gun barrel rise slightly. "Mrs. Hatfield?"

"That's right, and unless you're mixed up with Eddie and his bunch, you better let us get out of here."

He seemed confused, and I figured it was the perfect time to confuse him more. I opened the door and stepped out, letting the gun I had fall to the bridge. "Hand me the rifle, Mama," I said, thinking that in a million years I would not have guessed I would utter such a phrase, but there it was.

She put the gun through the window and I let it fall, then helped her out of the car. "We're unarmed now. We're not a threat to you."

"Lie facedown on the bridge," he called.

"Bobby Ray, I've known you since you were this high," my mother said. She turned to me. "Taught him in second-grade Sunday school." Then, to Bobby Ray, "I don't think you're mixed up with these people, but if you are, you'd better ask God to forgive you right now because judgment is coming."

"I don't know what you're talking about, but I want you two to just get down so we won't have any more trouble."

A car screeched around the corner, and one headlight sped toward us.

I grabbed my mother's hand and pulled her to the middle of the bridge. "Stay down. I don't think Bobby Ray'll shoot his Sunday school teacher."

There were holes in the wood, and a couple of times I thought we would both fall through, but we made it to the far end of the bridge as Eddie pulled up beside Bobby Ray. He said something and Bobby Ray pointed to us. Eddie ran toward our car and bent down beside it.

"What's he doing?" Mama said.

Eddie picked up the handgun I had dropped and examined it. He took a few steps back and surveyed the area. The front of the bridge was illuminated by one fluorescent light.

When he retreated toward the police cruiser, I faced Mama. "Walk straight up this hill and get to somebody's house. Hurry."

"But what's he doing?"

"Go!"

Before she could move, the Glock exploded on the other side of the bridge.

"Mercy!" My mother knelt on the soft shoulder and covered her mouth as the boy she'd taught in Sunday school slumped to the ground in the circling lights of the cruiser.

I stood at the end of the bridge, in plain sight, as Eddie turned and walked toward me.

"He shot him," Mama said, her voice trembling. "He just killed Bobby Ray."

"Mama, you have to get up."

"I'm not leaving you." She put out a hand, as if trying to grab a railing, and her eyes were misty. "Honey, I could never bear to go to the trial and watch. It tore me up inside. I hope you can forgive me because—"

"I never blamed you. I wouldn't have been there if I could have helped it."

"End of the line, Will," Eddie said, stepping around our car. "It would have been better if you'd have stayed in Clarkston instead of coming back here. Mrs. Hatfield, stay right where you are."

"It's fitting we should be here—don't you think?" I said. "Last time we were on this bridge, you lost a tooth or two."

"What are you talking about?" Eddie said.

"Remember Karin? Remember coming out here with her? Thinking you were alone? When a girl says no, she means it."

He disappeared into the darkness of the bridge, silhouetted by the spinning lights. "So that was you, huh? I should have known you'd take up for that no-account. She wasn't worth all the trouble she caused."

"And this is where you got rid of Elvis."

"What goes around comes around," Eddie said.

The bridge creaked and groaned, and a rail split above him. Eddie jumped to the walkway as our car fell through—halfway at first, just touching the water, and then it plunged all the way in with a splintering crash.

"Now old Elvis will have him something to drive." Eddie laughed. "And you're going to join him."

"You're gonna shoot me with my own gun?" I said. "That won't make much sense in the report."

"You shot Bobby Ray with it, didn't you? When I cornered you, you turned it on yourself." Eddie walked closer, as I knew he would, and the river flowed below, swollen and muddy, carrying debris downstream. "And before you turned the gun on yourself, you took care of the skank who birthed you."

Of all the scenarios I'd thought of as a kid, of all the robbers and terrorists I had saved my church and school from, it had never crossed my mind that I would be defending my mother from the chief of police. I stood my ground and stepped to my right, blocking his aim. "You're not going to hurt my mother."

Eddie smiled. "Fine." He moved closer to the railing and looked me in the eye. "I've waited a long time for this."

People wonder what they will think of in the moments before they die. Children. Things left unsaid. Forgiveness. God.

I thought of Karin in the moment before the gunshot—the distant, otherworldly explosion. I thought of the house on the hill and the view of the valley and the trees in fall. A panoramic, maudlin rehearsal of my life. I thought of all the times Karin and I would *not* have together, the children we'd never have, the love we wouldn't make. The songs left on pause in the soundtrack of our lives.

The strange thing was, the gunshot didn't hurt. I realized why when I saw the blood in Eddie's mouth, running down his cheek, and the way his eyes rolled up as he drifted sideways, stumbling. And the railing on the bridge giving way, his body tumbling into the surging river, and the thin trail of smoke coming from Bobby Ray's gun as he staggered on the other side of the bridge.

Then, as if the world had seen enough, the whole thing collapsed. Boards that had been there since the Civil War washed away and broke in pieces, like a life splintering.

More lights swirled near the town, and my mother spoke over the wail of the siren. "You all right, Bobby Ray?"

"Yes, ma'am." He rubbed his chest and stumbled to his cruiser, grabbing the radio.

❧

They dragged the river for three days after Eddie was shot, but they didn't find his body for three weeks. A father and his son fishing for catfish seven miles downstream came upon him caught in a twisted mass of debris and sludge. It was not a pretty picture.

Bobby Ray arrested Randy, who gave up the others. The state police got involved and cornered Wes in a trailer that belonged to one of his estranged girlfriends. He wasn't taken easily and went out in a hail of bullets. Over time Bobby Ray discovered that Elvis had overheard a rather intimate conversation between Doris Jean and Eddie. As authorities had suspected, someone who knew the inner workings of the gentlemen's clubs up and down the valley had coordinated the robberies of those establishments. Doris Jean had been mixed up with the people at the meth lab at the end of the road. When she was late with a payment, she told them where they could get some "real money." The deal had turned sour for her and she went to Eddie, who was more than willing to take her information and anything else she offered. Doris Jean gave the meth lab's location because she knew there would be a sizable amount of cash on hand. Instead of arresting the men and breaking open the case that had stymied the state police, Eddie, Wes, and Randy had taken care of them, so to speak. Bobby Ray found their bodies buried on a hillside covered with ferns and rhododendron. The shallow graves were near the abandoned house at the end of Benedict Road.

The mistake Eddie had made was having a flat tire as he passed the Exxon station on his way back to the office. Elvis happened to be there and had removed the bags of cash from his trunk while installing a new tire. It took Eddie two days to piece together the truth and find evidence of some sort of explosive device Elvis had used to flatten the tire. Some didn't believe Elvis was capable of such a plot. Those people didn't know Elvis and how his life was inextricably tied to explosions.

The same workers who looked for Eddie's body in the river found Elvis a few hundred yards from the bridge, wrapped in chains and two cinder blocks. His body had decomposed, but it was in better shape than Eddie's.

Mama and I went to the funeral, closed casket, and sat next to his mother. It was the first service I'd been to with my mother since my release, and it felt like I was finally home. The preacher said as many good things as he could about Arron, even referring to his nickname and his penchant for singing. But no one even came close to capturing who he really was. Arron was one of the walking wounded, haunted by the choices he made, just like the rest of us. He hadn't deserved his fate, and I wished I could have been released earlier.

Bobby Ray came to the burial and spoke with Mrs. Spurlock afterward. He told her how sorry he was and that he wished there was more he could have done. She hugged him, and it almost seemed like she was giving more comfort than he was.

I reread Arron's will and tried to decipher his words. As kids we would come up with words with double meanings, producing a hidden message only we could understand. It was our "Elvis Code."

I have only one other thing of value, and it should all go to Will Hatfield because he's probably as tired of the police around here as I am. He'll know where it's at, and I think he'll know what to do with it.

It finally struck me, so one frosty Sunday morning I called Bobby Ray and we went down to the station and popped the trunk of Eddie's cruiser. Inside the spare was most of the money from the robberies still in their bank deposit bags.

"You know there's a reward for this," Bobby Ray said.

"How much?"

"I'm thinking it might be enough to finish that house you're working on."

The reward was slow in coming, and I was loath to keep all of it. As much as Arron loved his mother, I figured he would want her to have some, so I made sure the bank cut a check to both of us. Some people weren't too happy with my decision, but I figured you can live your whole life and not make everybody happy.

❧

Judge Henderson came to the house one day while I was working, and Mama drove with him up the hill. He looked at the wide expanse of hillside and stretched. "I suppose this is what kept you going over there in Clarkston."

I nodded and wiped the sweat from my brow.

He took a deep breath and let it out. "It would me too."

"Judge Henderson and I went to school together many moons ago," Mama said. "He lost his wife about this time last year, wasn't it?"

"Yes, it was."

"She was a fine Christian woman."

Henderson nodded. "Never could get her to do any target practice like I hear you've been doing with the local constables."

My mother laughed, and it was one of those sounds you dream about. Like life coming back into the body of Lazarus. Or a stone rolling away from a tomb.

"I never knew you were Coyote," I said.

"Didn't want anybody to know," he said. "It was something to pass the time, especially after my wife passed. Just to hear a few voices in the night made it a little easier."

"I'm glad you were listening that night."

"Not sure I did much to help. Wish I could have done more."

He informed me, on behalf of the town council, that the eminent domain issue was going away. "It was something Eddie was pushing on them. You shouldn't hold your brother responsible."

I showed Henderson the layout of the house, and Mama tagged along like a happy puppy. On the deck outside I told him I hoped one day to stand on that very spot and watch my children play in the front yard.

He ran a hand along the railing. "Will, I don't say this very often—don't have the chance to—but I think I was wrong about you."

"How so?"

"The way you acted in court. I've never had anyone just sit

there and take it like you did. I spoke with the warden at Clarkston, and he told me you were a model prisoner."

"Sounds good to you and me, but it doesn't look too hot on a résumé, Judge."

"After all that's happened, I think the town will accept you. I think it's the least they can do. Be a little more open to their prodigal son."

"I appreciate that."

Mama invited Judge Henderson to dinner that night, and I told them I had so much work to do that I couldn't see breaking away. Mama just laughed again.

47

Karin

Ruthie once said that life isn't pretty, so you gotta hug the ugly out of it. I hung on to that as the days passed. I talked with Richard and tried to sort things out, but I wasn't there for my children like I wanted and I was unable to reach Ruthie. She had now pushed me away as much as pushing me toward something.

I kept coming back to the thought of Will and the drive home from Cincinnati. I couldn't shake the awareness that I had been there when he had killed the children. Was it true? Or had he dropped me off beforehand and fallen asleep on his way to work?

I busied myself about the church, drinking my coffee in the atrium, thinking Ruthie would walk in and join me, but I drank alone.

I was in my husband's office, pouring my heart out about something, when a knock came at the door. "Come in," he said.

The door opened and Will Hatfield walked inside. Older, his face lined and sunburned from whatever work he had found. Immediately I turned to Richard in fear that he would think something was going on between us, but he welcomed Will, shook hands, and pulled up a chair for him.

"Hi," Will said to me.

I remembered his voice, and warmth spread through my body. "It's been a long time."

"Sure has. How are you?"

I looked at my husband again. He had taken a chair directly across from us, as if we were going to participate in some kind of three-way conversation. "I'm okay," I said. "Struggling with some things, but okay. What brings you to the church?"

Will looked at Richard, then back at me. "I wanted to talk to you about that night."

"Yes, the concert and the trip home. We were just talking the other day about whether or not I was still in the car when you . . . when the accident occurred."

"Right," Will said, rubbing his hands on his jeans. He had such strong hands, and muscles rippled up his arms. But he seemed nervous. "What do you remember?"

I told him what I had told Richard but that things were fuzzy.

Will listened, nodding and affirming my words.

"At some point," I said, "my father said you brought me home and carried me inside."

Richard crossed his legs, studying me. "Karin, sometimes you need permission to remember. There are things locked up inside all of us that we don't think are affecting us but have bearing on our lives every day."

"You sound like some psychologist." I laughed.

Richard smiled. "It's okay to remember. We're here to help."

"Okay," I said nonchalantly, "I'm ready."

Will leaned forward, his elbows on his knees, his hands clasped. "Karin, there's something you *don't* remember about that night."

We had gone the long way home, south of Cincinnati toward Kentucky, and Will had swerved to miss a deer crossing the interstate near Morehead. A late night/early morning fog had settled in, and he turned in to a rest area. I stirred and Will patted my shoulder.

"I need to sleep for a few minutes. My eyes are really heavy," he said.

I was hunkered down in the passenger seat, trying to shake off the effects of the wine. He asked if I wanted to stretch out in the backseat, but I said I was comfortable where I was.

"I can't stretch my legs up here," he said. "I'm going in the back."

The night drifted over us as 18-wheelers passed through the rest area. There were so many lined up along the on-ramp that I lost track.

An hour or two later, we began moving again as the morning mist fell, a coating of moisture on the windshield. Tired wipers squeaked as they moved back and forth.

My parents will be worried.

A blue sign welcomed us to Wild, Wonderful West Virginia. The trees seemed inviting, the hillsides exploding with green, and the air filled with that wet, earthy aroma. Morning traffic increased, people going to work at hospitals and factories and auto supply stores. We passed an old truck laden with junk, half of it hanging so loosely that I was afraid it would fall into the road in front of us.

The road hummed a soothing melody, and it was impossible not to think of sleep again. We were only a few minutes from my home, but Will had to get to his job, and I assumed he'd want to freshen up.

I turned and stared at him sleeping, then adjusted the rear-view mirror to look at his face. Peaceful. Sleeping the rest of a baby, soundly and unaware of the world around him. This was a boy—almost a man—who would make a good husband. With some work, of course. But a good, stable man, loyal and true. Not like many of the boys I had known.

Will was everything I had failed to be. I did not deserve a man like this or a life with love and kindness. I had tempted and tested the limits, and here I was, in the presence of this good son.

The first sign of trouble was a jerking feeling, bouncing and knocking at the right side of the car. I looked up, startled in that dreamy half-asleep/half-awake world of morning. The car was off the edge of the road, kicking up gravel into the wheel well, the steering wheel swaying violently.

Will sat up. "Karin!"

It was too late. I overcorrected and jumped from the edge of the pavement to the other side, stepping on the gas instead of the brake. No one was coming in the other direction, but when I swerved back into my lane, I overcorrected again and this time both tires went off the road.

"Brake! Brake!" Will yelled.

I put both feet down and we slid, but not before we hit something, then slammed into the guardrail.

Will climbed over the seat and out the passenger side. Steam came from the radiator. I thought he was looking at the front of the car, to check for damage, but the expression on his face was one of pure horror. He bent over, examining something. Then he moved to his left. When he looked up at me, his eyes showed a despair I had never seen, as if there were something deep in his heart he could not explain and could never share.

"No, stay in the car," he said.

But I was already out, walking to the front, looking at the damaged hood, dents in the metal . . . and streaks of red.

A doll lay on the ground, its face in the gravel, and I wondered who could have dropped such a lifelike toy by the road. Some child would certainly have cried herself to sleep when she couldn't find it.

And then I spotted another. Dark brown hair over the shoulders, masking the face. Something red oozed from her head. Arms and legs splayed.

I collapsed on the ground beside them, and Will picked me up—he must have because I awoke in the car, pulling into my driveway. He carried me from the car to the front door and put me on the couch.

"There's been an accident," he said to my father. "I've called for help, but I have to go back."

Like waking from a long, tortured dream, the truth of that moment engulfed me. I had been hearing a single note on a piano, and now I began to hear the strains of the symphony of sorrow, love, and living. I had not only been there in the car at the scene; I had been behind the wheel. It finally made sense that Richard would allow Will access to me, to break through with this terrible reality and what it had done to me.

"You were asleep," I whispered to Will, "and you told the police that you were driving." I turned to my husband. "I was the one who should have . . ." I put my face in my hands.

Will took one of my hands and held it gently. "Karin, from the time we were kids, I knew . . ."

"Knew what?"

"That we'd be together someday. And I couldn't stand the thought of you facing this."

"I haven't faced this."

"I mean facing the consequences."

The walls of the study seemed different. I had painted them a pretty lime green, but now they were a drab off-white, just like the shades. Richard sat in front of a steel desk, not the wooden one in his office. Was I in the church conference room? someone else's study?

"It's all right, Karin," Richard said. "We're here to help."

A woman wearing a thin sweater festooned with tiny bears

stood behind me, listening. Had she just walked in on us? Why was she here? When I asked, Richard said she could leave.

Richard uncrossed his legs, still staring at me. "We found your stash of pills in the closet. You haven't been taking your medication again."

I looked away, feeling both of their stares.

"There's something else," Richard said. "I know this is a lot to take in, but I think you can handle it. Are you ready?"

"Have I killed someone else's children?" Then the weight pressed me down. "It was me. I killed them, didn't I?"

Richard's face was full of love and compassion. "Someone once said the truth will set you free. Do you believe that?"

"Yes," I choked.

"This is not your church. I'm not your pastor."

"Of course you are. You spoke last Sunday on . . . the woman who was about to be stoned for adultery."

"I don't preach. I'm a doctor. You've been here since your parents worked it out for you to stay. They brought you to see your grandmother, and you bonded with a few people here."

"What are you talking about?"

"This is a nursing home. A managed-care facility. Because of your episodes—"

"Episodes? They think I'm crazy?"

"Your mind was fragile before the accident. You were vulnerable because of some things in your past. That trauma sent you into a world of your own. A reality that helped you cope with—"

"Where are my children?" I said, my voice shaking. "What have you done with the kids, Richard?"

"You have no children. They were in your imagination."

The room spun and I stood, a hand to my head. "That can't be true. I walked Darin to the bus this morning. And Kallie. Tarin will be out of preschool in a few minutes—I have to go."

"Don't you see?" Richard took the scraps of newspaper from

my hand and unfolded them. "The children of that family. Karla. Tanny. Danny. They start with the same letters as *your* children. Only they're not. You never married. You never had children."

"No! They are my children! I've cared for them and loved them, just like I've loved you and this church and the women and . . ." I turned to Will with pleading eyes. "Tell him this is nonsense. You know I have children, don't you?"

Richard's voice was behind me. "There are people here who love you. These are your confidants of the church. You sit in the day room and talk about banquets and special speakers. Some who know you play along, but—"

"Ruthie!" I shouted. I was up before the woman with the bear sweater could grab me, rushing by Will and out the door. Someone had taken the carpet from the hallway. It was just a tile floor, and there was an antiseptic smell. A rollaway bed with white sheets sat unattended. Women in similar bear sweaters stared at me, white shoes silently walking the halls.

"Ruthie Bowles!" I shouted. "Where is she? Where's Ruthie? Please tell me!"

"Miss Ruthie's right in here, dearie," a large black woman said. She pointed to a hall and a room on the left. Inside was a single bed with a curtain drawn around it. A TV was mounted on the wall, and there was a chair and a small chest of drawers. A large bathroom stood at the end of the room with silver railings around the toilet and tub. And a small closet.

I pulled the curtain and viewed the remnants of my friend. All our conversations. All her wisdom. Her face was drawn, and the skin on her arms pressed to the bone. A large tube stuck out of her mouth and attached to a machine that whirred and ticked, lifting her chest and letting it fall.

Someone put a hand on my shoulder. It was Richard. "Ruthie is real. Shortly after your trip to the penitentiary, she fell ill. She wasn't in good shape before that, but there's been a steady decline."

"I've been to her house," I protested. "I smelled her cooking. We went to Wal-Mart together."

"You were here. In the lunch room. And the little shop by the day room. Other than your trip to the penitentiary or a few days here and there with your parents, you've lived here."

"My whole life . . . is a lie. Everything—my kids, my husband, even God. It's all a big lie."

"No," Will said, coming close. "You chose a church and to be married to a pastor. You made up children you loved. That's a good thing. It's helped you. Somehow this other world helped hold you together."

"The human mind is a wonderful thing," Richard said, "but it can be damaged. I like to think this time has been spent healing, regaining your strength so those things that helped you cope can become a reality."

"How long have I been here?"

"You came here about eight years ago. I've come by to help you from time to time."

"Eight years," I echoed.

Then I looked at Will and knitted my brow. "If Richard isn't my husband . . ."

Will took me in his arms.

I pulled away, tears blurring my eyes. "I don't believe you. It's too much to take in. . . ."

"Shh," he said, gathering me in. "Take your time with this. I'll wait for you."

48

Will

Karin retreated to her room at the facility, her closet actually, and stayed for days, coming out long enough to go to the bathroom and eat. She carried a threadbare Bible and a journal inside the tiny space, along with a couple of books she'd borrowed from Ruthie's room.

Dr. Richard Welles had written to me at Clarkston explaining Karin's situation—not everything, but what he could piece together. Hers had been a slow slip from reality, making up relationships, her marriage, the children, not in one fell swoop but over time. A coping mechanism that overtook her and sent her spiraling further toward the unknown. It was her relationship with Ruthie that had been the beginning of the process of reclaiming her. A gentle, withered hand to lead her from her abyss and into varying degrees of light.

Dr. Welles had okayed the trip to Clarkston, with him and her parents escorting, keeping a distance behind the car, watching so nothing happened.

Ruthie had been in on the plan as well, believing all along that Karin had a future and a hope. She saw glimmers of life inside her friend and chose to lead her along quiet paths of truth hidden in the inner recesses of Karin's mind.

What Ruthie didn't know until she spoke with me in Clarkston was that her friend was the monster the town had wanted to expunge. Ruthie had lost her grandbabies on that misty July morning. After the initial grief wore off, she could tell it was time for her to move away from the home of her daughter and son-in-law. She chose the assisted-living wing and a few years later made friends with Karin. Ruthie sensed the delicate nature of Karin's problem immediately but didn't know what to do. It wasn't until she met with Dr. Welles that she formed a plan.

In the end, I believe Ruthie helped Karin the most. Not Dr. Welles or any of the drugs they tried. Just a compassionate woman of wisdom who did her best to listen and speak into a life that had fallen apart and needed mending.

When Ruthie finally slipped the surly bonds, as she often quoted, Karin and her parents came to the funeral. No one knew the truth about the accident but Dr. Welles, Karin, and the lady in the casket. I slipped into the back of the funeral home and left before the service ended. Karin just stared at the floor throughout the service and seemed content to simply go where she was led.

At the burial, I stayed in the shadows. Someone touched my shoulder and I turned.

A toothless man in dirty coveralls with a chaw of tobacco much too big for one cheek smiled at me. At his feet was an old dog content to stay beside his master. "Will," he said. Only it came out, "Whihh."

"Jasper," I said. "It's good to see you."

"I mihh yoo dah."

"Yeah, I miss him too. I miss him a lot."

The pastor said a few words about the old woman, and everyone hugged and walked toward their cars. Karin lingered at the casket with a handful of flowers, and I edged closer. Ruthie's daughter broke away from the others and returned. I was close enough to hear.

"My mother talked so much about you the past few years," she said. "She considered you her best friend."

"I don't know what I'd have done without her," Karin said, her chin quivering. "It's been a hard adjustment."

"She always wanted you to come to our house for dinner, but we never got around to it. I wish we could have done it while she was still here. Do you think . . . maybe you could still come? I think she'd like that."

Karin stared blankly at her, and then something clicked—as if a motion sensor had turned on somewhere in her mind. "Your children. They were the ones who were killed."

"Yes," she said, not in pain but with a certain air of security, as if she were glad someone had spoken of them. Glad someone had mentioned their existence. Perhaps others feared bringing up the subject, but here was Karin laying it out straight. No illusions, just the truth. "They're right over here," she said, pointing.

She led Karin to the gravestones and Karin knelt, holding the woman's hand. She placed the flowers in front of the marker and ran her fingers over the letters of the three names.

"Tanny was such a rascal," the woman said. "You would have liked her. She had her grandmother's personality. My mother loved all my kids, but I think Tanny was her favorite. She was just always into something."

Karin nodded and stretched herself on the little graves and wept.

∽◯

Each of us makes a world of our own where we live and breathe. Mine had been in Clarkston. Karin's had been just as real to her. Neither of us wanted to stay in those places. We just needed a way out.

The sun set in the west and cast a golden glow on the hills. I had mowed the field with my father's tractor, and the field glistened in the sunlight like a child's haircut. I hadn't moved much furniture into the place, only a bed and a table for the kitchen. The new carpet made it smell like a showroom, and I always kicked off my boots before coming inside. My routine was to sit on the porch and toast the sun's demise another day. Sometimes my mother joined me, though, as it turned out, she was spending more time with Judge Henderson.

When Carson and Jenna came to see the place, they both had the same reaction. "Why would you want to live way up here away from everybody in the world?" Jenna said.

"I don't want to live away from everybody," I said.

She shook her head.

Carson said, "You're gonna need a good dog to keep the animals away from your trash cans."

"Expect I will."

He showed Jenna the arrowhead stuck in the tree and put a hand on her belly. "Our kids are going to get a kick out of seeing this."

❧

The ice in my glass left a wet ring on the porch concrete. My body ached, and I leaned back and took in the last gasp of clouds settling in the sky. The wind rustled the grass and I closed my eyes, picturing my father tossing a ball at this same time of day. *You'd like this house. You'd absolutely love it up here.*

Another rustling of the wind and I noticed movement among the trees. Deer frequently passed in the field. But this was no deer. A person walked around the curve at the limestone and approached like a child kicking at grasshoppers. The gait was familiar, a dancer's body, brown and agile, and the hair, the color of winter wheat, hung softly to the shoulders.

I stood on the porch, waiting, as I had promised. It seemed fitting that I not run to her and embrace her in the field but simply wait. I had let her come to me in her own time. Her own way. It was what she needed.

"I heard you built a house up here," Karin called to me when she got closer.

"I've got quite a view. You should see it under a blanket of snow."

"Big too. How many bathrooms?"

"How many you need?"

"Just one, I guess." She smiled.

She was at the walk now, taking slower steps, turning to see the valley, then looking back at me. The sight of her on the hillside sent chills through me. The sight was like a dream.

"I think I know you," she said, pushing a strand of hair from her eyes.

I took a step down and met her on the walk.

"How long have you been waiting here?"

"Not long. Not long at all."

Karin leaned into me and put her head on my chest, and it felt like the sun had melted the whole world. I put my arms around her and pulled her close. "I would have waited a lifetime."

She looked at me with eyes that were deep pools of hurt and love and memory. "Didn't you make a prediction a long time ago? About us?"

"I did."

Karin turned and looked at the last fingers of sunlight streaking through the clouds, the stars almost ready to begin their show. Then she slipped her arm around my back and leaned close again. "It may take more time, but I honestly think I could get used to this."

49

Danny Boyd

I told my counselor about my grandmother's funeral and seeing the guy standing by the trees. And the woman who stretched out on my sisters' graves. I told him I'd figured it out. Pieced the whole thing together. She was really the one driving, and he had taken the punishment. A loving thing to do. Sacrificial.

My counselor nodded. How are your parents holding up?

I think they're better. Not that they're over it, but, you know. It's been a long time.

Any more questions about your life?

I shook my head.

He stared at me. I guess he saw me sweating and figured something was wrong. I looked around for a thermostat but couldn't find one.

He stroked his beard and glanced at my shoes. What are you thinking?

About my sisters. Being at the cemetery kind of brought it all back. Regret that I was a lousy brother.

What would you say to them? If they could be here right now?

I thought for a long time and finally said, I'd tell them I'm sorry for letting go. I'm sorry I jumped out of the way. I wish I'd held on.

If you had, they'd still be alive? Or if you hadn't let go, you'd be with them, right?

I don't know.

Not a good answer, he said.

Yeah. It's what I'm feeling.

Okay. Fair enough. He leaned forward and put his hand on mine, like he wanted to say something I should remember. Getting ready to pull some curtain back and ask me to choose from three boxes or doors like they did on *Let's Make a Deal*.

I want to show you something, he said. If you're ready.

How can I know if I'm ready if I don't even know what you're gonna show me?

He stood and opened a door. A bright light shone from the hallway, and I had to shield my eyes. Two women walked in, both of them pretty, with long hair like my mother's. Not as old as Mom but definitely out of high school. Maybe even college.

Hi, Danny, the brown-haired one said. There was something familiar in that smile.

The other said hello and giggled.

Hi, I said.

My counselor turned to me and stared.

What? I said.

The two women knelt on either side of my chair.

What? I said again to him, but he wouldn't speak.

The brown-haired one, the one with the dimple in her chin, took my hand gently. You didn't let go, she said.

I squinted and said, What did you say?

Danny, you were there with us, the other said. Don't you see?

My mind spun like one of those amusement park rides you want to get off but can't because the guy who's running it can't hear your screams. Or won't. I closed my eyes and heard the roar of the engine, heard the skittering gravel. Tires off the pavement. The car rushing toward us. We had a second, maybe half a second.

The impact threw me over the guardrail.

It took them a few hours to find you, Danny.

I opened my eyes. I was standing with them, hand in hand, not in a room with bookcases and paintings, just an open vista overlooking a sparkling city, clean and pure.

Like what paradise is supposed to be.

The counselor leaned close to my ear. Welcome home.

I couldn't take my eyes off the scene in front of me, but I could tell he was smiling. He took a breath and put a hand on my shoulder. A scar. A big one, like I had seen on my uncle after they drove the pitchfork through his hand by mistake.

Why did you show me? Why did I go through all that?

Many questions are unanswered. Here there are answers. And tears are wiped away. Pain is gone. You see, Danny, our stories are like rain, dropping into streams, rushing forward, gaining momentum. They're flowing together, trying to reach the end. But there is no end now. Your story and theirs will be told again and again, worked out in so many ways.

But you gave me this. You showed me.

And you'll tell others. You'll understand more deeply.

I felt a tear well up. I looked at my sisters, then back at him. I didn't let go, I said. I didn't let go.

The tear fell harmlessly to the ground.

It was my last.

With Gratitude

I'd like to mention a few people who helped make this book a reality. Kathryn Helmers was a true friend before she became my agent. I am blessed to know her as both. Karen Watson at Tyndale gave this book a chance and thus has given me one. Thanks also to Lorie and Stephanie, who had a passion for the story, and to everyone at Tyndale for standing with our family through some challenges the past year. Also, thanks to Jerry B. Jenkins, who has answered questions about writing and life and even provided time at his writing cave for this book. My children have provided many story ideas, motivation to keep working, and much love. And to Andrea—you have been a constant encourager, reader, sounding board, and confidante. Thanks for walking this road.

About the Author

Chris Fabry is a 1982 graduate of the W. Page Pitt School of Journalism at Marshall University and a native of West Virginia. He is heard on *Chris Fabry Live!* each weekday on Moody Radio, the Love Worth Finding broadcast, and other radio programs. He and his wife, Andrea, live in Colorado and are the parents of nine children. Though he has written more than 50 novels for children and young adults, *Dogwood* is his first novel for adults. You can visit his Web site at www.chrisfabry.com.